EYE of the PARROT

Anthony F. GANTNER

NORFOLK PRESS
2203 Newcomb Avenue
San Francisco, CA 94124
www.norfolkpress.com

Anthony F. Gantner
Eye of the Parrot

Cover illustration: John Mattos
Interior illustrations: Susan Bearden

Website: eyeoftheparrot.com

Publication date: March 2018
Printed in the United States of America

ISBN: Softcover 978-1-60052-138-6

EYE of the PARROT

Anthony F. GANTNER

NORFOLK PRESS

TABLE OF CONTENTS

NAPIER LN

CHAPTER ONE: BIRDS OF A FEATHER

THE SCREECH OF PARROTS HERALDED McCABE'S NOONDAY WALK.

The parrot ensemble was indecipherable babble, except to one man—Tom McCabe. He was blessed with a talent only one in a million possessed—perfect pitch—a particular ability through high-level cortical processing to identify a musical note without having another note with which to compare it. The neural fingers in his brain sensed the intrinsic identity of the parrots' jagged syncopation—its spiky dissonances and jarring chords—much the same way the photo pigments in the human eye could distinguish Newton's corresponding spectrum of colors–red, orange, yellow, green, blue, indigo and violet.

Over the years he had decrypted the basics of the parrots' sonic realm, working their raucous vocalizations into a linguistic matrix that revealed the twisted world of these avian jokesters. There was a distress call, a look-here call, a rally call and a fight call. A treble **D** warning call indicated a predator hawk or falcon lurking above. A crashing **E** major chord straight out of *Sgt. Pepper's*, "A Day in the Life", might signify a feral cat looking for a kill, or feigned surprise at a twilight raccoon rummaging through a recycling bin. Occasionally, it represented the funeral note when a parrot passed away, not always guaranteed to raise a smile. A tree of ripe berries produced a high-pitched **C** major, excitable chatter. There were also the expressive **B/D** calls when McCabe's bowl of sunflower seeds was empty or when a blue jay was hogging the space. A chattering **B/C** prattle meant a human was walking nearby, while a **D/G** modulation involved a discussion whether the person was a stranger, a neighbor or Catz the mailman. The parrots also used varied octaves in calls to their offspring, by which McCabe identified the parrotlets before they were fully-grown members of the avian tribe.

McCabe was a strange bird himself—a left-hander born on a blustery leap day not all that long ago. In leap years he had reached the age of ten—still rapier thin, sweeping brown hair, brambly brows, a turquoise stud in his ear—lithe and lanky from his favorite sport—walking the hills and hollows of San Francisco. Quadrupling his leap years, McCabe had entered his forties without ever marrying, ostensibly free to govern his fate—clinging to his well-constructed, solipsistic life. He did however, share his bedroom with select male and female lovers, and the dream of the great American novel. His amorous liasons had authored his collection of first edition American literature, many in mint condition dust jackets—from Hawthorne, Melville and Twain to Hemingway, Fitzgerald and Faulkner, as well as contributors to the San Francisco literary scene—Robert Louis Stevenson, Jack London, Bret Harte, Dashiell Hammett, and the Beats. McCabe enjoyed playing with all of them, his slow hand pulling a random first edition from the wall of books to feast on the evocative dust jackets from the Lost Generation or the Harlem Renaissance—as erotic to him as stripping the clothes off a woman he intensely desired. He was untroubled by having such a precious collection of literature in a house that could go up in flames in minutes, consuming every word. He had been burgled twice, his first editions left undisturbed. The clueless intruders considered his foxing books, worth their weight in gold, as little more than musty wood pulp whose only value was to fill a shelf.

McCabe lived in a cottage of saw-cut bargeboards just above the sandstone cliffs of Telegraph Hill at the northeastern edge of San Francisco. His dwelling had originally been built by a bilious, one-legged sea captain just after the War Between the States. It had survived the Great 1906 Earthquake and Fire through the divine intervention of a dissolute squad of recently emigrated Italian peasants and Irish warehousemen. With the water mains ruptured, no water to be had, they covered the cottage's shingled roof with wine-soaked blankets and burlap, splashing buckets of vino rosso on the sides of the tinder-dry home, inoculating it against the holocaust of sparks and embers that consumed most of the hill.

The cottage was located just off the Filbert Steps on Napier Lane, a passageway that had once gently trailed down to the bay. Now it was a dead-end alley with a sheer hundred-foot drop to the streets below. The transformation of the hill began during the Gold Rush of 1849. For the hundreds of vessels whose crews had not jumped ship and lit out for the goldfields, a few blasts of black powder set in the hill yielded the sandstone ballast needed to stabilize the empty ship's return voyage home—leaving behind an armada of abandoned ships rotting in the bay.

The indiscriminate dynamiting of Telegraph Hill continued after the Gold Rush, its sandstone used for landfill, seawalls and grading of streets. Collateral damage was extensive. Houses were showered with rocks and debris. Streets and alleys collapsed into gullies and ravines. A secret plan by the quarrymen called for gradually buying up undermined houses for pennies on the dollar, then to completely flatten the hill, selling off the newly leveled land at premium prices. But after pitched battles between homeowners and the quarrymen, adjoined with lengthy court proceedings, all went quiet on the eve of World War I.

A former Hollywood stuntwoman, Grace Marchant, greened-up the hill after World War II, transforming the dynamited outcroppings into a dreamscape of ferns, fuchsias, trumpet flowers, midnight jasmine, banana palms, and the occasional explosion of red and purple rhododendrons—a gentle reminder of the scofflaw quarrymen who had nearly dynamited the hill to oblivion. As Marchant closed in on one hundred years of age, she too, passed from the garden. Her ashes were buried in her stairway paradise just down the alley from McCabe's home, where she now appeared in the form of a magenta rose—a burning bush nourished by her inspirational remains.

Napier Lane was the only surviving wood-plank street in San Francisco, running between a handful of cottages and a riot of garden greenery. It also served as a catwalk, each house having its signature cat, including McCabe's own black and white feline, Squad Car. It had wandered into his garden as a kitten, hiding underneath a loquat tree, mewing for a compassionate soul to come to its rescue. An older, emboldened Squad Car used to accompany McCabe along Napier Lane to the Filbert Steps, following him through Grace Marchant Garden to Montgomery Street. But lean and loathsome feral cats gradually curtailed Squad Car's excursions, unlike the mellow clowder of cats that lived on Napier, snoozing on the wooden planks warmed by the sun. It had been years since Squad Car had cruised beyond the sheltering verdure of Napier Lane.

Just when the cherry-headed parrots—Coneurs—arrived on Telegraph Hill, no one was certain. They were part of the avian order, Psittaciformes, that included not only parrots, but parakeets, macaws and cockatoos as well. Nomadic and adaptable, the parrots acclimated to ecological niches formed around exotic urban and suburban plantings of trees and shrubs. The brainy schmoozers had found a bowered niche around McCabe's cottage, their luminous green feathers camouflaged in the luxuriant loquat trees that grew in his garden. The parrots lived off the hill's non-native and subtropical foliage—a cornucopia of pine nuts, flowering eucalyptus, toyon and juniper berries, blackberries, bottlebrush, cherry blossoms, pear, plum, figs and apples—and most exquisite of all, the succulent pectin rich golden fruit from the loquat trees themselves.

By city ordinance, it was illegal to feed the parrots, but McCabe ignored the prohibition, setting out bowls of sunflower seeds and diced apples—just as he occasionally fed the raccoons, foxes, skunks, possums, even the occasional coyote, that inhabited the hill and crept through his nocturnal garden.

As to the clownish parrots—Red Headed Coneurs—they were a foot in length, differentiating splashes of red on their shoulders, sporting droll, down-curved hooked bills, tensile toes, and orange eyes with impenetrable coal-dark pupils. McCabe could identify every parrot by their distinctive markings. Often the parrots paired up, preening, grooming and bickering with each other for life. Sometimes they would dissolve their bonds and separate forever.

There was also a larger Coneur called Athena by the hill dwellers—her head the color of lapis lazuli. Despite the difference in the color of her crown, she was the leader of the contentious pack, and like McCabe, had always been single.

The parrots were originally from the tropical forests of northwestern Ecuador and Peru. Theories abounded how they arrived in the city—escaped a warehouse of smuggled birds, perhaps set free by a couple who were leaving town, or thrown out of the house for irascible behavior and general insubordination. Colonies of parrots lived in other parts of the country as well—in Florida and Louisiana over to Texas and Southern California. Similarly, their cousins the Monk parakeets, inhabited New York City. Peach-faced lovebirds from Africa established thriving colonies in Arizona. Down south in Los Angeles County, enclaves of feral parrots—lilac-crowned Amazons, macaws, cockatiels and rose-ringed parakeets put on a Hollywood show.

The parrots had gradually come to intuit McCabe's circadian rhythm, beginning with his workday as a columnist for the city's leading daily, the

Bay City Clarion. He rarely went to the *Clarion* offices in the old brick building just a few blocks away on the waterfront. Instead, he wrote his column in the afternoons at Vesuvio Café on the other side of the hill in bohemian North Beach.

When the siren on the waterfront's Ferry Building wailed at noon, the parrots roused their fractious selves, summoning McCabe even on the rainiest of days. Their rising crescendo signaled a collective determination that as soon as he left for North Beach, their traveling carnival could take flight across the city to Mission Dolores where food was also plentiful.

McCabe needed but three items to begin his workday—laptop, pen and cell phone. Occasionally he would forget letters to be mailed, curse his absent-mindedness, and return to the cottage. Such unexpected reversals caused frenzied invective among the parrots. Was this some sort of game? Was he really not intending to leave? Should they return to the garden? Ultimately, the flock had adopted a coordinated flight plan, looping round Coit Tower at the summit of Telegraph Hill, waiting to determine if he actually made it to the top of the Filbert Steps and continued on his journey. Once they were certain he was on his professional rounds, the flock as one interconnected mind would shriek a raucous farewell and fly off in ragged formation to Mission Dolores.

For McCabe there was no finer way to begin his workday than walking the carless wormhole of Napier Lane, up the Filbert Steps through Grace Marchant Garden. This day, upon reaching Montgomery he took a last inhale of Eden's air as the magic portal closed behind him.

Overhead, the parrots screeched good-bye.

CHAPTER TWO: NORTH BEACH CITIZENS

At Filbert and Montgomery lay the *Dark Passage* hideaway where Bogart and Bacall engaged in their secret assignations. Falsely accused of murdering his wife, Vincent Parry played by Bogart, had escaped San Quentin in a barrel. He was cut a new face by a plastic surgeon to foil the police while he searched for his wife's murderer. It was McCabe's favorite *film noir* movie, providing a mild frisson each time he followed the trail of bandaged Bogie struggling up the Filbert Steps. A life-size cardboard cutout of Bogart in a double breasted suit and fedora, front brim tilted downward, now stood in the window of the second story retreat, impassively staring him down.

Past the *Dark Passage* safe house McCabe reached the summit of Montgomery Street where the fault line of Victorian buildings from the post-Gold Rush era overlooked the financial district's high-rises below. He took the switchback stairs back down to a three story Victorian building at the corner of Green and Montgomery. The apartment had been the setting for the steamy trysts in *Basic Instinct.* Michael Douglas played Nick Cannon, a sex-addicted police detective. He and Catherine Tramell, an erotic writer and serial killer suspect, played by Sharon Stone, met at the apartment for their kinky cat-and-mouse games. McCabe savored the interrogation scene at police headquarters of Stone in tight white dress, sans panties, casually crossing her legs, revealing her most private and beckoning parts to the befuddled *Ess Eff Pee Dee* detectives. It always induced in him a wry smile. ***Fabulous money shot!*** thought McCabe.

Driven by his own basic instinct, McCabe turned right on Green and began walking down to Grant. The grip of the tropical side of Telegraph Hill gradually evanesced as if he were floating down from a gentle mescaline high. McCabe himself was no stranger to psychedelics, his last trip having been taken a decade earlier, a few months after joining the *Clarion*. The morning following that final excursion, still experiencing aftershock hallucinations, he thought ***Why not rip out a column on the discovery of LSD?*** As written below:

> LSD was by all credible accounts providentially discovered in April 1943, by Albert Hofmann, a modest, self-effacing research chemist at Sandoz Pharmaceutical in Basel, Switzerland. While experimenting with a rye fungus called ergot which could enhance memory function in the elderly, the unseen hand of God intervened, guiding Hofmann in synthesizing D-lysergic acid diethylamide tartrate. Inadvertently absorbing a small amount through his fingertips, the multiverse blinked open to Hofmann or so it seemed, presenting a glimpse of "an uninterrupted stream of fantastic pictures, extraordinary shapes with intense, kaleidoscope-like play of colours." More experimentation was obviously needed. Immediately! On himself! Days later he ingested 250 mcg of LSD at his laboratory, then hopped on his bicycle to return home to ride out the effects of his second visitation to this new and fantastical frontier. Hereinafter known as "Bicycle Day", Hofmann insouciantly pedaled through the streets of Basel, as the cobblestone streets began rippling beneath him. Upon reaching home, the mechanistic reality of his Swiss timepiece dissolved like the melting clocks in a Dali painting, "I lay down and sank into

a not unpleasant intoxicated-like condition, characterized by an extremely stimulated imagination."

The mind-altering genie, along with its atomic cousin, was out of the bottle. After the war, LSD was made available to research institutes and physicians as an experimental drug. The Deep State was not far behind. In the early fifties, the CIA began "Operation Bluebird" to investigate mind-control techniques using LSD, soon transforming the little bluebird into the secret program sinisterly named "MK-ULTRA". LSD unmasked its darker side on CIA employee, Frank Olson. Clandestinely given LSD, Olson believing he was going insane, freaked out and committed chromatic suicide, flinging himself from a New York City window.

By the mid-fifties, LSD characteristically slipped through the fingers of the CIA and began its civilian breakout. Aldous Huxley, having taken mescaline in 1954, published *The Doors of Perception*, and then tried LSD a year later. In 1957, Humphrey Osmond, who had been treating alcoholics with LSD, coined the word, "psychedelic". International conferences followed in 1959, and in that year Allen Ginsberg who had already written *Howl*, ingested LSD for the first time.

As the 50s passed into the 60s, Timothy Leary experimented in Mexico with magic mushrooms—psilocybin—his first psychedelic experience. Leary was a devotee of the Harvard philosopher and psychologist, William James. Several generations earlier James had authored *The Varieties of Religious Experience* exalting nitrous oxide that stimulates "the mystical consciousness in an extraordinary degree." Leary returned from Mexico to his tenured position at the Harvard Psychology Department. There he established along with Richard Albert, the "Psychedelic Research Project". At the same time, Ken Kesey on the West coast joined a parallel research project, volunteering for psychedelic drug experiments in Palo Alto.

In 1962, Leary took LSD for the first time, conducting the "Good Friday Experiment". He tried using it on prisoners to determine if it would reduce recidivism among the criminal element. It didn't. Terminally ill Aldous Huxley died in 1964 upon receiving his last request—an IV injection of LSD administered by his wife. And as to Mr. Leary? He was kicked out of Harvard.

The first illicit commercialization of LSD occurred in 1965 when Augustus Owsley Stanley III succeeded in synthesizing crystalline LSD. Mass production of "Owsley" acid soon followed. He charged two dollars a hit and became a LSD millionaire. Fueled by Owsley acid, Ken Kesey and his Merry Pranksters began holding Acid Test parties that morphed into a three day "Trips Festival" in San Francisco—Haight Ashbury becoming planet earth's short-lived psychedelic capital. But the legal production and use of LSD was as fleeting as a firefly. On October 6, 1966, one hour before a new law took effect outlawing the manufacture, sale or consumption of LSD, hundreds of hipsters gathered in Golden Gate Park dropping single, double, quadruple hits of acid. The *Ess Eff Pee Dee*, alerted to the protest celebration, looked on abjectly, some on contact highs. Neither mass hallucinations nor internal possession of LSD were crimes against the state.

The following year, Owsley came out with a special varietal—"Monterey Purple" for the Monterey Pop Festival at which Jimi Hendrix purple-hazed the crowd with a guitar–burning finale to the golden years of LSD.

At the corner of Grant and Green, a Weed on Wheels van, emitting a discordant aroma, both floral and skunky, was serenely parked, a luminous marijuana leaf bountifully emblazoning its sides. Weed on Wheels was a former MCD—medical cannabis dispensary—now selling recreational marijuana, and the only outlet that didn't have a fixed location. It floated round the city, neighborhood to neighborhood as it pleased.

Weed on Wheels held a question-and-answer session at lunchtime—an opportunity for the curious to inquire about the nature and benefits of the miraculous herb which was now being legalized in one form or another throughout America. A sign was propped up on the van, "Closed for Lunch. Open for Questions." Today, there were about a half dozen curious men and women waiting for the session to begin. The vendor was a spare, wiry man somewhere in his forties, long brown ponytail, goatee, a chandelier earring swinging from his ear. He wore a cool-tinted purple-blue cap emblazoned "Weed on Wheels", a green day-glow band looped round his neck. Just the week before, McCabe had devoted his daily column to door-to-door delivery of cannabis in the "Cool Grey City of Love".

A police car blithely slipped by as the cannabis marketeer began his lunchtime presentation. "Ladies and gentleman, I'm Dr. Bud. Thanks for stopping by today to hear about our town's newest rush—it's not the gold rush, and it's better than the silver rush—folks this is our very own Green Rush! Some even think of it as our newest bubble—a green bubble—a pot.com boom! As part of our *cannabusiness* selling recreational marijuana, we're asked by the city to provide outreach and education, to act as a guide to our unique homeopathic frontier. As you can see, we're a one-stop operation readily accessible to all. We're even ADA compliant—you can bring your wheelchair right up to our van for a buy! Talk about getting high, soon we'll be delivering direct to your bedroom window with our Green Hornet drone force!"

"We sell over thirty strains of high-quality cannabis: Juicy Fruit, Super Lemon Haze, Maui Wowie, Cannatonic. And we got a lot of other cannabis products too—edibles like brownies, pretzels, candy bars, teas, drinks, space cakes and Gummy Bear pops—*Bong Appétit*! And our vaporizers will evaporate your anxieties and our patches soothe your muscle pains! We also got extracts: tinctures, creams, balms, and sprays. And how about hemp wearables—shirts, hats and hoodies? Or our hemp infused shampoos for a little head tingle? And for those of you who are paranoid about the heat, we got specially made baggies, like the kind you doggie lovers use to keep our sidewalks clean—they hold in the odor—perfect for weed when traveling abroad or to an unfriendly state. There's no other plant remotely like it on the planet!"

"But this isn't a sales pitch—it's our educational outreach to the people of this beautiful city and to the millions of people who visit every year. Allow me one off-note: don't take edibles across state lines! And keep them away from kids—especially the candy colored edibles; it can take hours to produce a maximum high, so don't gorge out wondering when that high is gonna' kick in! All right, I'm here to answer your questions—make you *cannasseurs.* So don't be shy, what would you all like to know?"

An elderly black lady in a marsala-colored dress barked out in a deep South patois, "Young man, young man, where did all dis diffrent stuf cums from? Mah husband wuz a jazz musician. He smoked a little in the 50s and 60s. Gots yuz a little high, made yuz cough, burned yoz throat, nothin' fancies. Hear what I'm layin' down?"

"Bless you, Ma'am! It was folks like your husband who were the pioneers. Yeah they had it rough—the stuff they smoked I mean! And I know the Man was lurking—ready to pounce!"

"Wells, a matter of fact mah old man did gets busted once—in de early 60s at the Black Cat—downs da street—where he wuz playin' a gig. Between breaks dey'd goes out in de alley, relax, yuz know—take de edge off. De pawlice busted him! Only carrin' two reefers! Six months in Quentin he did for dat!"

"Ma'am, in a narrow lane beware your enemies! The *cannabigots* are still putting people in jail just for hanging with Mary Jane! It's because of people like your husband—jazz folks—that pot jumped to the Beats—a lot of them from right around here."

"Daz right," she snapped.

"They kept the flame alive. But the stuff was pretty much the same—comin' out of Mexico. My father was in college in the 60s. His favorites were Acapulco Gold and Panama Red. Then things began to change—you know the hippies..."

"Nothin' but white negras, dey wuz," she said imperiously.

"Those Bo-Ho hippies lit out for all parts of the globe. They walked the earth: Nepal—Kathmandu—Machu Picchu—boated up the Mekong."

"What's dat gots to do with mah question?" she asked sharply.

"Well, when they returned to America, they became *ganjapreneurs*—brought seeds–wondrous seeds—the spawn of marijuana from all over the planet. The plants were interbred by modern Mendelians. Now we have over 700 strains officially recognized in California alone."

"Well, I'll be! I wishes mah man wuz still alives!"

McCabe broke away and continued on his journey down Grant. His old friend, Stark was sitting on a beat up wooden chair with a sagging wicker seat in the doorway of an abandoned pizzeria. He was a "shopping cart soldier" from the Vietnam Era. At night he slept in the doorway on layered cardboard, covered in dirty blankets, his shopping cart parked diagonally at his feet creating a protected sleeping space. He had run through a small family inheritance. Now he made his living as a North Beach bard typing out poems on his old Olivetti Lettera 22 portable typewriter—streamlined, light and easy to use by reporters on assignment in the 50s. He called it "improv poetry". A hand-painted sign listed prices from simple haikus to sonnets. From time-to-time, McCabe ordered up some poetry that occasionally made it into his column for which Stark would receive a twenty-dollar bonus. At the moment, Stark was breezily typing out an obscure haiku on the Japanese Red Crown Crane Dance for a tourist from Sapporo.

McCabe nodded a quick acknowledgement and moved on. The police car from moments earlier had circled the block and pulled up beside him. Officer High was at the wheel. The window on the passenger side of the cruiser slowly slid down revealing a ventriloquist puppet dressed in a police uniform with a miniature police hat, a yellow badge sewn over his heart. Woody was his name. He called out to McCabe, blue eyes bobbing in his cherubic face, "Morning Daddy-o! Can you dig it?"

"Hey Woodster, what's happening?" laughed McCabe, game to the show as the police car meandered off down Grant, leaving McCabe without his usual opportunity at full-out rejoinder.

The saga of Officer Woody was one of the very first subjects McCabe had covered in his *Clarion* column. The police department began experimenting with "community policing"—engaging neighborhood groups in a dialogue about humane methods to fight and prevent crime. The *Ess Eff Pee Dee* had a long line of eccentric police officers, beloved by the neighborhoods but derided by the brass, among them, Officer Bob High who worked as a ventriloquist in his off-hours. High walked into the North Beach police station carrying his sidekick puppet dressed in a police uniform, declaring that he had the solution to community policing—Officer Woody. But it was not to be. After a few days riding shotgun with Officer High, Woody was silenced as if someone had put a bullet through his oaken heart. Police Chief I. M. Frost, bloodless as an ice cube, declaimed the puppet held the *Ess Eff Pee Dee* up to ridicule and disrespect. Woody was banned from appearing in the police station, riding in a police cruiser, or masquerading in a tiny police uniform. Impersonating a police officer they raged—a ludicrous charge that deeply offended Woody. If the *Woodster* ever showed his face at the station again, he would be exiled to the evidence room to languish forever until the termites reduced him to sawdust.

Hundreds of letters poured into police headquarters pleading for *Sir Woody*'s reinstatement. But the chief was unmoved, he couldn't see the wood for the trees. Defying the police brass, Officer High called a press conference presenting his *Woodiness* in full police regalia, pledging to take the matter to the ballot. Only the good people of San Francisco could make things right! On Officer High's dime, college students were paid to collect signatures for a simple one sentence advisory measure on the November ballot, "Should Officer Robert High be allowed to use Woody the Puppet in his police work?" The petitions were submitted to the Registrar of Voters, and the matter qualified for the ballot. High and the *Man of Wood* vigorously campaigned throughout the city—at candidate endorsement nights, bingo games, parades, and neighborhood festivals. That November the compassionate people of San Francisco granted a reprieve; by a vote of 52% to 48%, Woody was allowed back on the police force. At his victory celebration he spoke his own, most unwooden Gettysburg address:

> "My friends and supporters, tonight we have sent a message to our police department and to police throughout America. You may think me a dummy, but suspend your disbelief! Am I not a thinking, feeling person just like all of you?
>
> Don't I share the same aspirations and hopes as any normal human being? Would the city deny me my rightful place on our police force because I'm made of wood, not flesh and bone?
>
> You've given me back my freedom—restored my faith in democracy. Tomorrow we ride again!"

Farther along Grant, the aroma of Caffé Trieste's freshly ground coffee came floating on the breeze. It was here the howling, "angel headed hipsters" of the 50s had established their west coast hub. This noontime, it was filled with tourists lined up at the counter. The regular Trieste crowd showed up when the café opened at six, vacated by ten, and later returning at five. For the remainder of the day, tourists or the lone writer seeking inspiration from the hipster history patronized the café.

Many of McCabe's pals hung out at Trieste—*habitués* with political opinions stronger than a double espresso—mostly on the left, a few on the right, there being no moderates of any political stripe. Many were artists and poets earning less than ten thousand dollars a year, some on mental disability supplemented by the sale of poetry and paintings. There were also lawyers and politicians, architects and designers, house painters and handymen, physicists, astronomers and bug hunters, mendicants of marijuana and mad verse—espresso scholars all.

On the unusual day that McCabe rose early, he would join his pals at Trieste, buy a cappuccino or espresso, then squeeze into a spot at one of the tables looking out on Grant. The early morning men and women of Caffé Trieste were human incarnations of the parrots that lived by his cottage—chattering, commiserating, surreptitiously filching sections of each other's newspapers. McCabe was allowed but a few breathing moments before a question, observation or insult flew his way. He was expert at scanning the paper, picking out a headline, reading a paragraph or two, commenting on a comment, nodding in apparent agreement at the wildest speculation, perusing a few more paragraphs, sucked into a political disagreement between the far left and the anarchists, pose a question, triumphantly find a word for a crossword puzzle, stand up and shift places to allow someone to leave or sit down, sneak another look at the paper, be drawn back into communal brickbats—finishing off his coffee an hour later.

As McCabe crossed the intersection at Grant and Vallejo to Trieste, Loki jumped up from her outdoor table and embraced him. Named after the Norse god of mischief, she was in her late twenties—violet eyes, freckles on her forehead like the milky way, sandy blonde hair with mint green highlights. She wore a coat-of-many-colors vest, tight blue jeans and scuffed pink pumps. Loki organized beatitudes for artists and poets at the Live Worms Gallery just up Grant. She was the sole woman in North Beach who hugged him whenever they met. "McCabe, how are you?" She laid her head on his chest as if to check his heartbeat. "Are you good? The only person in San Francisco who has a café for his office. And your commute down the hill—the congestion, the road rage, the lack of parking! How do you manage?"

Loki was a practitioner of BDSM—in the west coast capital of kink. Occasionally, McCabe served up light BDSM in his column, including tales of Loki who inhabited a distinct subculture. She was a "bottom" or "submissive", but in fact was the "dominant". She particularly enjoyed performing public wax play, her putative "dom" lighting different colored candles, dripping them over her silk sheet stomach, rose sorbet breasts, modestly peached aureoles, and firecracker nipples, creating an endorphin induced high of sublime sub-frenzy. She adored as well—often indicated by her hanky codes—black sheet parties, pet play, cock milking, strap-on play, sensory deprivation, feet worship, tease & denial, and for occasional cash she would indulge in diaper porn—but no fisting, front or back—it was strangely discomfiting—a bit of a stretch. She would only engage in submissive exercises with a "service top"—the "top" only having apparent control, while in reality following instructions by the "bottom".

Loki's BDSM was based on the motto, "Safe, sane and consensual"—a clear delineation from sexual assault or domestic violence. The most important element was consent, a full awareness of potential risks and results, and the ability to make coherent judgments before entering into the arrangement. There was an implied contract on accepted practices and behavior, including a safe word: "Red!" or if gagged, a shaking of the head: "*Ah, Ah, Ah!*" by which the "dominant" would cease the action objected to by the "bottom". The most serious misconduct was ignoring the utterance of the safe word, the "sub" having revoked consent to continuing play by the "dominant". But the concept became somewhat muddied when the person uttering the safe word was in fact "topping" from the "bottom".

McCabe and Loki ritually dry-kissed as he administered a flinty slap to her taut blue-jeaned ass. Relinquishing her with a wicked smile, he went into Trieste, bought a double espresso, and threw it back like a shot.

It would soon be leavened by wine.

CHAPTER THREE: VESUVIUS ERUPTUS

Leaving Trieste, the scramble lights at Columbus and Broadway limned green, McCabe crossing over the boulevard to City Lights, the first all-paperback bookstore in America. City Lights was founded in 1953 by Lawrence Ferlinghetti, publishing anti-war, libertarian, and humanist works in the anarchist tradition of Thoreau. Its literary impulse was Buddhist as well, emerging from the World War II camps for conscientious objectors located in the mountains of Northern California and Oregon. From these post-war Bohemian seeds sprouted 50s Beat, which in turn provided the countercultural roots for the psychedelic 60s lurking just around the corner.

Across the alley from City Lights was Vesuvio Café where McCabe spent his afternoons as a *Clarion* columnist. Warm cool Kerouac ran beatitudinally between City Lights and Vesuvio—the alley that is—Jack having sloughed off his mortal coil in 1969. The alley was a mere stone's throw in length, honoring the Beat generation and its literary inspirations. It was proof as Beat author Herb Gold once observed, "Like ailanthus, the tree of heaven, Bohemia grows in any alley where there's a bit of fertile dirt and noninterference."

At the portals to Vesuvio was a reassuring epigram that greeted the wet-brained, hallucinating sojourner:

> When the shadow of the grasshopper falls across the trail of the field mouse on green and slimy grass as a red sun rises above the western horizon silhouetting a gaunt and tautly muscled Indian warrior perched with bow and arrow cocked and aimed straight at you it's time for another martini.

Kerouac had one such experience shortly after publication of *The Dharma Bums*. He received a complimentary letter from Henry Miller inviting him to visit his convict shack in Big Sur. Kerouac began his trip by fortifying himself with a drink at Vesuvio, then called Miller to say he would be slightly delayed, then hoisted another, made another call to Miller, continuing to drink until he was poleaxed. The two would never meet.

At the back of the Vesuvio was a narrow staircase leading to a tumble-down balcony that overlooked the bar scene, Impressionistic as absinthe drinkers in an 1880s Paris café. Tulip lamps sprouted from beneath the balcony, rivulets of flowering luminescence leaking through the stained glass windows onto Kerouac.

The women's bathroom was secreted off the balcony unlike the more spacious men's bathroom down an easy flight of stairs in the basement. The Beats had a misogynist streak, manifested in the woman's birdcage bathroom at the summit of Vesuvio. The ladies were forced to climb the vertiginous stairway, then upon entering the encapsulated space, duck or suffer a blow to their head from the low-slung ceiling.

The misogynist message was reinforced by a warning just inside the front door of the café, "BEWARE PICKPOCKETS AND LOOSE WOMEN." It was amplified by a sign beneath an arch-backed black cat sculpture above the back bar, "IT WAS A WOMAN WHO DROVE ME TO DRINK AND I NEVER HAD THE DECENCY TO WRITE AND THANK HER." Further to the status of women in the 50s, patrons were warned on the bar register itself, "OUR CREDIT MANAGER

IS HELEN WAITE. IF YOU WANT CREDIT GO TO HELEN WAITE, WE SERVE *DRINKS* NOT *DRUNKS*!"

Vesuvio also served as McCabe's office, where for more than ten years now, he had cranked out his columns each weekday afternoon, ensconced in the alcove looking out on Columbus Avenue. The alcove was reserved exclusively for him between noon and 5PM and for which his column was named—*McCabe's Corner.*

Upon entering Vesuvio, McCabe bee-lined to the alcove, set down his laptop then walked over to the bar. Ward, the daytime bartender was holding court to his minions. Like all North Beach bartenders he was a formidable psychotherapist as well, believing everyone was worthy of at least some level of pub analysis. Ward was a fixture in North Beach—a Viking god—barrel-chested, massive arms, tree trunk legs, curly grey hair, light blue eyes, and a trimmed grey beard. At 300 pounds, he was bigger than a Frigidaire, a fire hydrant of a man. He had spent several tours of duty as a Green Beret in Vietnam, engaging in special ops around the DMZ. His favorite weapon had been his Bowie knife, which if notched for kills would have exceeded a score or more. He still possessed the weapon two generations later. Now he used it in more peaceful pursuits: peeling strips of lemon rinds for martinis, using the butt end to mash down mint in his rummed-up mojitos. His favorite move was striking a match off the knife's granular handle, lighting his other hellish Martinique "rhum" concoction of sugar cane dynamite—"a flaming savage motherfucker"—equal notes of despair and debauchery.

The Green Beret in Ward still lurked within him like a crouching tiger in the twilight shadows of the forest. His predator nature occasionally emerged when called upon to enforce a ban on those permanently denied entry to the café. Etched into the concrete by the front door was Vesuvio's 86'd list—all those permanently barred from the establishment—fallen regulars. It included the names of Beat writers and poets—Gregory Corso and Bob Kaufman—also a convicted murderess named Janice Blue—and other miscreants whose behavior had so enraged the owners that they were exiled forever from the café. A test of whether the 86'd list was still a lifetime ban had occurred earlier that week. Jimmy Thudpucker, now in his sixties, strode into the café after a thirty year absence. Living on the streets had rendered him virtually unrecognizable. He ordered up a Kerouac—a madras and tequila. The drink had been concocted in honor of Jack's 1949 visit to Mexico City to meet up with gentleman junkie, William Burroughs who had fled the US to avoid a drug charge in New Orleans by an overzealous DA. As Ward mixed the Kerouac, he spied Thudpucker snake a ten-dollar tip from the bar. Ward feigned ignorance, casually serving up the drink. Thudpucker thanked him by name, paying with the snaked bill. Ward growled with a most delicate malice, "Jimmy, is that you?"

Thudpucker acknowledged same.

"Can't you read, fool? By the front door, you were permanently 86'd years ago! Sorry pal, there's no parole!"

Thudpucker pleaded for clemency, bleating, "Man, that was another lifetime! Come on, *amigo*!"

"Jimmy, there's no statute of limitations for murder, kidnapping, nor ungovernable behavior at Vesuvio! As far as I'm concerned they're all the same: heinous crimes for which there can be no redemption. You're outta here!"

"Hey man, I haven't even had my drink!"

"Which you didn't pay for, you petty-ass thief!" Ward came *rhumming* around the bar, grabbed Thudpucker by his rawboned neck and dragged him out the door like a wounded gazelle. Pointing at the 86'd list, Ward bellowed, "This is your tombstone, Jimmy! Your Boot Hill! You're just a shitty name in concrete that people walk on every day—for eternity!"

Today, the violence of men was far from Ward's mind as he engaged in flirtatious banter with Noë and Zoë, students at UC Berkeley Graduate School of Journalism. They often frequented Vesuvio when

McCabe was writing his column. Occasionally, he helped edit their stories, but had never gotten to know them well. Noë was of English and Portuguese descent, long brown curly hair, aquamarine eyes, lips of fire, full round breasts. Zoë was shorter than Noë, an intriguing mix of German and Japanese, vulnerable and supple, medium length chestnut hair, almond eyes, delicate nose and cherry lips. Today she wore a tight sweater that accentuated her smaller breasts. They shared a Macondray Lane apartment on Russian Hill overlooking North Beach, commuting to their classes at Berkeley.

McCabe rapped his knuckles on the hard beauty of the mahogany bar. Ward glanced up from his conversation with Noë and Zoë, "Hey, McCabe, good to see you, pal! One o'clock, you're cutting it close! If they knew you put your stuff together in a coupla' hours from here, *roguifying* with the likes of me, they'd slash your salary to a dime on a dollar and you still wouldn't deserve it!"

McCabe looked over at Noë and Zoë, nodding in their direction, then kicked some sand back at Ward, "I write it in my sleep—in the shower—when I'm walking down the street—by the time I get here, I'm beat right down to my socks!"

Ward jibed back for Noë's and Zoë's entertainment, "Hey pal, you skulk the bars of North Beach, your drinks paid for by wannabes passing on some pitiable rumor, hoping it will end up in your scurrilous column. Swells invite you to their Pacific Heights parties. Politicians buy you dinner. Women offer their bodies without precondition. You take god knows how many vacations. You stay up to three in the morning, rise late, get here in the afternoon, work till the five o'clock whistle blows, then kick back and suck off the urban chaos you helped create! I bet more readers of that scandalizing fish-wrap of yours have jumped off the bridge than I ever..." Ward paused, looking for the right diplomatic phrase, "than I ever—ever took care of in Nam."

McCabe throttled Ward's out-of-character circumspection, "Don't you mean disemboweled and left for dead?"

Ward ponderously leaned over the bar, Bowie knife gripped in his wrench of a hand, "McCabe, what do you want to drink?"

"Glass of Zin," reproved McCabe, believing he had jiu-jitsued Ward and won the match.

As Ward poured the glass of wine, Noë and Zoë moved down the bar saddling up to McCabe. Noë's eyes flicked up at him and dropped all in one motion, her mascara making her eyes pop, "McCabe, we're wondering if we could work with you in the alcove today?"

Zoë looked over Noë's shoulder, giving him a Gioconda smile, bright lips with a warm undertone, "We really won't bother you."

Noë slid her hand over his baby finger giving him a curious tingle. She pushed out her chest, enough to make McCabe pretend he hadn't already noticed. Her lips slowly curved, "We have pieces due tomorrow about how you old-media types write on deadline. You're the only person we know like that."

McCabe replied derisively, "The old media works just fine for me. Write what you know–a few facts, some narrative and editorial comment–boom and out."

Noë made a disappointed mouth. "Your columnizing sounds a little boring!" then cooed, "How about a corollary: let sex in?"

McCabe chuckled, breathing back his own breath. "Like I said, write what you know, Sweetie."

Zoë sat down on the other side of McCabe, the barest impression of her nipples hinting through her sweater. "We need to know everything from a column like yours to blogging, crowd sourcing, aggregating, social media, multimedia packaging, web design, content management, editorial and business dynamics. We have to master it all—from print to digital."

McCabe immodestly mocked, "I'll stick with my carbon-soaked

writing. What ever happened to good old Homeric storytelling, or is it AI producing journalism now?"

Noë batted the question back with a hard laugh, "Homer was a mnemonic journalist, who through tricks of memory recited his epic, and the thousands of years of evolution since then in how to tell a story. We need to be flexible enough to create a new paradigm beyond your Jurassic journalism."

Zoë added impulsively, smiling feintly, "Just let us see how you write your column. We'll link our laptops. Follow along. Maybe we could throw in a few words for the fun of it. Then we'll take our versions of your column to class, show how you work, our own interpretation. It won't be an intrusion." Zoë glanced furtively at Noë for assistance.

Noë's voice rose an octave, "McCabe, a coupla' hours watching you write. Come on, it's not a big deal! Your version goes to the *Clarion*, our version we take to class."

Ward slapped his hand on the bar, intoning, "Time is wasting," then did his John Donne takedown, "No man is an island, not even you, McCabe!"

Siren song, tie me to the mast, mused McCabe, ensorcelled. "Alright, what the hell, but remember, I'm on deadline!" But there were no salty shipmates to tie him to the mast.

Surprised at the ease of their apparent good fortune, Noë and Zoë dutifully followed him to the alcove, blithely setting down their laptops on the table, then sliding in on either side of him on the leather couch. McCabe warmed to their proximity. With a flicker of uncharacteristic nervousness, he took a quick sip of his Zin letting it tease his tongue, then popped up his laptop and powered on. Glancing over at Ward, he called over for the WiFi code which was changed each day to thwart the slackers who came into Vesuvio to use the WiFi, never buying a drink.

"B-E-A-T-5-7," barked Ward.

The year* On the Road *was published—created on Kerouac's old

typewriter on a single long roll of paper, ripping out his American odyssey. Now I got Word and the web at my fingertips anywhere I go. What a long strange trip, he reflected.

Even before reaching the café, shards of thought began forming a mental mosaic of the next day's column in McCabe's left brain. Upon crossing the threshold of Vesuvio, he transferred over to his "write" brain, which in a few hours time translated the fragments, bits and chips into a linear progression of paragraphs. Though he had written several thousand columns, there were times when his thoughts didn't cohere even for the most quotidian of subjects. Often just before deadline, the stress induced his best writing—bearing out his editor's admonition, "Write, don't edit!"

McCabe mumbled to Noë and Zoë, "Turn on. Tune in." ***They won't get it.***

Zoë replied with pretend offense, "We've studied the 60s! We know about McLuhan and that *Robespierre on acid*, Leary!" then turned it back on him, testing, "Is the *Medium the Message* or the *Massage*?"

McCabe retorted matter-of-factly as if in a batting cage, swatting out balls, "*Content* is the message. It's not eyeballs."

Zoë gently countered, looking at him through the tail of her eye, "We are what we type, McCabe, you're definitely not on fact-overload."

Noë moved even closer to McCabe, "Let's link our laptops. You have the collaborative writing program right? If not, we do."

McCabe nodded, went online, then clicked on his writer's collaborative app. The program was simply a blank page that linked through the same principle as instant messaging.

Noë and Zoë popped up their laptops, powered on, then went online. "What's your email, McCabe? I'll link us up," said Noë matter-of-factly.

McCabe smiled to himself. ***Careful, do it the other way.*** "*Ahh*—you give me your emails."

"Geez McCabe, you think we're going to put a bot on your computer or something?" sputtered Noë.

"What color?" asked Zoë calmly.

McCabe grunted, "Black"

"Mine's red," blurted Noë as if to grab the best sushi on the plate.

"Then blue for me," chimed Zoë.

"So what are we writing today?" asked Noë growing bolder.

"*Hah*—we? The mayor's race is this November. I want to write my impressions of the leading candidates," replied McCabe.

"How long is your column?" queried Zoë.

"About a eight hundred words, not counting anything you sneak in," snorted McCabe. "Column in final by 5PM—AND sent to the paper. So a good draft by 4:45, then quick edits and corrections. Out by five. If you want to throw in stuff, don't go overboard. I might keep some of it if it's any good. OK?"

Noë and Zoë nodded enthusiastically, ready to sail.

McCabe, began typing his column:

> God is in the firmament, and we don't begrudge the movement of the stars, but our fate is here with the fallen angel, in the Devil's playground—North Beach. The city has not one god, but many. Each follows his own, seeking not some universal meaning that holds for everyone everywhere on our urban playground—no single principle or set of values to which we should all play and pray. Three hundred neighborhoods on and between our forty-eight hills make up our discordant, beautiful city and each of them has a god.

A minute had elapsed. McCabe looked up, smiling smugly, "Anything to add, ladies?"

Noë and Zoë gave each other blank looks as if lost at sea.

McCabe laughed self-approvingly, "Thought so–writer's block?" He continued writing:

At the westernmost edge of the continent, San Francisco is the epicenter of earthquake country, at the edge of a tectonic plate that uplifts and shifts from generation to generation, continually renewing itself: funneling adventurers and vagabonds, robber barons, money drunkards and profiteers, painted ladies, romantics and dreamers into its peninsular melting pot. Oscar Wilde wrote that it is an odd thing, but everyone who disappears is said to be seen in San Francisco.

Noë emphatically hit her keyboard:

Funneling Actors and Absintheurs, Bloggers, Beatniks, Bohemians, Bibliophiles and Boulevardiers, Cooks, Critics, Comics, and Cynics, Gourmets and Gourmands, Poets, Playwrights, Programmers, Pimps, and Politicians, Rogues, Rebels and Revolutionaries.

Then Zoë followed on:

Singers and Songwriters, Wanderers and Wastrels, Cuisine Weenies and Oenophiles, Hell's Angels and Green Berets.

McCabe chuckled, "'Cuisine Weenies'? Now that's a keeper!" He began typing again:

Crammed onto a tiny finger of land at the end of the sunset trail, our bay-windowed city is an operatic stage, built on the fortunes of gold and silver. It can't be measured by its length and width, but by its texture and tapestry. It's a walking town. A fold-up bike nirvana. A sourdough city. A lubricated bubble of dark web entrepreneurs. A tech company conurbation of blue-jean billionaires. Its fog-swept state of mind carries the anguished groans of shanghaied sailors, arias of marooned opera singers and the conspiratorial whispers of turn-of-the-century oyster pirates.

Noë's and Zoë's fingers remained motionless over the keys, ready to engage.

McCabe continued:

In the mayoral race this November, the leading candidates are as diverse as the city is tolerant. There is our incumbent mayor who after a much publicized office affair trysting with his appointment secretary—the wife of his closet advisor—paid her off with funds earmarked for catastrophic health emergencies, ostensibly gave up drinking, quit the single life, and married beauty and wealth. He hasn't given up affairs...Our girlfriends say he's great in bed! Kinky too...Sign me up! Is there a waiting list? The mayor recently undertook a "major" initiative to combat global warming: Won't stop Mass Extinction...Or Ecocide! banning bottled water in city hall and outlawing plastic bags. While the earth burns! And drowns too... He needs a second term to further his long-term goal of moving onto Washington and the White House. Undemocratic malevolents... Plutocrats! Day-to-day administration of the city is but a weigh station on the road to higher office. Meetings with department heads are a nuisance and distraction from the dozen daily events designed to burnish his image to a red-hot glow.

Closing in on the mayor is the city attorney. He finds himself in the paradoxical role of having to represent the mayor and by extension the city for all the challenges and problems brought on by the mayor's personal and political indiscretions. He is the mayor's attorney who wants to be mayor himself—but if he became the next mayor, would he have a fool for a client? Don't think so...He'd no longer be city attorney, McCabe.

The third leading candidate, the city council president, ran for vice-president on the Green party ticket. A lesbian utopian socialist and romantic environmentalist, she has made her office a gallery for street and performance art. She is more poet than politician, too honest to be a public official, may lack the ego to win for mayor. We deserve the government we get...then Blow it up!

So far these are the three leading candidates vying for the office of mayor, unless a dark horse candidate joins the race. With five months to go to Election Day, we've rounded Cape Horn. There's dirt in the streets and the mines are played out. Wait...Social media is our Golden Age. A century ago, like a phoenix rising from the ashes, the city rebounded from the earthquake and fire that leveled and burned two thirds of the town—fiero de oro, a boom and bust metropolis. We need leadership that will speak to us of shared sacrifice, Don't pile more of your obligations on us...We won't be slaves to the Boomers! bringing out the best we have, Don't trust any politician...over thirty! appealing to the higher spirits of our nature, We're being proletarianized...One worker for every two retirees! Free us from the iron heel! Was that Kerouac? No the other Jack—London...showing us the future with honesty and clarity, Student loans paid off by sixty...We'll never afford a house! Social Security gone...Medicare too! making the painful cuts that are necessary, Continually raising our tuition...It's generational theft! restoring trust in city hall. Tax the rich...Then eat them! Take it to the streets...Like they did in the 60s!

Closing in on 5PM, McCabe concluded his column, "You keep your draft for class. My editor may give mine some tweaks. You'll see the final in tomorrow's paper." McCabe spent the next few minutes refining and streamlining *McCabe's Corner* then emailed it to the *Clarion*. With a flush of satisfaction he proclaimed, "It's a wrap. I kept Noë's 'beatniks, bohemians, bibliophiles and boulevardiers' and Zoë's 'cuisine weenies'. Now, can I get you guys a drink?"

Zoë: "Buttery Chard."

Noë: "Peppery Cab."

McCabe returned shortly with three glasses of wine, including an old vine Zin for himself, ready to lubricate. "That's how it's done—*bang, bang,* and out." He took a taste of his wine, swirling it in his mouth, picking up hints of jammy wonder and naughty schoolgirl. Noë took a quick sip of wine, and began typing again. He glanced at his laptop, still on:

Noë: McCabe let us be your muses!

Then Zoë typed: Caress your imagination...

Noë: Play with your writing!

Zoë: Be your laptop...

McCabe smiled and typed: The new journalism?

Noë: Tease our keys!

McCabe took a large sip of wine, then typed: QWERTY.

Zoë: Something more solid McCabe...

McCabe: The CONTENT is the message.

Noë: Hit our keys harder McCabe!

McCabe: !!!!!!!

Zoë: Who do you like? Give us some opening lines[1] from your favorite novels...

McCabe: *Lolita, light of my life, fire of my loins.*

Noë: We're twice as old as her, McCabe!

McCabe: *It was a bright cold day in April, and the clocks were striking thirteen.*

Zoë: 1984—it's back again...

Noë: Tell us everything!

McCabe: *If you really want to hear about it, the first thing you'll probably want to know is where I was born, and what my lousy childhood was like, and how my parents were occupied and all before they had me, and*

1. See End Notes, pp. 222-223.

all that David Copperfield kind of crap, but I don't feel like going into it, if you want to know the truth.

Zoë: Oh yes, Catch Us in the Rye…

McCabe: *All children except one grow up.*

Noë: Peter Pan McCabe?

Zoë: Are we your heroines?

McCabe: *Scarlett O'Hara was not beautiful, but men seldom realized it when caught by her charm as the Tarleton twins were.*

Noë: Oh Rhett, carry me up that staircase every time!

McCabe: *Time is not a line but a dimension, like the dimensions of space.*

Zoë: In a Cat's Eye it is…

Noë: Book us McCabe, book us hard…

McCabe: What about my column?

Zoë: We feel your beautiful column…

Noë: Yes, yes, give us your hot, hot column!

McCabe: %=========>>

Zoë: Ohhh! We barely know you…

McCabe: &&&

Zoë: How did you know? Our favorite position too…

Noë: Don't stop, don't ever stop!

McCabe: No deadlines???

Zoë: How do we look?

McCabe: *It was love at first sight.*

Noë: You're a good Catch Two Two, McCabe!

Zoë: We're getting close McCabe…

Noë: We can feel your end!

Zoë: Fill us up—every last drop…

McCabe: ^^^^^^^^^^^ *Arrgh!*

Noë: It doesn't get better than that!

Zoë: Give us your ink, McCabe…

Noë: Every last drop!

McCabe: ***It was the best of times, it was the worst of times...***

Zoë: Something more modern, Dick...

McCabe: *In my younger and more vulnerable years my father gave me some advice that I've been turning over in my mind ever since.*

Noë: The Great McCabe!!!

Zoë: Soft commas,,,,

McCabe: *How,,,,,,I love thee,,,,,,let me count,,,,,,the ways,,,,,,*

Noë: DEEP CAPITALS!

McCabe: *A SCREAMING COMES ACROSS THE SKY.*

Zoë: We love Gravity and Rainbows too...

McCabe: *A story has no beginning or end; arbitrarily one chooses that moment of experience from which to look back or from which to look ahead.*

Noë: Never End our Affair!

McCabe: *Call me Ishmael.*

Noë: Great White Obsession!

McCabe: *In the late summer of that year we lived in a house in a village that looked across the river and the plain to the mountains.*

Zoë: Farewell, always keep us in your Arms...

CHAPTER FOUR: SEMPER FI

His column completed, McCabe kicked back and gazed meditatively across Columbus at the afternoon light shimmering off the gabled windows of Tosca Café. Traffic was thrumming.

Ward lumbered over to the alcove, setting a glass of Zinfandel down on the table. "More libation from the wine dark sea to fuel your mad Odyssey!" McCabe made for his wallet but Ward waved him off.

Noë and Zoë were in animated conversation with a couple of spruce guys at the bar. Proustian ripples of memory flooded his brain, cueing up grooves of things past—to return to the lighter gravity of his twenties—his *La Bohème* period before the long march of a thousand columns into his forties.

There was a rap on the alcove window. It was Max Kepler, senior editor at the *Clarion*. Vesuvio was the watering hole of many reporters from the paper. Max looked distressed, in a panic. He'd started at the *Clarion* in the mid-70s after serving in the marines, covering sports, entertainment, local politics. Max edited people, not copy. He valued writers who led with their personality.

Max had written a family biography of his Montana upbringings. As a boy he had known Ernest Hemingway who hired Max's father as a fishing guide during America's Golden Era of Fishing. When Max turned ten he accompanied them to the headwaters of the Yellowstone River fishing for cutthroat trout. Hem had given Max a hand-made rod that he found too stiff for his style of fishing. The rod lacked the whip-like flexibility for the sinuous casts to put the fly down in the bubble lines and distant pocket water where the elusive cutthroats hold and feed. Now Max had the rod displayed above the fireplace in his living room on Telegraph Hill. It served better for catching conversation.

Max bowled through Vesuvio's double doors, unhinged. His face was craggier than Montana's Bitterroot Mountains, softened by a salt and pepper beard. He shot a wild look at McCabe, apoplectic, "Give me a second, I need a drink!" He ordered a bourbon and water, then walked over to the alcove, slumping down at the table across from McCabe. He hissed like a cornered timber rattler, "Remember a couple of months ago when we were told our jobs were being 'redefined' and we all had to reapply for new positions and complete job applications?"

McCabe replied tentatively, "Yeah, I just wrote down, 'Columnist'. Never heard another word."

"We aren't you, McCabe! They're afraid of your sad ass! Anyway, we had to justify our existence at the paper, explain our 'new media skills', be interviewed by human resource consultants. Groupthink Twitter mobs and meme wars, tweet first, think later mentality—turning us into digitally focused bits and bytes—everyone in their own little self-absorbed niche!"

"At least they didn't ask you to bend over," quipped McCabe.

"Yeah, well we did today," Max replied brokenly. "We were summoned to the publisher's suite. If they handed you a thick envelope it meant you were gone, explaining your lay-off and severance. A thin one offered you a job. I got the fat one! Hell, we've all been laid off: news editors, copy editors and backfielders—editing layers gone—and bureau chiefs, a bunch of reporters—over a hundred people! They put us through this excruciating process! Toyed with us! Covered their ass! Then threw us under the bus!"

The impact of the *Clarion* layoffs ricocheted off McCabe. He had no family, no siblings, no children. His parents had passed some years before. His *Sanframily* friends at the paper were it—a tribe of street-wise writers and reporters he had labored with for years. "A goddamn print apocalypse—shit!" was all he could muster, his throat tightening, the pillars of the temple of journalism seeming to collapse round him.

Max began to calm as the bourbon entered his veins. "Thcy explained it as 'critical cost-saving measures…a comprehensive restructuring plan.' They expect major concessions from the unions, probably more layoffs. Ramp up the digital side. Dumb down the paper. Consolidate editing and layout. Share production and administrative costs. Abandon some beats entirely, eliminate some sections, merge others. Draw in big, addicted online audiences—hook 'em on short news cycles turning it into visual journalism—no such thing as print deadlines anymore."

"They even told me only half in jest that journalists are killing journalism! What the hell does that mean? Give readers what they want? Really want? When they want it? How they want it? Not wasting money on what they don't really want? A disinformation ecosystem? Bot-based manipulation? In which case, why believe anything? What are we supposed to do, stop writing in-depth pieces, stop investigating, stop probing, stop asking questions? Never leave the office for on-the-ground journalism? And if their digital realignment doesn't work, they're threatening more layoffs—even close the paper. Maybe it's all a bluff to extract concessions from the Guild—all I know is that I'm out of a goddamned job!"

There was a pause, Max catching his breath, before he continued to rip away, "They gave us one-month severance—one lousy month—didn't even offer us buyouts! Some of us may find another job, but where media priorities are—slim chance! I'm ready to retire anyway, but the others have years left." Max paused, "Years...", his cracked voice trailing off.

Several more ink stained wretches from the *Clarion* straggled into Vesuvio, marinated in gloom. They ordered drinks then joined McCabe and Max in the alcove. April, who covered the port and parks for the *Clarion*, sat down next to McCabe, squeezing his hand, giving him a deeply wounded look. She was in her early sixties, twenty years McCabe's senior, with the cutest dimpled cheeks as if still holding onto her childhood. They had an affinity of which few were aware. Shortly after joining the *Clarion*, he had attended a boozy holiday party at the newspaper offices. Later that evening the newbie and April had ended up flopping around in bed back at her North Beach apartment. Since that encounter they had settled into a friendship colored by the memory of that one night of sloppy holiday passion.

April had two grown children, raised after her husband had died in a bizarre car accident following the birth of their second child. Her husband had also been a reporter at the *Clarion* where they had met. He was a hard charging, whiskey-loving investigative reporter who had driven in the early morning hours the wrong way onto the Peninsula Ridge highway just south of the city. In an irony that had added to the tragedy, he had been struck head-on by a newspaper truck—a *Clarion* truck.

April had never remarried. Her hair, now gone grey, hung down to her waist in a long braided ponytail. She was barely five feet tall. Her old fashioned horn-rimmed glasses reinforced her utter lack of vanity. She was dedicated to writing for the *Clarion*, often working twelve, fourteen hour days, always clutching a reporter's notebook. April was notorious for never getting her pieces in on time, always searching out that one last fact, one more interview, plodding and careful to a fault. She asked McCabe in her sweet Northern Mockingbird voice, "So I guess you heard. What about you, Tom? Are you part of the saved or the damned?" smiling in mock concern.

VESUVIO

McCabe responded vaguely, assuming he wasn't part of the massacre, "Haven't heard anything, sent in my column, nothing, not a word..."

"McCabe they'd never let you go," interjected Joyce, who had been the *Clarion*'s lifestyle editor. "You're money, we're not."

Robert, the movie and music critic, added dispiritedly, "She's right, McCabe. You're syndicated—part of the *Clarion*'s brand. How many people actually read our by-lines or remember our names? None of us are immune, maybe not even you. Readers are getting younger—skimming your column off their cell phones, and while doing something else at the same time. They want things fast and short which makes your column ideal, I guess. But good lord, ask them to sit down and read a paper for an hour or so would be equivalent to a month-long trip down the Amazon."

"Combine that with real-time analytics—they know exactly how many people are reading our stuff and for how long—if you don't make the grade you're gone—expendable!"

April joked ruefully, glancing at McCabe, "Next they'll offshore the columnists!"

Max slipped back into the conversation, now with the first hint of the phlegmatic, "Look, we can't go backwards. Traditionalism can be an albatross I suppose, but that doesn't mean print is doomed. It's a question of how news is gathered and disseminated. Television and radio still piggyback on us. We're still the gatekeepers of content. Digital platforms are useless without content!"

Robert shot back, "Brave rhetoric, Max—the *Clarion* used to be fat and happy, now it's losing a million dollars a week. Its fixed costs are unsustainable. Print is a drag on earnings. Pure play, undiversified print companies won't last much longer. Reader metrics will drive coverage."

"Look back to the birth of print. It wasn't some lofty humanist medium. Gutenberg never found a way to profit from his invention. He needed huge amounts of capital just to publish his bible. He died bankrupt. It took decades for someone to figure out how to make money off movable type. All those inflammatory pamphlets, ignorant screeds, religious tracts, posters and handouts required hard news—sensation—excitement. Once they figured that out, a decentralized, street-oriented press that could actually make money evolved."

"How many people under 30 actually read a daily? It's tweets, blogs, and YouTube clips. Do you really think when they get older they're going to start paying for dead tree journalism? We're just part of the old brick and mortar. Look around this café—WiFi séance and laptops!"

Max removed his glasses, massaging his temples as if trying to alleviate a severe migraine, dispassionate, "This isn't about pixels over print. It's not how you read, but what you read. Newspapers are an indispensable organ of free society. We make order out of chaos. We're sitting here in a café. Do you think cafés sustained themselves over a cup of java? Hell no! They proliferated because that's where people came together to read newspapers—a conscious pause to consider a coherent representation of reality—as they're now calling it tautologically: "fact-based" journalism. It was a revolution in thought, shaping the way people felt about their own lives, and what they expected from their government. News wasn't only read but spread, like internet discussion forums. By the 1680s coffee houses were considered seditious."

"Some still are," quipped Joyce looking round Vesuvio.

Max rolled on, beginning to feel refueled, "This old media, new media dichotomy isn't it. The truly old media began around 50 BC in Rome with Cicero and his wax tablets: the first iPads. For longer distances, papyrus was used: lightweight, informal and as about as secure as WiFi. The onset of printing left monks adrift in their scriptoriums with their illuminated manuscripts. The sixteenth century had their handwritten poems: Twitter of the day. The Age of Luther had its ballads and woodcuts: early YouTube. The 17th century had its pamphleteers during all those religious wars: the early bloggers. Thomas Paine's *Common Sense* went viral. The invention of the steam printing press allowed for ad-heavy, cheap papers: our media. Then the browsers gave us access to the web. It took a couple of decades to really take over, and here we are crying in our beers and out of a job!"

Robert snapped at no one in particular, "We're screwed! Information is free! That's its natural tendency! Like water. You can try and restrain *Free.* File lawsuits to protect your stuff, but in the end *Free* is the future. Infinite disorder—it's a bunch of bloggers: ephemeral, unedited, confused, distorted—click bait—reading a sentence counts as much as reading the whole article. A tweet from President Groper makes *Newspeak* headlines around the world! Who cares if it's unrefined and unreliable? They sure as hell don't! Everyone his own alt-reality editor! Unless we adapt, we're all going to share the same fate! No newsprint. No news racks. And we'll be as broke as Gutenberg! Who wouldn't want their news served up *Free* on a digital platform—searchable, aggregated and repackaged as original content—pictures and video, interactive, linked to background material and other news stories—hours, minutes old?"

Max's storm clouds began to part, "You know damn well web content can't make it without paid reporters. The Internet is still subsidized by the old economy. We'll always be the backbone of journalism. What's a city without a newspaper? How can you tell which town you're in without one? Papers paint the city. The presses will always roll and the news is always gonna break. But when it comes to straight up reporting we're in a transition between evaporating print prosperity and questionable digital profits. Come on, we need to brainstorm, come up with our own model! We could start our own paper: owned and operated by us!"

Robert retorted, "And lose a million a week like other *newsosaurs*?"

Max's eyes narrowed, "No, a smaller paper, maybe sixteen pages."

Joyce queried the table, "What about grants, subscriptions?"

Robert grimaced, "By the time we got that kind of start-up financing, we'll all be dead. You have to try and make it on *Free* somehow."

Max double-clicked his fingers, "Remember that guy who ran for city council last year? He took public campaign financing and used it to put out a paper. He hired a bunch of writers. There was no advertising—no profit and loss. The city paid for most of it, matching private contributions at ten to one...ten to one! It was basically a city-funded operation."

Robert smirked, "I vaguely remember, and the guy got his ass kicked in the election. His paper was so well disguised it didn't even look like campaign literature. No one ever got the fact he was running for office."

"You're missing the point," replied Max. "He published a paper and never lost a cent. He put out whatever he wanted with enough about his own campaign to justify using public financing to underwrite it."

Robert slapped an oar in, catching Max's drift, "In other words we leverage *Free*?"

"Exactly! It was a beautiful thing—perfectly legal—pretty much all freelance journalism with a page or two of his campaign ads, which of course he didn't actually pay for—the city did. It was basically a free paper with writers letting it rip."

"We could do the same thing?" asked April, her curiosity kicking into gear.

Max nodded emphatically, "We find someone who's game, got some credibility, run him—or her—for office. We take public campaign financing. Pay ourselves a salary and put out a paper!"

Perplexed, "Run for what office?" asked Joyce.

Max didn't miss a beat, "Why not mayor—this November?"

Robert scoffed, "Who'd do that? We'd need someone who can at least look like they've got a fighting chance. And they're going to do it for us? Ain't no such person. Doesn't exist."

McCabe had drifted into another zone as the discussion went back and forth across the alcove. Suddenly he began tensing like his cat, Squad Car, awakening from a doze on the warm planks of Napier Lane, hearing some far-off sound—straining to determine if it portended danger.

Joyce gave McCabe the briefest of looks, "It would have to be someone who knows city politics, knows the players, isn't intimidated by city hall!"

The lightening of their mind storm illumined the alcove. As if a clap of thunder had jolted him from a reverie, McCabe realized too late that the opportunity to redirect the discussion in another direction had been lost. He pursed his lips, looking around the table: ***Maybe I'm wrong—maybe they're not thinking what I think they're thinking—maybe.*** But all eyes were upon him. ***God almighty! So who is going to broach this insane idea, which one of you, jokers?***

It was sweet angelic April, a virgin to all evils. "Tom, why don't YOU run for mayor? What material you'd have for your column—an insider's look at running for mayor of San Francisco, with all the farce and pageantry of a three ring circus!"

McCabe gave April a skeptical eye. ***Here comes the pile on.***

Robert's dour demeanor changed to sunny-side-up, "Intriguing idea!" adding collegially, "We all got time on our hands."

Joyce jumped on the freight train, "It'll give us some breathing room till we find something else. We'd be our own bosses—our own editors!"

Then Max lassoed them in, "You all can't be a bunch of journalistic cowboys doing unedited stuff! It wouldn't be that loose for god's sake! We still need editorial oversight—good clean writing!"

McCabe was aghast. ***Max has already started running the paper.***

Max expanded the beach head, "We'd have to find some inexpensive space. We'll put out a weekly, or maybe three times a week—do daily updates on our website."

Robert cheerleaded, "Sounds doable."

April closed with a simple directive, couched as a question, "Tom?"

McCabe muttered, outgunned, "I appreciate being consulted."

Joyce pleaded, "Come on, this will be your show!"

"That's ludicrous! I'd have to whore myself for contributions. Walk precincts. Do bus stops. Candidate forums. A thousand questionnaires.

Kiss everyone's ass. Go to brain-dead endorsement nights all over town. Listen to every self-indulgent complaint and off-the-wall gripe imaginable. I'd have to debate—can you imagine me debating? I'd lose my weekends—my weekends! I'd have no free time! You're out of your minds!"

Max tried softening the cram-down, "McCabe that wouldn't be the game plan. You'll be the publisher, or your campaign would be, that's all. Don't worry about all the other stuff. Just cruise through it, write about it in your column."

April nursingly added, "Suffering is optional, Tom. You might actually enjoy it!"

Max's demeanor continued to brighten, "You wouldn't really run for mayor, just pretend to. We'll help you raise an initial ten grand, then we apply for public campaign financing. The city matches it ten-to-one. *Bam!* We got over a hundred thousand right off the bat! Then we use the paper to raise more campaign contributions, matched again by the city—like a perpetual money machine!"

McCabe trying for a desperate 15th round knockout countered, "The *Clarion* would object to me publishing my own paper."

Max quickly assured him, "Who cares? We'll run the shop. You don't have to do a damn thing!"

McCabe fell back, regrouping, "But I'd have to run to lose. If we undertook this bizarre scheme of yours, I'm sure as hell not going to try and win! We'd have to make sure I lose!"

Max smirked, "If you actually say what you believe, and we write what we think without having to worry about publishers or advertisers—taking it to the margins—we'll look so nutty, no one—*no one*—except a few kooks, will vote for you! People don't want the truth! Right now we sugarcoat it: the graphics, the photography, columns like yours, food and wine sections, sports. It all makes reality go down easier." Max clenched his jaw, "All that's really out there is PAIN—*PAIN*, and the voters don't want to hear about it!" Max seemed to be taking malicious pleasure in throwing out the word "PAIN", like the old marine he was. "If you speak the truth on PAIN you won't get elected. And, if you suggest a bunch of utopian ideas to alleviate the PAIN, they'll think you're crazy and won't vote for you either! You can't possibly win! It's guaranteed!" concluded Max triumphantly, if not quite believing his own analysis.

April took the hand-off, looking for closure, "Will you do it, Tom?"

McCabe waved them off, "A bailout for laid-off reporters paid for by the city? Not exactly a sustainable model!"

April gave him a reassuring look, "We run it till the election on city monies, then maybe try to turn it into a sustainable enterprise. We have enough time to build a paper that will survive on its own—or just move on. A few months—it's not that long!"

McCabe looked over to the bar for respite, but Ward was staring him down, his admonition from the afternoon still reverberating, "Time's awaiting, no man is an island!" Ward the Green Beret, Max the Marine, April of the briefest affair, his other colleagues at the *Clarion* had him surrounded. Once they were with you they never left your side. *Semper Fi*. His pals were in trouble. He might be too, he just hadn't taken a bullet yet.

A fire engine careened by, followed by a police car. Both stations were located a few blocks up Columbus. The sirens faded. Desultory conversation continued round the table. Men and women in a palette of khaki and grey-colored suits walked by, migrating from the financial district. McCabe slipped into unsettled rumination. The *Clarion* to its credit had never tried to censor him, never spiked a column. But, he'd been churning out a column for years now and was growing restless with his performance art. Why not write less hurriedly, de-emphasize all those active verbs, be less of an opinion writer, write with more reflection, drop out of the 24/7 news cycle for a time? He stared distractedly at the traffic on Columbus. ***Why not, why the hell not?*** He impulsively stood up and with a glorious sense of indiscretion mounted the dock to plead insanity. "Let's jump through the looking glass!" he yelled exultantly.

Everyone was momentarily stunned, incredulous at McCabe's apparent commitment to the crazy enterprise. Settling down with the assistance of several more rounds of drinks, there ensued an extended, chaotic discussion on starting the paper, raising campaign monies, putting together some kind of campaign platform.

The conspiracy had been launched.

The streets began to darken. The *Clarionistas* slowly decamped from the alcove. He was alone again in *McCabe's Corner*, feeling magnificently free—and hungry—ready to split Vesuvio. People were two and three deep at the bar. Another bartender had taken over for Ward. Noë and Zoë emerged from the crowd. They had already heard the news about the *Clarion* lay-offs and his agreeing to run for mayor.

"Hey, McCabe," said Noë.

He was surprised they were still at Vesuvio. "Hi guys, what's up?"

"You need–*ah*–you need…" said Zoë hesitantly.

In almost the same breath, Noë completed their thought, "Campaign managers!"

CHAPTER FIVE: CHINATOWN

The following day, the city's newest mayoral candidate unaccustomably rose with the East Bay sun. The parrots chattered deliriously in the backyard loquat trees, having heard the news of McCabe's dark horse candidacy. Squad Car, curled up on the bed, barely raised his head, irritated by the early rise.

After showering, McCabe cleaned up the kitchen, washing a few dishes. Above the sink, Charlotte the spider had woven an intricate web, hanging unconcernedly among its silken threads. It had been living there for almost a year now, catching the occasional insect that flew into the house. The arachnid's name had originated with the book, *Charlotte's Web*, which had been read to McCabe by his kindergarten teacher, affectionately called the "Spider Lady". At the end of the school year she had admonished them, "Never harm a spider," reinforced a few years later when he learned from *Huck Finn* that killing spiders is bad luck. He had assiduously followed Huck's and the Spider Lady's advice ever since. Each month he applied a wet cloth around Charlotte's lair, leaving the web and recent catches—a sustainable arrangement that required no food be bought, no vet bills paid, no refreshing the water bowl. The spider wasn't a nuisance to be exterminated. It was as much part of the tree of life as McCabe himself, the parrots, his cat Squad Car—and all the wild creatures on the twilight side of Telegraph Hill.

McCabe went to his front yard and picked up a copy of the *Clarion.* There were no edits to *McCabe's Corner.* Noë's and Zoë's additions had survived.

Next to *McCabe's Corner* in bold headline was an article about the paper itself—"Clarion Lays Off Hundred Employees". The paper described its worsening financial situation, the depressed conditions of the newspaper industry, competition from web-based advertising, contemplated cost-cutting actions, including the sharing of printing and distribution facilities with other Bay Area papers. Hearing nothing from the *Clarion*, McCabe's vague concern that he might have been laid off had waned since Vesuvio.

He left his cottage around eight, walked down Napier Lane, up the Filbert Steps, over Montgomery to Green, then down to Grant, turning left to follow the smell of Caffé Trieste's roasting coffee. A peregrine falcon shadowed him in arching circles, knowing that parrots were often nearby. The falcons loved to cleave the parrots almost as much as the plump pigeons that brainlessly pecked at bread crumbs outside North Beach cafes and bakeries. Occasionally, McCabe had watched delightedly as a flotilla of parrots passed noisily overhead, only to witness their formation skewered by a lightening snag of a falcon or hawk. No one was invulnerable to a blind-side hit.

Caffé Trieste was the first espresso house on the West Coast, opened in the Beat 50s. Across the street was the shrine of St. Francis. Poets Plaza ran between the café and shrine. The piazza was created by Lawrence Ferlinghetti who had a vision of an urban plaza, a secular yet spiritual oasis dedicated to the poets of the world. Located on Vallejo Street between Grant and Columbus, it was a curious combination of street names for a plaza of peace—Grant, head of the

Northern armies in the American *Götterdämmerung*, Columbus, the lead voyager on the Spanish *apocalypto* in Mesoamerica, and Vallejo, the last *comandante* of the Mexican province of Alta California.

The plaza honored poets ancient and modern, including Homer the Blind Bard, as well as St. Francis, considered by many the first Italian poet. Incised in the paving stones were quotations from Shakespeare, Whitman, Shelley, Keats and Yeats, Angelou and local Beats—Rexroth and Kaufman—and Dante, "Abandon All Hope, Ye Who Enter Here". The plaza, only one hundred fifty feet in length, was set in alternating bands of grey and white sandstone pavers patterned after the great Umbrian piazza of St. Francis of Assisi. The design had been kept simple, avoiding visual noise and architectural distractions. Olive trees were planted on each side of the plaza. At either end were granite benches, one to watch the sunrise, the other to watch the sun set. Marble benches lined the sides of the plaza including a couple of stone chess tables. A podium of burnished brass stood in the center of Poets' Corner near the entrance to Trieste, used for poetry slams and recitations, and occasionally by a drunken poet without audience engaging in a midnight howl.

Max was sitting on the sunrise bench, africano in hand, reading the *Clarion*. A flock of pigeons meandered about the plaza searching for pastry crumbs. McCabe crossed over Grant, greeting him, then went into Trieste. Iolanda, closing in on eighty, was working the counter. She had emigrated from Trieste forty years before and took a few of the morning shifts. She peered at him through her oversized tortoise glasses, "*Bello*, what are you doing here so early? Espresso, yes?"

"*Grazie, Bella.*" McCabe looked round the café. He nodded to his pals then took his espresso back outside joining Max on the bench. At the foot of the bench was an admonitory Ferlinghetti poem in brass lettering set in the sandstone pavers:

POETRY AS INSURGENT ART.

MAKE IT NEW NEWS. WRITE

BEYOND TIME. REINVENT

THE IDEA OF TRUTH. REIN-

VENT THE IDEA OF BEAUTY.

IN FIRST LIGHT, WAX POETIC.

IN THE NIGHT, WAX TRAGIC.

LISTEN TO THE LISP OF

LEAVES AND THE RIPPLE OF

RAIN. THROUGH ART,

CREATE ORDER OUT OF THE

CHAOS OF LIVING. IF YOU

WOULD BE A GREAT POET,

DISCOVER A NEW WAY FOR

MORTALS TO INHABIT THE

EARTH. IF YOU WOULD BE A

POET, SPEAK THE TRUTHS

THAT THE WORLD CAN'T

DENY. IF YOU WOULD BE A

POET, INVENT A NEW

LANGUAGE ANYONE

CAN UNDERSTAND.

Max appeared curiously relaxed to which McCabe cautiously observed, "You look better than yesterday, my friend."

Max raised the palms of his hands skyward and smirked, "Is there a choice?"

McCabe caressed the granite bench as if it were a woman's supple back. He looked over at the fading yellow rectory next to St. Francis church. On the roof stood four weathered wooden owls, stoic sentinels intended to frighten away pigeons—accomplishing the opposite, providing convenient perches for the birds. Underscoring the owls' impotence, the sidewalk below the rectory was speckled with pigeon droppings. The peregrine falcon, color of smoke, barred feathers on its chest, flew above the plaza. Spreading its wings to break, talons curled, it alighted on one of the gold crosses atop the twin spires of the church. The angel of death briefly angled its head in McCabe's direction, then in an effortless sally sprung from the cross. Space compressed, pigeons scattered across Columbus Avenue leaving in their wake a talon-clenched explosion of ticker tape feathers and the choked screech of an older, incautious pigeon. Seconds had elapsed.

Max smiled unawares, "I love this plaza, it's so peaceful in the morning."

"I read about the lay-offs in the *Clarion*," McCabe said simply.

"Yeah, I never thought I'd be reading about my own layoff," countered Max mordantly.

"Nor will you be reading your own obituary," joked McCabe.

Max smirked resignedly, "Unless I'm Twain." He added more seriously, "Are you still up for this venture?"

"We're already down the rabbit hole, Max."

"Good, I figured you were still game!"

"You're mad as a hatter, what do we do now?"

"We need to find some space. I figure we'll have about a dozen people working for the paper in one capacity or another, maybe a half dozen working full time, the others as necessary. We don't need a bunch of offices, just one big space we can divide up as necessary."

"I want to be able to walk there."

"Agreed," said Max. "I may have found some space a few blocks from here."

"Space around here is expensive as hell. We'll use up our campaign money on rent."

"Not where I'm thinking."

"Where's that?"

"Chinatown."

Surprised, McCabe sipped his espresso, pondering Max's suggestion.

Max continued, "Pelican Design has offices in Chinatown. They had to lay off most of their staff. They're down to a couple of people. Don't expect to do much if any rehiring in the next six months, so we can have most of their space, almost an entire floor."

McCabe countered skeptically, "And the cost?"

Jubilantly, Max responded, "Zero, zip, nada!"

"Nothing?"

"Not one thin dime. In exchange we hire them to do the layout and design of the paper. This morning I spoke to John Nattos the head of

CAFFE TRIESTE
ESPRESSO
ONE WAY
VINS
CLARION
ANNOUNCES
LAYOFFS
S.B.

Pelican Design. He likes you McCabe. Don't know why," Max added sarcastically. "He's up for helping us out, and getting some work out of it for what's left of his firm."

"Sounds too good to be true. Where's his office?"

"On Waverly Place, off Grant. Want to check it out?"

"Sure, why not?" McCabe gamely replied.

They returned their cups to Trieste, Max throwing his copy of the *Clarion* in the trash. Walking down the short block of Grant to Broadway, they crossed over to the Shanghai Gate, carved with dragons, Chinese temples, and misty mountains—a gift from the people of Shanghai to their sister city, San Francisco.

At the corner of Kerouac Alley, the Ming Kee Game store was advertising a turtle soup special. The customer had a choice—buy the soup there, or take a turtle home, alive or dead, and cook it up. Further along Grant at the Lucky Dragon Gift Shop they turned right onto Washington and walked up a half block to the Imperial Palace restaurant. Crossing over to the Wong Fook Hing Book Store, they entered Waverly, walking by the Blossom Bakery and Pot Sticker restaurant to a sooty four-story brick building. Rusting iron porches, connected by a fire escape, adorned its facade. The door was ajar and led up a long narrow flight of worn wooden stairs. Over the doorway was a dirty marble plaque with chiseled gold lettering, a barely legible, "Buddhist Association of America". To the right of the doorway were two newer signs, "Pelican Design"; another read, "Kung Fu Martial Arts Foundation".

The first floor landing was lit by a fifty-watt bulb, the barest light at the end of a steepening tunnel. They warily climbed the first flight of stairs. An open metal gate led to the upper floors where the Kung Fu Foundation and the Buddhist Association were located. To the right of the gate was a door with a hand-painted sign, depicting a line of pelicans flying in formation over the Golden Gate Bridge. Max rapped on the door. After a time, John Nattos, a great bear of a man with a tinsel beard appeared. He was holding a cup of green tea, greeting them thoughtfully, "Hey fellas, come on in," joking, "welcome to our town." And indeed the space was expansive—an abandoned village of empty work stations, Aeron chairs and a scattering of tables. It was only at the very front of the space that John and his partner, Bruce Alaska, had their own desks overlooking Waverly.

"We've been expecting you for awhile," continued John. Max and McCabe gave each other perplexed looks. "Take a look around. See what you think."

Max and McCabe wandered round the space. The only natural light came from the front of the office overlooking Waverly. There was more than enough room to accommodate a small newspaper. It was as if the whole operation had been planned some time before, waiting for the next set of players to appear and begin their simulation.

John had settled back down to his desk and was looking absently into his big screen computer. Above his desk hung enlarged duck stamps that he had designed for the federal government, a dozen stamps in all, purchased for hunting licenses. It was a curious paradox as John was a vegetarian. He invited them to sit down, "So what do you think?"

Max replied, "It's a great space. What will it take to reserve it?"

"All we need is your word. And you pay us for layout and design of the paper. We'll even split the utilities."

McCabe interjected, "That's really generous, but there are no guarantees on anything here. We're assuming decent cash-flow that keeps everyone working on the paper till the November election."

John gave an easy nod of approval, "Fine, great, works for us."

Bruce Alaska wheeled his chair around, "What's the name of your paper?"

Max turned to McCabe, something he had yet to consider as things were moving so fast, "Got any suggestions, Boss?"

McCabe smiled at Max's feigned humility, knowing full well that Max was driving the train, then proferred, "Something evocative—something that envelops the reader—something stealthy—subversive."

Max added, "And something San Francisco."

Bruce countered with an amused smile, "Sounds like Carl Sandburg."

The fog creeps in
on little cat feet.
It sits on silent haunches
looking over harbor and city,
and then moves on.

McCabe laughed, "*The Weekly Fog*"?

John snapped his fingers, "You got something on the fog, something, something..."

McCabe gave him a blank look—even after an early morning shot of espresso, his mind wasn't so quick before noon.

"Yeah, fog—*fog* something..." continued John, seeming to play McCabe for everyone's amusement.

McCabe eyes widened, "How about 'horn'—the *Foghorn*"?

"*Ahh*, sounds goooooooood!" Max punned.

Bruce coughed out a laugh, "The fog creeps in on little cat feet and so will your paper."

Max clapped his hands with uncharacteristic delight, "Well then, we're set with the office. We got the name of the paper. We'll start pulling a team together, figure out how to make it look like a campaign paper. And we'll do a fundraiser as soon as possible." He looked at McCabe, "Am I missing anything?"

"Yeah, the most important element of all."

"What's that?"

"Our intent is to lose."

John and Bruce gave each other the briefest of looks, then burst out laughing. "You mean," asked Bruce, "by not really trying, you'll win—reversing your tactics—because if if you really tried to win you wouldn't, but doing the opposite, you'll get elected?"

Mystified, John exclaimed, "Like walking backward in the same direction you normally would walk forward—reversing all the normal stuff you think would get you elected to win?" John shook his head in wonderment, "Now that's different, McCabe!"

Max attempted to undue the knot, "No, no, really, we actually don't want to win! No desire to! It's just provides us work for a few months, that's all. The paper will be so over-the-top that no one takes the campaign seriously. And since we have no advertisers we don't have to worry about staying within certain editorial limits. The city will be paying most of the bill. We'll have a free hand to write anything—anything at all. Let the First Amendment rip. No way he'll win!"

John gave McCabe a skeptical look. "No telling what might happen, given where we are. You're doing the opposite may have the opposite effect of what you actually intend."

McCabe laughed clueless, "How Zen of you. Anyway, that's the plan."

"This is good, really good: 'The Plan'! Oh that's rich, McCabe, really rich!" hooted John. "Well, we'll do what we can or is it what we can't?" He turned to Bruce, "Why don't you take these guys upstairs? They're going to need all the help they can get, or can't get? Success or is it failure? Whatever!"

"What's upstairs?" asked Max.

Bruce grinned, "Buddhists—our landlords."

"You mean we need to sign a lease with them?" asked McCabe, lost.

John and Bruce fell over themselves again in spasms of laughter. Bruce composing himself exclaimed, "This is too much! You guys are something! A lease? Can you imagine? It's not written, not even oral. You just kind of need their blessing or at least no objections to your being here."

Bruce grabbed a bottle of peanut oil from a nearby shelf. Max and McCabe followed him up the stairs winding round a corner to a door that said "Kung Fu Marital Arts Foundation". To the left of the landing they continued up to the Buddhist Association of America. Bruce knocked gently on the door, then with no apparent response, knocked again slightly louder. Shortly, a time-worn monk appeared at the portal giving them the briefest of bows and barest of smiles.

Bruce beamed back a beatific eye, "We have some people who would like to join our space downstairs. They wish to visit your shrine."

The old man gestured for them to enter. Greeting them just inside were a series of restored statues from the centuries after Alexander the Great's invasion of Afghanistan. The statues looked like perfectly muscled Greek gods, except they were Greco-Bactrian Buddhas, among the earliest representations of the Buddha in human form. Beyond them, orange banners in Chinese script hung nearly to the floor. A hand-carved black Buddha face wall panel hung above a long monkey pod wood table with flickering tealight candles. 1st century Buddhist incantation bowls of silver-bronze alloy from the Indus Valley were filled with oranges, apples and pears. Another wall depicted bright colored drawings of the Buddha's life beginning with his quest for enlightenment. In the middle of the room was a large teakwood Buddha sitting in a lotus position, his right hand uplifted in a nothing-to-fear gesture. His left hand held a multi-green, planet Jupiter onyx ritual bowl. There were rose petals at his feet where a wooden gold box lay, said to hold an infintesimal quantum of ash from the Buddha's cremated body.

Bruce nodded to Max and McCabe in the direction of the donation box near the door, McCabe putting in some bills. The old man apprised McCabe, "Please contemplate the Buddha if that is your pleasure. Light a candle if you wish. Spritual consolation is greater than all the pleasures of the world. But be careful thinking you have achieved understanding—the meaning of nothing is the beginning of everything. There was a young monk who pointed his finger at the moon and thought he was enlightened. He didn't achieve enlightenment until someone cut off his finger." He tittered and shuffled away.

Bruce sauntered over to the Buddha and poured peanut oil into the bowl of his outstretched hand. He took three small round candles in aluminum containers from the monkey pod table and placed them carefully in the oil. They floated. He lit one of the candles with a taper, handed the taper to Max who lit another, passing it onto McCabe who lit the remaining one. They stood with their hands clasped, staring intently at the candles serenely floating in the pond of peanut oil.

After a time they drifted away from the Buddha, the lit candles still floating in the oil. Looking through the antique carved wood panel window shutters, Waverly appeared curiously remote. Bruce took an apple and bit into it, "Tasty," he sniggered. As they left, the monk handed Max and McCabe each an apple, a sign of acceptance.

Returning downstairs to Pelican Design, John joked, "You guys sign that lease?"

As if testing the laws of gravity, McCabe pitched his apple in the air, "*Hah*, I asked the Buddha for success in our little project." The apple levitated momentarily at minimum complexity, seemingly hung by an invisible thread, Newton then returning it to his hand at maximum density.

"Did you wish for success or successful failure?" quipped John.

McCabe shrugged, "I didn't make a distinction."

John laughed uproariously. "Take a bite of that apple, McCabe! May you achieve *Satori*!"

CHAPTER SIX: BURNING BRIDGES

Max remained at the new campaign headquarters to work out the details of setting up the office. McCabe hiked back through Chinatown.

Just before Broadway, he took a right down Kerouac Alley to City Lights bookstore. A clutch of people was gathered around a sinewy middle-aged man known as the "naked yoga guy". Today he was just that, butt-naked except for a Golden State Warriors cap with campaign pin, "Davidson for Mayor". Behind him a campaign poster was taped to the wall of City Lights, "Davidson for Mayor—Make City Hall Clothing Optional!"

Davidson also took occasional nude walks around San Francisco, wearing only his basketball cap and a pair of orange tennis shoes. McCabe had often seen him drinking coffee outside North Beach cafés—fully clothed—looking like an architect or a high school teacher, quite modest, even shy in speech and demeanor.

But this morning, freed of his clothing, Davidson stared unabashedly at the curious throng and started speaking, "You know we already have annual semi-naked days all over America when winter turns to spring and women change into sundresses. Until 5,000 years ago, people in hot, even moderate climates went naked. In ancient Greece and Rome, in Persia and India, people only wore clothes as a necessity or for ceremonial reasons. Then the pagans were overthrown. Theocratic religions took over. They controlled the people through body shame. They made sex and sensuality sinful. Imagine the re-introduction of naked yoga to the mainstream cultures in India and China, the transformational impact on cultures like Iran, Saudi Arabia, Afghanistan! Imagine naked yoga available not just here in San Francisco without threat of arrest, but to our brothers and sisters all over the planet!"

Today, Davidson would show off his side crow pose. He began with a mountain pose, arms at side and feet together. He inhaled, lifting his arms over his head, then exhaled placing his hands in front of his chest. Bending his knees, he lowered his hips into a chair pose, then lifted his heels and rested his weight on the balls of his feet. Keeping his hands together in a prayer pose, he twisted them to the right, hooking his upper left arm on the side of his right thigh for a twisted chair pose. Then spreading his right arm to the right, he brought his arms into a chaturanga pose—dropping his hands to the ground, resting his body weight on the back of his upper left arm. The crowd had quickly doubled in size and was sure to double again. As he came out of the pose, placing his feet on the ground and lifting his hips skyward, a police car pokied up and came to a lazy stop. This was no bank robbery, no need for police reinforcements—it all seemed quite routine, practiced. It was Officer High and his sidekick, Woody.

Mr. Woody stuck his head out of the cruiser. "Hey, Rooster, enough of the Sticky Grenade! Put your clothes back on!"

Davidson waved him off, "I'm campaigning for mayor on the Nudist party platform!" He motioned over at his campaign poster, "I'm exercising my constitutional right to run for office!"

Woody yakked back, "The Constitution doesn't say anything about being naked in public with your Water Gun!"

"What about the pursuit of happiness?"

"Different document, pal. It should be self-evident, Lil' Dickey, your One-Eyed Monster isn't making me real happy right now!"

"Public nudity isn't a crime in San Francisco!"

"It's called indecent exposure, Hot Dog! Your Pocket Rocket sure looks indecent to me!"

Someone from the crowd called out, "You got my vote, Davidson!"

Another in the crowd shouted, "Mine too! Vote Davidson!"

The crowd began chanting, rhythmically clapping, "Vote Davidson! Vote Davidson!"

Woody was undeterred, "I don't care how many supporters you got, Hollow Point! Get your Trouser Snake dressed!"

The naked yoga guy removed his "Davidson for Mayor" campaign button from his Warriors cap, walked over to the police car and pinned it to Woody's uniform. "Come on officer, join my campaign!"

Woody went limp, slumping from sight. Officer High bolted from the cruiser, enraged, "You know I was going to let you go, Boomerang, till you got smart with Woody! Never disrespect a police officer—even Woody! I know you and your Slut Slayer have been arrested before and the DA refuses to press charges. I don't care! In my book you and Mr. Wang are breaking the law! I'm taking you in! The DA can do what she wants with your Little Toy Soldier!" Officer High flung open back door to the cruiser, "I won't cuff you! Put your clothes on, Peckerwood!"

Davidson puckishly retorted, "I'm not getting dressed. Nudity isn't a crime in San Francisco. I can only be arrested for being lewd or blocking traffic."

"You got to be kidding, Half Mast! If your Philly Cheesecake isn't lewd, what is?"

"War," said Davidson simply.

"That's it! Your Lil' Buddy had its final chance! You're naked on my beat, Turtle Head! Now move your Johnson in the car before I cuff you!"

Davidson gamely picked up his clothes, and still naked as a jaybird, climbed in the cruiser onto the cold-ass leather seat. Officer High slammed the door behind him. The crowd started chanting, "Free Davidson! Free Davidson! Free Davidson!"

Through the commotion, Officer High saw McCabe at the fringe of the crowd. A resurrected Woody popped back up in his seat, hung his head out the window and shouted, "Now put that Wangdoodle in your column, McCabe!" The police car pulled away, Woody's blue moon eyes bouncing wildly in his head.

The jazzed crowd dispersed in a cloud of mutterings, McCabe venturing into Vesuvio. Ward greeted him at the bar, "McCabe are you mad? It's 10:30 in the morning. What happened to the afternoon check-in time?"

"You all got me running for mayor, remember?"

Ward laughed, "Yeah, I saw some of your mayoral competition out there doing his naked yoga stuff. You hot pockets are crazy as loons! What a freak show!"

McCabe shrugged off Ward's jibe. Despite it still being mid-morning, he ordered a glass of red, walked over to the alcove, popped up his computer and powered on. The naked yoga guy and free body culture movement would be a good subject for his next column. He sipped his wine, Googled the subject and columned-up:

> The modern-day nudist movement began in the late 1800s in Hamburg, Germany as a protest against Victorian culture. It sought to remove taboos on nudity and to promote nudism as a mainstream cultural phenomenon in sports, recreation, public affairs and the home.
>
> I've seen a lot of nudity all over town. There's the Folsom Street Fair where the naked and the leathered—fetishists of every stripe—act out their sadomasochistic fantasies—slave masters with their dog-collared slaves, public whippings, and myriad forms of

> bondage with slings, chains and ropes. A close runner-up is the Bare-to-Breakers, a naked run cross-town from San Francisco Bay to Ocean Beach. Added to the mix are the annual cross-city Naked Bike Ride and the Gay Pride parade that feature many participants in various states of undress. There is also an official nude beach where I've actually spent time on hot summer days.
>
> A few years back, I had a lady friend who participated in the city's nude golf competition. She wanted me to be her golfing partner. But even though it was for charity, I passed on the opportunity. I figured if it was a cold and foggy day, my morning wood might embarrass me, if you follow. As far as I know in all these instances, no one was ever arrested for public nudity.
>
> Organized nudity requiring an official permit from city hall is left alone, whereas the lone scofflaw practitioner like the naked yoga guy is hauled off to the slammer, held for a few hours, then exonerated by the district attorney, Kamala Harris, who always opines, "Simply being naked on the street is not a crime in San Francisco. All San Franciscans have a natural right to be nude."

Upon completing his column, McCabe impulsively added a final paragraph:

> This will be my last column for a while. I will be taking a leave of absence from the *Clarion* to run for mayor of San Francisco, joining a number of my recently laid-off colleagues in starting a new neighborhood-oriented campaign paper to support my candidacy until the election is over.

What the hell, I can't be working for two papers. He pondered the last paragraph. He hadn't consulted the publisher of the *Clarion* who clearly wouldn't be pleased–no–totally pissed. McCabe had no contract with the paper. It was an employment-at-will arrangement that either side could terminate at any time. He'd been writing *McCabe's Corner* for nearly ten years. A sabbatical could be an opportunity to slough off an old skin. The publisher might not accept his leave of absence and simply fire him. But McCabe knew better, he was a franchise, way too valuable to be let go.

McCabe hit the send button, his column landing at the *Clarion* as he raised his fingers from the keyboard.

The afternoon was not yet old, his column having taken only a few hours to write. He left Vesuvio and walked up Columbus to Stockton, stopping by North Beach Restaurant. At one of the outdoor tables, the owner, Luciano Peroni was taking a break, the lunchtime crowd having begun to thin. He was a large man of ample girth, in his early seventies. He was dressed in a dark blue pinstripe suit that matched his curly grey hair and light blue eyes. His family was from Lucca, having immigrated to San Francisco in the second great wave of Italian migration to Northern California in the 1880s.

Luciano was a showman, a third generation San Franciscan who still cultivated a slight Italian accent. Today, he was sitting by himself staring reflectively at the people walking along Columbus. At his right hand was a bottle of his own red wine, Brunello di Sonoma. Luciano's Brunello was taken from cuttings of Sangiovese grapevines in the Montalcino region of Tuscany. Brunello, meaning brownish, inspired by the dark color of the wine—was the local name given by Tuscan wine makers to their Sangiovese Grosso. The Brunello, like Luciano himself, combined muscularity with elegance.

Luciano had a hard right political attitude that he wore on his sleeve. But his sentiments were pretty much a lost cause on the Left Coast as frequent patrons of his restaurant included the leading figures in the California Democratic Party—congressional representatives, senators, mayors, governors—as well as prime ministers and presidents spanning the globe.

Upon graduating from high school, Luciano worked his way up the restaurant business at the finest Italian restaurants in town. By 1970 he had saved enough to open his own restaurant, North Beach Restaurant, specializing in Lucchese-style cooking. Much of the food and wine was supplied by his farm and vineyard located in the hills above the Sonoma Valley: eggs, walnuts, honey, seasonal vegetables, radicchio, Porcini mushrooms, figs, and pears. He grew thousands of olive trees harvested in late fall. Each table at his restaurant had a bottle of his dark green, spicy oil. Cheeses also were produced on his land—the fleeting beauty of burrata with its creamy quivering center, as well as sharp and salty pecorino cheese from his wild fennel and clover-fed sheep.

Luciano looked up from the table as McCabe approached, "*Bello*, I hear you're running for mayor. Are you nuts?" Luciano knew everything in North Beach before it became public. "Sit down, talk to me, have a glass of Brunello." He motioned expansively to Nino, a waiter, to bring out a wine glass. "You have a good life, *Bello*, why ruin it with politics? A columnist, yes, but run for office? It's not for you," he said distastefully as if he had sampled a vinegary wine. "*Bello*, you've made enemies as a columnist, no? Everyone you've insulted will be out to get you. Why didn't you talk to me first?" With Luciano, you had to let his harangues run their course, then edge in a short piece, before he smacked you with another gale of remonstrance.

McCabe laughed to himself. ***After the thunder, so little rain.***

Nino returned with a wine glass and poured the Brunello. McCabe vigorously swirled the wine. It hung high on the glass, leaving a thin ruby gloss as it receded back down the edge of glass. ***Years in the bottle, minutes in the glass, what fine long legs!***

McCabe had his own small Cabernet vineyard above St. Helena in the Napa Valley on the eastern side of the Mayacamas mountains. Luciano's much larger vineyard was fifteen miles away on the western slopes of the Mayacamas, a few miles outside the town of Sonoma where much of the catastrophic conflagration of 2017 had occured.

McCabe nodded his satisfaction with the earthy Brunello, "I'm not really running for mayor, not in the normal sense."

Luciano arched his beetling eyebrows, "*Bello*, what are you talking about. Now I know you're *loco*."

"We're going to publish a paper. Staff it with some of the people who were just laid off from the *Clarion*. Put it out a few times a week with a regularly updated website. We'll run it till Election Day. The odds of my actually winning are problematic, obviously." But McCabe didn't totally level with Luciano—in fact the campaign was designed to lose.

Luciano exclaimed more throatily this time, "What? Why do it then, *Bello?*"

"I'm going to help out my friends who've been laid off, Luciano."

"How's it gonna help them?"

"They'll get paid a salary till the election is over. We raise some initial contributions, get ten-to-one matching funds from the city, then use the newspaper to raise more money, matched by the city and so on. I need to try something different. It's only a few months."

Luciano intuitively understood the code of supporting old friends. He shrugged, "I don't know *Bello*, I don't know. So I should help you then, no? What can I do? I'll give you a fundraiser, we'll have it here at the restaurant. We can have it downstairs in the Prosciutto Room." He clapped his hands, imagining the evening, and no doubt turning it to some unseen financial advantage. "We'll have my Brunello, we'll give away bottles of my olive oil, serve some appetizers—bruschetta, maybe some of my burrata—a little prosciutto and melon, fried calamari. How much do you need to raise?"

"To qualify for city matching funds, ten thousand. Then we get the ten-to-one match, so a hundred grand more from the city, and we're up and running."

"Of course, we can raise ten easily. I've known you, what—thirty years, since your father began coming here, bringing his little squirt of a son? He was a lot shrewder than you, *Bello*, a sensible man! He'd never do something crazy like this! But if this is something you must do, then I'll help you."

"*Mille Grazie*," said McCabe, genuinely pleased at Luciano's unexpected generosity. He leaned back in his chair, his mind dancing in the dusty aroma of the Sonoma Sangiovese. It was the briefest blissful drift. His cell phone rang, caller ID indicating it was Snellgrove, publisher of the *Clarion*. The phone rang again. At five rings the call went to voicemail. McCabe stared at the screen, a third ring, then the fourth.

Reluctantly he answered the call, "Hi Snellgrove, I was just not thinking of you."

A torrent of the vilest invective poured through his cell phone. He said nothing. There followed another barrage of twisted fulminations. McCabe smirked. ***The swiftest runner cannot overtake a harsh word once spoken.*** Snellgrove realized he was in a one way conversation, "Are you there, McCabe? *McCabe?*"

"Hey, Snelly, yeah I'm still here—barely." Luciano who had remained at the table immersed in his own thoughts perked up and looked over at McCabe. He conspiratorially poured McCabe another glass of Brunello. "*Mille grazie*," McCabe whispered.

"McCabe, what it is you're trying to accomplish," screamed Snellgrove.

"What don't you understand? It's there in my column. I'm taking a leave of absence to run for mayor. That's clear enough isn't it? You're lucky I didn't mention the huge pay raise you took right before firing all my friends, you prick!"

Snellgrove reversed course, playing the victim—the short notice given by McCabe, the need for the paper to adjust, how these were difficult days for the newspaper business, the need to check with his partners about McCabe's future status, how hurtful this was to him personally, even a betrayal.

"Snelly, what about your fifty percent staff cut effective immediately? Now that's a betrayal! Look it, I'm taking the leave. Accept it, fire me, whatever! I've made my decision."

"Dammit McCabe, you can't do this, not now, not after we just let so many people go!"

"Turn it to the paper's advantage," McCabe countered, "how open-minded and tolerant you all are—the sacrifice the paper will be making—my temporary leave as a contribution by the *Clarion* to the political dialogue in the city—how I'll be writing a column for my own campaign paper." McCabe realized he had just played a wrong card.

Snellgrove's heat blasted through the cell phone, "You're what? Writing a column for another paper!"

McCabe took a large sip of wine, swallowed quickly, "Easy, easy! It'll just be a weekly column in the paper published by my campaign."

"It's still writing a column for another paper! A lot of people take the *Clarion* just for your column." Now Snellgrove had blundered. "Well, what I mean to say, part of the reason some people enjoy reading the *Clarion* is your column."

McCabe took another sip of Brunello, a respectable buzz infusing his head, "Alright, I tell you what. Any column I write for my campaign paper, you can run for free in the *Clarion*—don't pay me a dime. That's damn generous."

Snellgrove replied tentatively, "*Hmm*, that might work, that might calm the waters."

McCabe smiled. ***Got him.***

Then Snellgrove spit out the hook, "Wait a minute, then every other kook running for mayor will demand equal time too! *Nah*, that won't work."

'Other kook'—Snellgrove's a jerk, thought McCabe. "If you want free columns you got it. But, I'm on leave. I appreciate your–*ah*–concern," ending the conversation.

Luciano had known Snellgrove for many years and he dined at his restaurant occasionally. "Are you sure you want to do this, *Bello*? Every day a fistful of unpleasant conversations. Swimming with the sharks. The worst SOB's in town. I know, politicos eat here every day. This isn't for you."

McCabe laughed, "You make it sound like Dante's *Inferno*."

Luciano intoned theatrically, "No *Bello*, more like a trip up the river to *The Heart of Darkness*."

McCabe took another sip of Brunello, closing his eyes, welcoming the sun. "Yeah, sure feels like it," he muttered sarcastically.

Jagged thoughts of Snellgrove soon were forgotten in the rolling hills of Tuscany.

CHAPTER SEVEN: BANDOOCH

McCabe's Mediterranean daydream was the briefest sojourn. People began stopping to say hello, forcing a return from his languorous journey. He ordered a double espresso with a twist, wiring up.

He casually mentioned to those who paused to talk that he was running for mayor—information that would go viral through North Beach and beyond, guaranteeing within hours word of his candidacy would reach city hall where the mayor, running for a second term, was bound to hear of it. McCabe had begun campaigning for the office of mayor of San Francisco fueled by hillside wine and shade-grown coffee.

Shadows lengthened along Columbus Avenue. A slight breeze began ruffling the American and Italian flags that hung from the utility poles bracketing the entrance to the restaurant. McCabe walked back down Columbus past Caffé Trieste to the Condor on the corner of Broadway—its now decommissioned Grand piano, visible through the open curtains, secured firmly to the ceiling like a *Desmoda draculae*—a giant vampire bat.

As the Beats had faded into the hipster sixties, the sluggish North Beach Broadway strip needed a gimmick to revive itself. The Condor lead the way—Go-Go dancing! The phenomena lasted a few frantic years before its novelty wore thin. The ever-flexible Condor laid down an ultimatum to its entertainers—mostly coeds who crossed over the Bay from UC Berkeley or stealthily made their drive-of-shame up the Peninsula from Stanford to earn tip money to help pay for college—dancing for tuition—certainly better paying and playing than sorority volleyball.

"Ladies you still can Go-Go, but it's gotta be topless!"

And that's where the Grand piano's rise to fame began. McCabe recalled a column he had written for the *Clarion*: it was on top of the Grand that the topless Go-Go dancers were lowered by a hydraulic motor from a trap door in the ceiling to the stage below—their sassy breasts gently pulsing to the incantations of Jimi Hendrix's psychedelia—"*Foxy lady I'm comin' to get you!*" At the conclusion of the dancer's show, a switch on the side of the piano was activated, the dancer lifted back up through the ceiling's trap door exit.

The Condor's most famous topless dancer was Carol Doda who made headlines worldwide in 1964 when as a 19-year old, she performed wearing only a Rudi Gernreich topless "monokini" swimsuit—a teeny, close-fitting bottom with two thin straps. With her silicone-enhanced twin forty-fours that would have even given Wyatt Earp some pause, she regularly mutated the hormonal college crowds into a frenzy of unpredictable consequence that often brought the North Beach police careening to the Club. It was unimaginably fun for the *Ess Eff Pee Dee* to muscle their well-oiled nightsticks on the callow collegians as the Condor's foxes fled screaming to their cloistered undressing rooms.

But with all the intimations of heavenly sex atop it, the piano was never granted due credit for its nightly up-and-down leg and back work. Through the 60s and 70s it toiled, steady and dependable as a mule. But no one ever considered playing its ivories. With the arrival of the 80s came its sweet revenge served cold and clandestine.

Topless had gone bottomless, they showed it all now. The Condor had closed for the evening. The piano was dozing on stage not yet tucked back onto the ceiling for the night. Atop the piano, the Condor's bouncer, a small-time Mafioso who had lit out from Chicago, was in the heat of *flagrante delicto* with a questionably legal dancer when the piano's lift inexplicably activated, the piano making its quiet rise—its bare back riders oblivious to the Dark Angel's upward trajectory. The trap door was just that—the debauchees' rumpy pumpy pinned to the ceiling. El Grande pressed inexorably upward. The well-upholstered bouncer still on top of the lithe girl of pleasure began to choke, no longer bouncing. The dancer shrieked, gasping for help in the closed and darkened club. The bouncer's locomotive grunting came slower, the nymphet's cries less emphatic. The piano's hydraulic lift quietly purred away, squeezing them like ripe oranges for the morning's Mimosas.

When the janitor arrived at dawn, he was greeted by the moans of the elevated dancer, still pinned under the bouncer, cranked firm and hard to the ceiling. The bouncer had suffocated—like a beached sperm whale atop the cutest Monterey Bay otter. Whether it was an accident or a mob hit—the bouncer strangled before being laid on top of the drugged dancer—was all speculation. The indecorous dancer disappeared later that day, taking an immediate break for "reasons of health", never again returning to strip in the City by the Bay.

Not even a tune-up would bring back Mr. Grand for an encore now...

McCabe moved on from the Condor along Broadway to Enrico's, the outdoor restaurant and café named after Enrico Banducci. "Bandooch" had passed away several years earlier and had been a good friend of McCabe's. There was no one that had made more appearances in his column.

Enrico had been an American impresario, opening the first cabaret on the West Coast in 1949—*the hungry i*—spelling it with lower case letters, the *i* being short for *id*. The *i* showcased the leading comedians in America, where many got their start. There was fast-talking radical Mort Sahl. Nebbish, neurotic Woody Allen and nineteen-year-old funny girl Barbara Streisand appeared on the same bill at the *i*. Dick Gregory, radiating cool positive vibes, cracked the color line. Gregory contrasted with the sunny optimist and storyteller Bill Cosby who ignored race and whited it out—though some were years later having "black-outs". There was frenzied hipster Lenny Bruce. The *i* often headlined go-for-broke Jonathan Winters whose career took a strange detour after one night's performance when he climbed the mast of the Balclutha, a three-masted schooner at Fisherman's Wharf and announced to the world, "I'm in orbit man! I'm a moon cat on Cloud 9, from outer space!" He was hauled off to a sanitarium, temporarily shutting down his quicksilver comic madness. Mike Nichols and Elaine May worked their improv satire along with telephone comic, Shelley Berman; and later Richard Pryor raced it up, offsetting late night talk show host, temperate Dick Cavett. Scores of other well known comedians appeared at the *i* along with the early folksingers and a bewildering array of pop and jazz performers.

The hungry i had been the leading edge of the comedic revolution of the 50s and early 60s. It had presented a universe of entertainment just a stone's throw from Lawrence Ferlinghetti's City Lights. Despite their proximity, they represented separate cultural break-throughs, neither feeding off the other, both challenging the mores and values of the Eisenhower era—then merging into the cultural rebellion of the 1960s.

A year before Banducci died, McCabe had walked with him one evening along Broadway after having dinner at Enrico's. As they passed the Marconi Hotel, Banducci's eyes darkened. He tapped his shoe emphatically on the pavement, "Lenny fell here—right here!"

McCabe, steadying the old man with his arm, was confounded, "Lenny? Lenny Bruce? Here—you mean he tripped? Probably wired out of his mind!"

Enrico pointed at the second story window, "No man, up there! It was that window—that window! Lenny was in his room after performing at Ann's 440 around the corner. We'd just closed Enrico's for the night.

I was walking to the parking lot just like we're doing tonight. I heard a window shatter and someone screamed, *BANDOOCH! Whoosh!* A body hit the ground right in front of me! No kidding! The impact was a hideous muffled sound. The guy almost landed on top of me! It was Lenny! He moaned, shouted some profanities, not at me but at the terrible pain he was in. He looked up at me, gasping, he was unbelievably distorted! Wild! Gone! He said he wanted to talk to me, saw me walking down Broadway and just wanted to say hi. I asked him why he didn't take the goddamned stairs? He said he didn't think he had to. What a shortcut!" Banducci belched a depraved, industrial-strength laugh. "He nearly killed himself and he just wanted to chat!"

Bandooch slapped on the relish, "I went back to Enrico's, called an ambulance—found a blanket. I laid it over the poor son-of-a bitch. Lenny was frothing, spewing all sorts of unbelievable crap. He wouldn't shut up, but he couldn't get up, he was hurt bad. The cops arrived before the ambulance. They knew Lenny well. He was no friend of theirs because of the obscenity trials and hassles they'd put him through. When he saw the coppers, he swore at them, called them pigs and other foul stuff. They didn't care, Lenny was down, he'd done this awful thing to himself. They hung around, joked with each other, enjoying Lenny's predicament till the ambulance arrived. The police never even took a report. Lenny broke both ankles, fractured his pelvis. They put him in a body cast for a month. In the emergency room, Lenny put on a performance so sick the doctors slapped a bandage over his mouth just to shut him up!"

There were several variations on the story—that Lenny slipped while standing on the sill, crashing through the window high on LSD. Another version had Lenny, who was bi-sexual, giving or being given a blow job—or fighting off or making a homosexual advance—shoved through the window. The one true fact was that Banducci had witnessed Lenny's fall to earth.

A year later in 1966, Lenny Bruce died under mysterious circumstances, ruled accidental from an overdose of morphine. A journalist fellow-traveler of Lenny's wrote, "Dead at forty. That's obscene."

This evening, Enrico's outside patio was filled with young professionals, cool and healthy in their expensive attire, glossy hair, faces smooth as a baby's bottom except for an occasional laugh or frown line. In the corner of the patio, he noticed a reporter from the *Clarion* talking to Galen Newman, the mayor, a couple of very young women sitting on either side of him. The mayor just recently turned forty, was the same age as McCabe. He was preternaturally handsome, shiny visage, tall and thin, gelled hair, perfect teeth, relaxed and self-deprecating. He spent a lot of time in North Beach and lived at the top of Russian Hill, a ten-minute walk from Enrico's—not that the mayor ever walked. He went everywhere in a limo with police bodyguard.

The mayor didn't appear to be engaged in deep conversation, casually throwing off well-rehearsed lines to the reporter in an impromptu interview. McCabe squeezed between the tables over to the mayor's corner. The mayor looked up in mid-sentence, then finished off his comments to the reporter, "So, yeah our budget is in meltdown—that's off the record, at least the word 'meltdown'. And we need to cut a couple thousand jobs, get the unions to give back on their agreements, maybe furlough workers, do across-the-board 15 percent cuts in department budgets. Then we'll see—probably have to do more cuts later in the year."

The reporter threw out a final question, "Will that include cuts in your own staff?" The mayor's staff was loaded with assistants whose primary focus wasn't running city hall, but helping leverage the mayor to higher office.

The mayor replied, "Absolutely not! My staff won't take a hit! *Hah*—that's off the record too. On the record, no area of the city budget is immune from cuts." He finished off the interview, "Got any more questions, call my director of communications."

As the reporter left, the mayor laughed, jock-voiced, "Hey, McCabe, you here to ask questions too? Every time I get into a conversation with you, my comments get twisted like pretzels in your column."

"Bad editing," McCabe deadpanned.

The mayor motioned in his gravelly voice to an empty seat, "Sit down."

McCabe hesitated, cryptically eyeing the mayor and his companions.

"Sit down McCabe," then mocking his manhood, "they won't bite! My *ahh*–aides–interns from UC Berkeley." One woman, shoulder length blonde hair, looked Scandinavian, high cheekbones like a Norwegian fjord. The other woman was Caucasian-Asian fusion, long dark hair, maybe Shanghai blood. They smiled politely but said nothing, evidently disinterested.

McCabe pulled a chair from the oval table. Nothing in Enrico's contained a straight line–the tables, windows, walls, counters–explained by Enrico as, "The world we live in is curved, isn't it?"

As McCabe sat down, the mayor smirked, "Ladies, this is McCabe, who has been a thorn in my side since I became mayor. He writes the most scurrilous column west of the Mississippi, only matched by the misery Mark Twain inflicted on politicians and poseurs when he lived in San Francisco and wrote a column for..." The mayor paused, realizing he didn't have that arcane piece of journalistic history at his fingertips which he knew would have impressed McCabe.

McCabe filled in the historic record, "*Morning Call—San Francisco Daily Morning Call*. Clemens of the *Call* pissed off a lot of people with his daily beat—didn't last here—jumped like a bullfrog to the Sierra foothills."

The mayor guffawed, "You take after him I see, except nowadays, you don't get run out of town!" The mayor's demeanor grew more serious, drilling McCabe with a grey-eyed stare, "You're running for mayor I hear."

"News travels fast. I was just going to inform you of that. Surely you're not worried?" asked McCabe in jest.

"I'd trade my job for yours, McCabe. You have your freedom," the mayor said ruefully. "I have to watch every word. I don't get edits or rewrites. You'd never make it, your balls in a cage like mine. You'd quit in a week."

The mayor's ladies gave each other pleased looks at the imagery of the male anatomy, now giving McCabe some curious attention.

The mayor mused, "There are times when I want to leave public life. There are some really bad moments, a lot more of them these days. The city finances are phonied-up—you know that—underwritten by bond issues that used to be paid out of the general fund. I can't fix it, no one can. It's just gotta run its course. You wouldn't want my job."

McCabe countered, "Then why run again?"

"Why write another column?" asked the mayor rhetorically. "You know as well as I, we don't just walk away." He slipped his hands under the table. Both women's eyes widened abruptly as they feigned innocent smiles.

"I took a leave from the *Clarion*."

The mayor hooted, his hands sliding languidly over the womens' thighs, "Things are improving already!"

"They certainly appear to be," said McCabe, glancing at the two women, getting up from the table. "A pleasure to have met you ladies. Take care, Your Honor."

The mayor nodded unconcernedly, "See you on the campaign trail."

McCabe eased back through the patio and inside Enrico's. Max was sitting at the end of the bar talking to a couple of well-dressed middle-aged women, maybe in real estate or finance.

"Got you your first campaign contributions," Max said triumphantly waving two fifty dollar checks made out to "McCabe for Mayor". He introduced the two women.

"Pimping me already?"

"Get used to it! I know it goes against the grain."

Of that there was no doubt. McCabe couldn't quite get his hands around the ethically vague concept of asking folks to give him money to run for public office. "Max, I know the maximum contribution is a thousand dollars, but let's limit it to a hundred. The city will be kicking in most of the money anyway."

Max shrugged, silently questioning McCabe's high-mindedness. More contributions meant more matching funds from the city and better salaries for the former *Clarionistas*, including himself.

Buying a round of champagne, McCabe proclaimed with a splash of irony, "To November!"

CHAPTER EIGHT: HANGING HOGS

McCabe's first fundraiser would be held in the Prosciutto Room at North Beach Restaurant. The goal was relatively modest—$10,000—in order to qualify for the city's campaign public financing. Between McCabe's acquaintances, his newspaper pals and Luciano's Rolodex, several hundred people were expected to drop by.

The Prosciutto Room was named for the hundred prosciutto hams hanging from the ceiling—used in the restaurant's appetizers and pasta dishes. The hams suffused the room with a pungent odor. Vegetarians shunned the place. A table had been positioned at the entrance for receiving campaign contributions. McCabe had preferred to dispense with a gate toll and allow people's conscience and goodwill to generate a contribution before departing, but he had been persuaded otherwise by Luciano, "*Bello*, I'm giving you this beautiful room, lovely appetizers, the best wine, free bottles of my olive oil. People can eat and drink as much as they like. But don't be a fool! If you don't get the contribution up front, you may get nothing at all."

McCabe arrived at 6PM, freshly showered, dressed in a blue blazer, red silk tie, pressed blue jeans and his beat-up walking shoes. Luciano greeted him at the upstairs bar, "*Bello*, what are you doing? Are you running for mayor or playing in a rock band? There'll be some wealthy people here tonight. They want to feel confident about you running. Go home and put on a suit!"

McCabe brushed him back, "No one is being asked to give more than a hundred bucks. I'm not looking to empty their wallets, come on."

Luciano shook his head, "*Bello, Bello.*"

Max and several *Foghorn* reporters were hovering like honey bees around the bar. Max fraternity-slapped McCabe on the back, "You're looking sharp, pal!"

"Anyone else here yet?" asked McCabe, dreading that no one would show.

Max scoffed, "This thing doesn't start for another half hour. Get this man some wine!"

McCabe smiled wanly, mildly nauseous.

Luciano approached the bar and whispered conspiratorially, "*Bello*, check out the Prosciutto Room. Some of your campaign workers are setting up for you." A throaty laugh tumbled out of him, "It's hot down there!"

McCabe moseyed to the back of the dining room and down the stairs to the Prosciutto Room. April was at the doorway setting up the table to receive contributions. Her long gray braid was tied with festive red, white and blue ribbons. Luciano's observation escaped him, nothing seemed remotely hot. He embraced April, "Hey, sweet pea, how's everything going?"

"Just setting up the contributor's table," April chirpily replied. "Still a hundred dollar maximum?"

"Yeah, let's keep it at that." Still perplexed at Luciano's joke, he asked, "So everything looks good?"

"Tom, things are just fine on my part." April nodded her head in a slightly disapproving manner toward the other end of the room, "Your campaign managers are here."

The banquet table that normally went down the center of the dining area had been pushed to one side. On the bar to the right were plates of appetizers and bottles of wine. At the end of the room two women were attaching a campaign sign to the front of an imposing lectern. The sign proclaimed in red blockbuster lettering, "McCabe for Mayor". Flying over his name was a band of wild parrots. He squinted at the two women through the soft lighting—short skirts, high heels, silk blouses, hair spilling down their backs.

He rambled over, a little self conscious, uncertain what to say. He went anodyne, "Some makeover!" Noë hugged him, then Zoë joined the hug as well. Their bodies were firm, their breasts pressing into him, the lightest scent of orange blossom perfume.

"We got Nattos to do the sign. Cool, no?" said Noë. "It can be your official campaign sign too!"

But the poster brought on an unanswered question. What did his campaign actually represent? Tonight he had to come across as utterly sincere even though the unspoken design was to lose. But wouldn't his campaign, if not intending to win, be a fraud? Wouldn't bringing people together tonight, asking for contributions make him a charlatan? Was this simply a selfish endeavor by a group of unemployed newspaper people to secure work for a few months while sucking off city finances? And what of taking taxpayer money from the city when it was in the midst of a budget deficit requiring the layoffs of scores of city workers—nurses, teachers, street sweepers, gardeners—together with closure of homeless shelters, health clinics, and mental health facilities?

Shortly, the *Foghorners* tumbled down the stairway into the Proscuitto Room. Like thirsty water buffalo, they headed for the bar, stampeding past the contributions table. Max corralled them before it was too late, "Hey you bums, remember this is a fundraiser not a wine-tasting! Come on! Pull out your wallets and write some kind of check—even ten bucks!" Max motioned to April, "You should be taking the money, right?"

April said chidingly, loud enough for McCabe to hear, "Noë and Zoë, they're the campaign managers. Shouldn't they be doing it?"

"Funny, April," said McCabe impatiently. He called over to Noë and Zoë, "Ladies, would you come here for a minute? *Ahh*—we need someone to take checks at the door—starting with the *Foghorners*."

"We already have remittance envelopes printed up," said Noë pleased at her conscientiousness, gesturing at the stack of envelopes on the contributor's table.

Next to the envelopes was an empty jar to which she pointed, "We need to salt the mine."

McCabe gave her a blank look.

Noë laughed at his cluelessness, "Put some twenties in the jar. When people see the cash they'll be more encouraged to give." McCabe pulled out a bunch of twenties from his wallet and stuffed them in the jar, effectively contributing to his own campaign.

"Perfect," said Noë as she and Zoë sat down at the table. The *Foghorners* dutifully wrote out the smallest of checks, filling out the required information on the remittance envelopes: amount, name, address, telephone number, employer.

Soon the Prosciutto Room began to fill, Noë and Zoë extracting campaign contributions from five dollars to a hundred. Everyone was allowed in, even the few who couldn't afford a dollar. Many offered to write larger checks than $100, surprised at the modest amount.

McCabe had consumed two glasses of wine, his head now in the sweet spot of a perfect buzz. Luciano bulled through the crowd, "*Bello*, are you ready? I'll introduce you, no?"

"Good, Luciano."

Walking over to the lectern. Luciano yelled out in his rumbling voice, "*Signoras e signores*, please—quiet, *quiet*." The chatter in the room died off...

Grazie, grazie. We are here tonight to launch a campaign for mayor of San Francisco. Tom McCabe, who you all know, has decided to run.

I've known his family since I first opened this restaurant more than forty years ago. His father used to come here at least once a week. His papa had a Pinot Noir vineyard in the Napa Valley. He sold me a few cases of his wine every year. It was by far the most expensive wine on our list. When his father came here for lunch or dinner, I would suggest he buy a bottle of his own wine. Was that asking too much? He would look at me so shocked! Tell me no one in their right mind would order such expensive wine! Then he'd order a glass of the cheapest house red. McCabe, your father was a shrewd man. He never gave me an inch on price—not once! I bought his wine for years and never—*never*—did he buy a bottle of his own wine.

You, McCabe—you're *not* your father. But you have other qualities. You write about the people of this city every day. You know everybody in town. You love this city as a real lover should. And you know her politics. I don't know why you would want to put yourself through a campaign like this! But if you're going to do this, I will support you of course. I wish your father were alive today. He would enjoy being here and I would still be trying to get him to buy a bottle of his wine off my wine list—and he would be getting me to buy even more of his own! McCabe, I wish you luck.

Buona fortuna!

The room broke out in applause. McCabe reached in his coat pocket for his notes, then let them be:

Thanks, Luciano. I want to acknowledge your generosity in making the Proscuitto Room available for my inaugural fundraiser for mayor—the lovely wine produced from your hillside vineyards—the appetizers, your exquisite burrata, walnuts, dried figs, your olive oil. Beautiful, just beautiful, I can't thank you enough!

McCabe paused, catching April's eye, satisfied it was a decent opening:

Let me begin by sharing with you the person whom I take as my guide in running for this office—the Greek philosopher, Diogenes who lived 2,300 years ago. He was considered a cynic, not in its modern-day interpretation that ascribes the worst of intentions to outwardly good motives of others—rather his was a protest against corruption, luxury and insincerity. Carrying a lamp in the daytime, Diogenes sought to find one honest man. He never did. In that same spirit, my column has always protested hypocrisy, cant and duplicity in the blood sport we call politics.

As soon as the words left his mouth, McCabe was struck by the light of Diogenes lamp. ***I'm the one who's duplicitous, not revealing the true purpose of my campaign!*** He looked around the room to see if anyone could read his thoughts.

Max gave him a wicked grin. Several *Foghorn* reporters smiled cryptically. He briefly stared down at the floor, ensnared in his own hypocrisy:

I don't have a lamp like Diogenes, but I have something that will serve a similar purpose. We'll soon begin publishing a campaign paper—the *Foghorn*. It'll be run by my friends and colleagues recently laid off from the *Bay City Clarion*—and from which I've taken a leave as well. We'll shine a bright light on the politics of our city. It will be of, by and for our neighborhoods.

And what of our neighborhoods? Do you realize here in North Beach for example, there's one hardware store where we used to have three? We don't have a good grocery store—or a shoe repair shop—no stationary store—no consumer electronics outlet. We used to have a basket of bakeries—now we have a couple. We've been cleaved down to one butcher shop. No movie theater. One drug store—we used to have four. No manufacturing of any kind. The doctors' and dentists' offices have all disappeared. Have you seen a single plumber's or electrician's shop around here? No clothing stores that sell inexpensive clothes. No repair shops of any kind. Only a single bookstore—can you imagine that? A neighborhood as literary as North Beach that's a bookstore desert! This neighborhood used to manufacture pastas, salami, prosciutto, wine, press olives, bake bread. We had artesian wells and water bottling companies. Everything you needed was within walking distance. Cars didn't matter all that much. Now if I want to get a key made I have to travel over the hill—just for a damn key! If I want an ink cartridge for my printer I have to go downtown. If I want to visit a dentist I have to go halfway across town. I don't want to have to leave my neighborhood for a head of cabbage.

We need to bring a new vision to our city–creating a sustainable City on a Hill–empowering our middle class, encouraging families to remain here—livable solutions that engage and support San Francisco's many vibrant communities—bringing back neighborhood-serving businesses—implementing uses of the public realm for community supported activities such as art and music events, farmers' markets, movie nights, festivals with local food and wine...

We will begin with the transformative power of our political will—your vision, our vision—of a neighborhood City upon a Hill. We will do what we can, where we are–in this beautiful town–to let a thousand flowers bloom!

McCabe paused, his mind suddenly adrift without a planned closing. He lunged for the finish:

McCABE for MAYOR

I see there's still remains a lake of wine and a mountain of appetizers. So let's not only celebrate to our mutual endeavor but dedicate ourselves to having some fun in this campaign all the way to election day!

I thank you, Luciano for sharing the bounty of your land, and each of you for coming tonight.

Mille grazie!

The Prosciutto Room gave him friendly applause acknowledging his shaky jump from columnist to politician—adequate if a bit short on detail.

By the end of the fundraiser, McCabe had a toasted red wine glow. Luciano was feeling equally painless on his high octane Grappa di Cabernet produced at his Sonoma winery. As they walked outside the restaurant, Luciano slammed McCabe hard on the back in an overly exuberant gesture of camaraderie, "*Bello*, this was a good evening for you—a good start! I know you think you're an underdog, but you gotta try! You gonna have to campaign all day, every day! No leaving town on weekends like you usually do! You gotta be knocking on doors, greeting people at bus stops, café walks in the morning, merchant walks at noon, people's homes in the evening. You gotta be everywhere—all the time—all over the city! No staying up late tonight, *Bello*, I wanna see you shaking hands at a bus stop early tomorrow!"

McCabe gave Luciano a comparatively lighter pat on the back, the hidden currents of his campaign welling up to the surface but not revealed, "*Ciao*, Luciano."

CHAPTER NINE: THE PRESSES ROLL

The Proscuitto fundraiser had gone down well enough. The following morning, McCabe was much relieved walking down to North Beach. The *Foghorn* would shortly be funded and gone to print, the campaign launched. At Caffé Trieste many of the regulars who would have normally stayed inside on a foggy morning were outside sitting at tables on Poets Plaza, taking in the sun. There was the faintest wisp of marijuana in the air, but McCabe couldn't tell who was smoking weed—hidden in plain sight.

He bought an espresso and walked back outside onto the plaza. Sitting alone, drinking coffee and reading the paper was Lawrence Ferlinghetti. Lawrence had left the navy after World War II, settling in San Francisco, when in his own words, the whole continent seem to tilt up, shifting the population to the west coast. He joined the navy in 1939 and with the onset of the War was made skipper of his own submarine chaser in the Atlantic. Ferl participated in D-Day and upon Germany's surrender in May 1945, was transferred to the Pacific theater in preparation for the invasion of Japan. Then in August 1945, the atomic bomb was dropped on Hiroshima and a scant three days later, on Nagasaki. Two months after Japan's surrender, Ferlinghetti hopped a train to Nagasaki and walked the atomic ruins. Lawrence once described the experience to McCabe, "Nagasaki had been cleaned up a little by the time I arrived. Still there was devastation as far as the eye could see, charred ruins under every step mixed with human bones, burned bits of clothes, broken tea cups, the smallest human possession blackened and pulverized. I left the service in 1946. I had seen some of the most horrific scenes of World War II. That's where my pacifism arose."

Ferlinghetti was now in his late-nineties, still spry and a little shy. McCabe had written about him dozens of times. "So I hear you're running for mayor. Have you lost your senses?" asked Ferlinghetti in his timbrel voice.

"Yes to both," laughed McCabe. "We're publishing a paper using some writers laid off from the *Clarion*. The city will give us public financing to cover most of the costs of publication, including salaries for our writers."

"You mean the city will pay you to publish a paper?"

"Damn right," said McCabe, "and we'll pay our reporters, maybe not at Guild rate, but they'll get paid decently through the election."

Lawrence chuckled, astonished, rubbing his closely trimmed grey beard, "What a scam."

A young woman walked up to Ferlinghetti and introduced herself, showing him a quotation tattooed on her forearm—"I am awaiting perpetually and forever a Renaissance of wonder."

Lawrence smiled, ruddy cheeked, slightly taken aback, "McCabe, know where that's from?"

He vaguely recollected, but couldn't summon the answer, "Nope."

Lawrence good-naturedly instructed the woman, "Tell him."

"It's from his *Coney Island of the Mind*. She kissed Lawrence lovingly on the cheek, "It's so wonderful to meet you, Mr. Ferlinghetti. I knew I'd run across you someday! Would you mind signing your name under the quote? I can use it to trace another tattoo! "

Lawrence carefully signed his name on her arm in blue ink. "Thank you for your devotional," he laughed.

McCabe was flabbergasted, "Damn, Lawrence! Women are branding themselves with your poetry!"

Ferlinghetti nodded with a lifetime's contentment of poetical controversy, reaching back to the mid-twentieth century. In 1956, City Lights released Allen Ginsberg's *Howl* on the ACLU pre-publication assurance that it would defend against whatever charges that might be brought—and for good reason. In those olden Eisenhower days, the *Ess Eff Pee Dee* was quite a different beast—in this case raiding City Lights and confiscating *Howl* as, "not fit for children to read"—as if any child would remotely understand or be interested. Ferlinghetti on a retreat at his cabin in Big Sur was blissfully unaware of the ludicrous assault on his North Beach bookstore. Upon returning to San Francisco, Ferl surrendered, was fingerprinted and released on $500 bail. Ginsberg was far away under the sheltering skies of Tangier along with William Burroughs who was deep into writing "Naked Lunch".

In the *People of the State of California vs. Lawrence Ferlinghetti*, Ferl went on trial. The prosecution exchanges with defense witnesses, in this case, a book reviewer for a San Francisco daily newspaper, were legendary:

Q: Going down a little further...'who sweetened the snatches of a million girls trembling in the sunset, and were red eyed in the morning but prepared to sweeten the snatch of the sunrise, flashing buttocks under barns and naked in the lake.'

The Court: What's your question?

Q: Now, is the word 'snatches' in there, is that relevant to Mr. Ginsberg's literary endeavor?

A: Yes, I think it is—he's trying to convey an idea of fertility there, among other things, and thus this is his choice of language to convey the idea.

The case was submitted without jury; several weeks later in the Solomonic words of the Court, "*Howl* does have some redeeming social importance, and I find the book is not obscene." Ferlinghetti's courage had opened the flood gates to the Beat era, and helped free up other works of literature that had been banned from sale in states and cities throughout the country.

Now here sat Ferlinghetti sixty years later in Poet's Plaza, closing in on one hundred years of age as McCabe bid him good-by.

"*Ciao*, Lawrence."

"*Ciao*, McCabe."

McCabe walked round the corner to the Saloon at the corner of Fresno Alley and Grant. As early as it was for some, the Saloon had opened its doors for the day. It was the oldest bar in San Francisco, rubbed raw by more than a century and a half of drunken conversation. It shared a curious affinity with McCabe's cottage. Both had been saved in a similar fashion from the conflagration of the 1906 earthquake and fire. Then the Saloon was called Wagner's Beer Hall and it was the favorite watering hole of army regulars stationed at the Presidio military garrison. Let city hall burn, the Nob Hill mansions be consumed, the financial district go up in flames—to every last army man the only true imperative was to save Wagner's Beer Hall and the frisky hookers who played upstairs! With beer soaked blankets and a bucket brigade drawing from a nearby artesian well, the fire passed over the venerable beer hall leveling most everything else for miles around.

McCabe poked his head through the swinging doors of the Saloon into the gritty world of bent blues notes. Johnny Nitro and the Door Slammers were playing the "Brunch Blues", serving up sweaty rhythm and blues beginning at ten in the morning—except for Sundays when they began at noon in deference to the good Lord.

Screaming out the rawest human emotions—love, hate, jealousy—shame and humiliation—hard luck and hard times—misery and oppression—mournfulness and melancholy—the Blues had evolved from the melodic patterns of the West African call-and-response tradition, merging with American slave field shouts and hollers. Soon it was liberated and adopted by freed slaves—thence passed onto guitar toting Mississippi Delta musicians who hired onto steamers, bringing their improvisational Blues minstrelsy to Memphis and St. Louis. From there it spread to the hard streets of the south side of Chicago, and then drifted over the Great Divide, and through the peculiar sensitivity of a classically trained French horn player, Myron Mu, son of a Chinese immigrant who had bought the condemned Saloon—arrived at a run-down bar in the city of Saint Francis on the west coast of America.

In the Saloon's ragbag light McCabe spied Dreiss slouched at the far end of the sticky bar reading a beat-up paperback, evidently with no adverse ocular effects. Dreiss looked up without the slightest hint of surprise at his sudden appearance, "McCabe, good to see you, man. Hey, I'm a little short, can you lend me a few bucks?"

McCabe reached in his pocket with feigned displeasure, "Dreiss, you financial black hole," slapping a couple of dollars on the bar.

Dreiss offered up his usual ironclad assurance, "Appreciate it. I'll pay you back next week," which had never happened in all the years they had known each other.

After trading desultory rumors with Dreiss and the other Saloonatics, McCabe got up to leave. Johnny Nitro stopped playing his riffs, "McCabe, keep drinking triples till you're seeing double, feeling single and getting in trouble!"

McCabe thumbs-upped Johnny and did the walkin' blues out of the Saloon. His eyes dilated, adjusting to the sunlight. Daytime transition

HIST
SSOC
of
America
and
florist
waverly
PRINTING
GON

from the miners' glow of the Saloon back onto Grant Avenue required some acclimatization even if you weren't seeing double and fuddled as a foamy beer.

From the Saloon, McCabe hustled on down to the Chinatown campaign headquarters. In just a few weeks time a fully functioning newsroom had coalesced. Max was sitting at the center table with Bruce Alaska working on layout for the first issue of the *Foghorn*. A handful of reporters were involved with their laptops. Noë and Zoë were hanging out on the balcony overlooking Waverly.

"We're closing in on print," said Max jubilantly.

"Do we have any money to pay for all this or are we still running on fumes?" asked McCabe skeptically.

Max gestured to the balcony, "Talk to your campaign managers, they'll give you the rundown."

"Noë and Zoë?" asked McCabe plaintively, still not quite believing they were ostensibly running his campaign.

"That would be them—the honey trap," joked Max.

McCabe walked out onto the rusting iron porch. In the alley below, elderly Chinese men were chattering in Cantonese, some smoking, a few doing Tai Chi. Mothers with babies bundled on their backs were shopping the markets, overloaded with plastic bags of bok choy and groceries. "Morning ladies, how goes it?" He gave Noë and Zoë a quick once-over that should have been subtler.

"Hey, McCabe," said Noë and Zoë in the sweetest unison.

He couldn't deny enjoying their easy presence. "So how goes managing the campaign? You guys got time to do this and attend your journalism classes too?"

Noë squeezed his arm animatedly, "It's so covered! We worked it out with our dean. We'll get credit working for you—and you don't have to pay us anything."

Zoë chimed in, "You just have to certify, you know—write a letter at the end of the campaign attesting to our working for you, helping to publish the *Foghorn* and hopefully we can write a few pieces for the paper. The whole mantra in journalism school is to get innovative—be entrepreneurial. Your campaign paper is the perfect experiment."

"Speaking of experiments," said McCabe, motioning back inside, "we got a bunch of laid-off newspaper people in there who're going to need a paycheck real soon."

"It's in the bag," said Noë crisply. "You raised over ten thousand dollars at the fundraiser. We filed the first request with the Elections Commission for the ten-to-one city match. They turned it around in a couple of days with a hundred thousand dollar check."

McCabe was disbelieving, "Come on! You mean we already have a hundred grand in the bank?"

"Actually, hundred ten thousand counting the private contributions," replied Noë scrupulously. "And remember, since you're taking public financing you're initially capped at one million dollars. But people like the mayor won't take city monies. For them, the sky's the limit. Once they go over a million, it makes you eligible for additional money from the city at the same ten-to-one match, up to another million. You know the mayor is gonna blow right through a million, probably raise four or five—so all we have to do is privately raise a second hundred thousand and we get another million!

Zoë roller-coaster cheered, "*Woooooooh!*"

McCabe, echoed out onto Waverly, relievedly, "Yeah, we're good to go!" Elderly Chinese passers-by stared up at the crazy white man. What was becoming of the neighborhood?

Back inside the campaign office Max and Bruce had worked out the rough outlines for the initial issue of the *Foghorn*. At the top of the first page would be a four color banner designed by John Nattos—the *Foghorn* name in hues of red and blue flying on elongated stylized wings. Beneath the *Foghorn* name were the words "NEWS AND VIEWS,

PICKS, PANS AND NUGGETS". Balanced on either end of the wings were Chinese symbols with the English translation, "Wisdom" and "Good Luck". Below that was a drawing of the Golden Gate Bridge and a foghorn blowing through wisps of fog into a silhouette of the city's hills. Running from page one to page two was McCabe's new column. Also on page two was the masthead showing the writers, editors, photographers, designers and the "McCabe for Mayor" campaign as the publisher. There would be a couple of lead articles sharing page one, jumping to inside pages. Page three would have a full-page cartoon of a bay view blocked by mile-high waterfront hotels and office buildings drawn by Norman Quidebeau, who had been the *Clarion*'s editoral cartoonist until the lay-off. The remainder of the paper would be filled with articles and photos covering the mosaic of city neighborhoods, interviews with people on the street, sketches and drawings of the city. The *Foghorn* would present its vision of a sustainable city on a hill with the automobile as the dystopian enemy. The *Foghorn* could blow as loudly as it wanted—about anything it wanted—until the November election. The city's ten-to-one matching funding effectively underwrote the entire enterprise. The paper would carry no advertising–none–it wasn't needed, except for promoting McCabe's campaign as a ruse to get public campaign financing.

The *Foghorn*'s back page was laid out with a large photo of a beaming McCabe superimposed over the skyline of San Francisco. In the left-hand corner was an image of Coit Tower, and next to it the pyramidal Transamerica Building, the Golden Gate and Bay Bridge, a cable car winding up a hill, a Chinese street lantern and a band of parrots flying overhead. Underneath the candidate's photo in blockbuster, movie poster lettering was printed "McCABE"—and below that in good luck Chinese red, "for MAYOR" set above the campaign slogan, "Clean, Green Streets for a Livable City". The bottom quarter of the page provided a contributors box that could be clipped out, filled in and sent to the Waverly

Alley campaign headquarters. The clip-out provided boxes that could be checked—"Yes! I want to support McCabe for Mayor!"—choosing varying amounts from five to a hundred dollars, and also boxes for those that wanted to volunteer, host a house party, or display a house sign. Several lines were also provided for contributor information required by city law—name, address, phone, and occupation. In the last section people could write their concerns about their neighborhood and the city. The clip-out feature was Max's concept for a perpetual money machine. In effect, the paper would pay for itself from the clip-out contributions sent into the campaign, and those contributions in turn would immediately be used to obtain the ten-to-one matching money from the city to continue running the paper.

The first issue of the *Foghorn* led with McCabe's column, "McCabe Speaks Out". The column briefly summarized the articles carried in the paper, explaining how each piece fit within his vision of a sustainable city on a hill. There were articles on protecting the waterfront from rapacious development, creating a blue greenway along the bay, achieving a 100 percent recycling rate, bringing back the fishing industry to Fisherman's Wharf, refashioning city-owned golf courses to native habitat, transforming the city zoo to a wildlife rescue and refuge center, pursuing wave and tidal power at the mouth of the Golden Gate, subsidizing wind and solar power on city rooftops, providing grants for renewable energy job training programs, installing electricity charge points for cars and motorbikes, combining energy-efficient street lighting with mobile phone infrastructure, congestion pricing for autos entering the financial district, installing hundreds of miles of new bicycle lanes, and establishing a program for thousands of cheap rental bikes and zipcars throughout the city.

Last and most importantly for McCabe, there was a separate article written by him calling on city hall to give the parrots formal legal protection.

A hundred thousand copies of the *Foghorn* were to be printed and distributed throughout the city. A controversy erupted over whether to print the paper at one of the few remaining union shops or a cheaper non-union shop in Chinatown. Max and April were insistent that the paper be printed at a union shop.

McCabe wasn't convinced, "We're publishing a paper not trying to win an election, so whether labor supports me or not doesn't really make a difference, does it?"

April admonished him, "Tom, we can't forsake the Guild!" Then, almost as an afterthought she asked, "You're still trying not to win? I thought maybe you'd reconsidered?"

McCabe cut her short with a wave of his hand, "The paper is the win, that's it."

April dutifully nodded her head, "We'll do the best we can for the paper—and let the people decide." She turned and began walking away, knowing she had drilled down to a nerve.

McCabe snapped, "April." She whipped her head around, her long grey braid grazing his face. "The paper wins, I lose!"

April gave him a look of disarming acceptance, shielding her own conspiracy within the larger, "Of course Tom, of course."

CHAPTER TEN: THE PARROTS' CAMPAIGN

Volunteers for the "McCabe for Mayor" campaign spread out across the city to distribute the *Foghorn*. The paper was secreted into empty news racks, scattered on buses, at cafés, laundromats, apartment lobbies, every possible doorstep, and inserted into mail slots throughout the city.

The ruse of a free neighborhood-oriented paper was a resounding success. Even though the front page of the paper ran McCabe's column, it gave no immediate indication that it was actually published by the "McCabe for Mayor" campaign. Only in turning to the masthead on the second page was the true nature of the publication apparent, or on reading the back page featuring the full page "McCabe for Mayor" ad. While obvious campaign literature would not be allowed to sit openly on café tables or apartment lobbies, a neighborhood paper was often tolerated. With the *Foghorn*'s camouflage, McCabe's campaign had entered every home and shop in the city. A flood of requests flowed into campaign headquarters for the campaign sign with the parrots flying overhead. Soon commercial corridors were papered with "McCabe for Mayor" signs. Residential areas were tattooed as well, including high-rise penthouses—as if a squabble of seagulls, a murder of crows or a gulp of swallows—even a loft of pigeons—might see the signs and somehow support McCabe.

SCHOOL
FOGHORN McCABE
FOGHORN McCABE
S.B.

McCabe played electoral ball—as if he were out to win—knocking on doors, handing out the *Foghorn*, talking to commuters at bus stops—putting on the appearance of trolling for votes wherever they might be found. It was easy. As a columnist he had grown a corky rhytidome from many thousands of encounters with the psychotic, the schizophrenic, the inebriated, the drug addled, and worst of all, the garrulous know-it-all.

Then, a curious thing happened. McCabe was beginning a midsummer stroll down to North Beach. The parrots had stirred early as well, having adjusted their cross-town hustle to his early rise campaign schedule. Above Coit Tower, the parrots had simultaneously formed up for what looked to be their flight to Mission Dolores. Instead of racing off en masse across town, the parrots splintered into small squadrons of three or four birds. McCabe thought the parrots were taking evasive action against a predator, but none was in sight.

The parrots dispersed throughout the city, winging the commercial corridors, restaurants and cafés, proclaiming their presence—a Frisco cacophony. The "McCabe for Mayor" parrot signs displayed all over town and the screeching parrots were subliminally connected. The outward assumption was the crazed parrots were high after eating some exotic fermenting delicacy from a South American fruit tree or mildly hallucinogenic nut or berry—losing all sense of direction and purpose. The chattering cherry-headed squads flew over Russian and Nob Hills to the Polk Street corridor, around wealthy Pacific Heights, to the Marina by the Golden Gate Bridge, by the Civic Center and Hayes Valley, farther west to the Mission District and Noe Valley, the Castro, Portrero Hill, out to the fog belt of the Sunset and Richmond, Sea Cliff, back over Twin Peaks to the predominantly Black community at Bayview-Hunters Point, to Visitacion Valley, the Excelsior, Dog Patch, Bernal Heights, Mission Bay, Glen Park, the south of Market artists' colonies, the Western Addition and the gentrifying Tenderloin, the financial district, and lastly an encore in Chinatown where the tiny squadrons reassembled and did a ceremonial fly-over of McCabe's campaign headquarters.

Calls flooded local television stations.

That evening on local news stations the bizarre phenomena was given extensive coverage, with video of roisterous parrots racing up and down corridors, alighting in street trees, hopping on people's shoulders and squawking their salty fight song:

Maaaacaaab Mahyer,
Saaay a Prahyer,
Saaay a Prahyer,
Maaaacaaab Mahyer.

The parrots had become subversive soldiers in McCabe's campaign conspiracy. All the bags of sunflower seeds he had put out over the years were now being repaid. McCabe had helped fuel their flights across town—the least the parrots could do was support him—all over town. Simple karma from man to bird and back again.

That afternoon, Miles O'Riley, a reporter for TV station, KINK, did an interview with McCabe at Coit Tower on the top of Telegraph Hill, airing on the six o'clock news:

Miles: Today it was reported by people all over the city that the parrots of Telegraph Hill flew into their neighborhoods making what appeared to be campaign forays on behalf of the "McCabe for Mayor" campaign, screaming out his name. I'm here today with candidate Tom McCabe to try and explain this pandemonium of parrots.

There were reports throughout the day of the parrots screeching your name. Were you aware of that?

McCabe: Actually, I asked them to do it.

Miles: No kidding! How do you get wild parrots to do that kind of thing? Sounds kind of implausible?

McCabe: Absolutely not! We've been friends for a long time. They live in my backyard. I've helped them out in the past, now they're helping me in my campaign.

Miles: Wow! How exactly do you instruct them to do this?

McCabe: Well, I speak their language. They were happy to oblige.

Miles: Come on, McCabe! You mean to tell the people of San Francisco that you can actually communicate with the parrots?

McCabe: Oh yeah, parrot talk isn't all that complicated, I've been listening to them for years. I got a thousand word vocabulary, speak it all the time.

Miles: Really? How about showing us some parrot talk?

McCabe: *Ha, ha*. Good try, Miles. I'm not going there.

Miles: Oh come on, McCabe, be a sport! Just a couple of words.

McCabe: All right, a few won't hurt I suppose. *GAAAAA*. That means "Go."

Miles: Yes, really?

McCabe: *JAAAP*, roughly translates as "Jump."

Miles: You're kidding? Go on!

McCabe: *AAAN* is "In." And lastly...

Miles: Yes, yes!

McCabe: *BAAAK*...

Miles: What's that mean?

McCabe: "Bay!"

Miles: Funny McCabe, quite the comedian. We'll just have to take your word for it. This is Miles O'Riley with mayoral candidate Tom McCabe, reporting for channel **KINK** atop Telegraph Hill.

The parrot forays were a tipping point in McCabe's campaign. Throughout the remainder of the summer, the *Foghorn* flooded the neighborhoods with local news and insight, while in the air, the parrots' avian megaphones bombarded neighborhoods with the cackled screams of McCabe's name. That the campaign was actually having an impact on voter sentiment became apparent in August when private polls began floating around the city's political circles. The campaign for mayor was turning into a horse race.

McCabe was doing rather well.

CHAPTER ELEVEN: THE ROAD TO EXCESS LEADS TO THE PALACE OF WISDOM—BLAKE

McCabe rose with the coral daybreak. Before leaving his cottage, he pinned a "McCabe for Mayor" button on his lapel with a flock of tiny parrots flying over his name. The parrots had stirred early as well, forming over Coit Tower and flying away in disparate directions after determining that he had inalterably begun making his way down to North Beach. The day was particularly fine—no chilling fog, a moderate 70 degrees, crystalline blue skies scrubbed clean by breezes surfacing off the bay.

Approaching Caffé Trieste, the smell of roasting coffee induced a craving—but for a lighter hit than a double espresso—a cappuccino grande. At Poets Plaza the outdoor tables and benches were filled with regulars. Elvis Christ, a beanpole, tripped-out poet was feverishly penning epigrams of onomatopoetic clippety-clop on strips of masking tape, then neatly aligning his oeuvre on the stone pavers just outside the entrance to Trieste. The North Beach cops who patronized the café considered the portal to Trieste as the vortex of insanity, while the firemen from nearby Engine Company 28 adjudged it a black hole of ambition.

Inside Trieste, McCabe ordered a cappuccino grande to go. Paul, a cute gay, recently married Javanese was behind the counter working the massive copper espresso machine that had pounded out a million cups of coffee. He handed McCabe his grande, then eyed him slowly, pointing at the campaign button on his lapel, "Who's running for mayor, you or the parrots? Are they going to move into city hall if you win, Birdbrain?"

"To birds of a feather, my windows will always be open at city hall. But decorum will have to be maintained and that will be a challenge!" joked McCabe.

Paul handed him a biscotti, "That's not for you, Birdman, it's for the parrots."

"Guess I'm going to eat their breakfast," said McCabe with a droll smile, dipping the biscotti in his cappuccino.

Returning to Poets Plaza, McCabe's world seemed to be in balance once more. Money was flowing into the campaign, city matching funds came quickly, his pals were making a living—on borrowed time but making a living nonetheless. He was actually enjoying his role as a candidate, becoming more familiar with the city—a town he thought he knew intimately but actually didn't in certain respects. Many of the outlying neighborhoods were only vaguely familiar, now he was getting to know them better—the cafés, bars, grocery stores and restaurants where locals hung out and shopped. Each day McCabe went with either Noë or Zoë, sometimes both, to a different neighborhood, handed out campaign material at supermarket entrances, engaged in morning café walks, or Noë and Zoë's favorite—neighborhood bar crawls in the evenings.

He also went in for an occasional house party. These fundraisers generally lasted a couple of hours. The host would introduce him, usually in a jumbled, disjointed manner, "You all know him, he's been writing a column on city politics and culture for years."—"He brings a fresh voice to the mayoral campaign."—"He is unencumbered by political alliances, a nonpolitician who will shake things up."—"He loves this city more than himself and will do everything to make it better." McCabe used a copy of the *Foghorn* as a prop to launch into his stump speech on a sustainable city on a hill, sprinkled with humorous campaign anecdotes. After five or six minutes he would conclude, take some questions, then spend the rest of the time chatting up and thanking his supporters.

Around town McCabe's campaign buttons proved to be extremely popular. Scores of buttons were given away every day. They were so sought after that opportunists began selling them online. For the large three inch buttons the price started at five dollars, but in a few weeks rose to ten dollars, then to fifteen. The one-inch buttons that had been selling for a dollar simultaneously rose in value to five dollars. The fact that campaign buttons were being sold online should have been a clue to McCabe—a clue about the popularity of his campaign. But he was on cruise control—cruising toward the finish line.

That evening, McCabe was scheduled to do a meet-and-greet bar crawl with Noë and Zoë. He was the only candidate who did bar walks—the unpredictable could happen, something nasty, something ugly and offensive. It didn't concern him. As a columnist he had been challenged a thousand times in drinking establishments about his views and opinions, sometimes by the most drunk, aggressive patrons—always ending without incident.

McCabe arranged to meet Noë and Zoë at the Climax, a bar on Polk Street that catered to Millennials—young professionals, mostly heterosexual, mixed with gays who knew nothing of the plague, also genderqueers of various kinds: bigender, trigender and pangender. It could be hard to make a distinction on appearance or speech alone about a person's sexual orientation as they often went surprising directions in their gender fluidity.

Polk Street ran the seam between Russian Hill and Pacific Heights, and farther south, Nob Hill and Cathedral Heights. It was comprised of a mix of ethnic restaurants: French bistros, Thai noodle joints, taquerias, oyster bars, trattorias, Moroccan casbahs, Irish bars, Italian cafés and bakeries.

Polk was a former gay haunt that had changed in the past generation to a mostly young hetero scene. Paradoxically, the success of gay rights had tolled the end of pure gay culture. There could be no lust for the forbidden if nothing was forbidden. The Ramrod, Bathhouse Disco, Chaps, and lesbianville's Faster Pussycat, Female Trouble and the Box were all gone. Pink dollars had been exchanged for green.

The Polk Street crowd didn't know McCabe well. Many didn't spend time on newspapers. The old habits of reading the paper in the morning, at lunch with a sandwich, or on the bus to work, had pretty much disappeared. Many of the younger professionals walked to work or hopped on the bus glued to their smart phones, iPads or laptops. They were no more than ten to fifteen years McCabe's junior, but it was another generation in how they searched for news, if they even searched at all. McCabe might as well have been from the Paleozoic.

Old fossil McCabe was a brisk walker. He took hills of San Francisco fast having lived in the city all his life. The most direct route from his home to Polk Street was straight over Union. There was no way to avoid Russian Hill whose eastern flank ran down to North Beach, its western side down to Polk. Leaving his cottage, McCabe took the Filbert Steps to Montgomery then on up to the top of Union Street to Speedy's Market. The Spediachi family had run the small grocery store since the 1920s, barely hanging on as a viable neighborhood market. The rich folks on Telegraph Hill loved to talk about quaint neighborhood businesses, but most of them spent little in the nearby stores and restaurants. McCabe knew hundreds of people on Telegraph Hill, many with assets in the millions and tens of millions dollars, but he could count on his fingers the households that regularly patronized the restaurants, cafés and retail shops of North Beach.

Mr. Spediachi was nearing ninety—stooped and slow, still living in the apartment above the store as his parents and grandparents had done. What little hair remained on his head was uncombed, his morning shave uneven, hair grew prominently from his nose and ears. He had worked the precarious corner grocery store since he was a child, his grandparents having taken the store space and apartment above for $50 a month. A wholesaler had provided the initial stock on credit—canned goods, coffee, sugar—and with it a ticket into the merchant class. At one time, the family knew every household for blocks around, primarily Italian, often advancing credit until payday.

"Hey, Boss," said McCabe good naturedly, putting down a dollar on the counter, grabbing a pack of breath mints to ward off alcohol breath.

Spediachi squinted through his glasses perched unevenly on his protuberant nose, "McCabe is that you? Running for mayor are you? I know you, McCabe. You always were a mystery, never letting people in. Someone is going to crack that exterior of yours—*someone*—and you won't know what hit you! You can try to dodge your fate McCabe, but it'll still be waiting for you over the next hill!" Spediachi rang up the old cash register with McCabe's lonesome dollar.

McCabe, inattentive to the old man's wisdom, replied simply, "*Grazie*, Mr. Spediachi."

Outside the store, the news racks featured the *Clarion*, *New York Times*, *Wall Street Journal*, *Oakland Tribune*, *San Jose Mercury*. There was also a free stack of *Foghorns*. McCabe grabbed a few. He could use the paper during the bar walk on Polk to break the ice.

As McCabe started down Union, the streetlights serially lit from the top of Telegraph Hill down to North Beach then up to the top of Russian Hill. The sight of the streetlights coming to life had always induced a sense of wonder in him since he was a child, as if he were witnessing the secret clockwork of the metropolis.

He walked down Union to Washington Square. The small park in the heart of North Beach was precious and overused. Together with Chinatown, North Beach had the highest number of people per square mile in the city—and the least amount of open space. Pine and cypress trees lined the periphery of the park. Wooden benches were set along the park's circular pathway. A stand of poplars in the middle of the park enveloped a bronze statue of Benjamin Franklin. McCabe detoured into the park to say hello to the dogs, most unleashed and running about on the grass. Occasionally, he carried treats in his pocket. A whirlwind of dogs scampered round him, pawing at his pants. Tonight they would be disappointed—he had no treats.

His cell phone vibrated in his coat pocket—a subtle sex-text from Noë, "Where r u? Cum McCabe!!"

He hustled up Union, then took a left on Leavenworth to Green. At the crest of the hill was an old Victorian firehouse that was now a residence.

As a child, McCabe used to walk with his neighborhood pals the couple of blocks from his Russian Hill home to the firehouse. Clustered expectantly at the entrance, they would tremulously ring the doorbell, a young fireman sheepishly granting them entry. Scrambling up the stairs to the second story sleeping quarters, they slid down the brass pole to the fire engines below, then back upstairs for another pole slide until they tired of the game. But one day, a visiting fire captain with ribbons on his chest and gold stripes on his sleeves answered the bell and blocked their way. They weren't allowed in the firehouse, it was against something called "regulations." McCabe marked the end of his childhood at that moment. The first order issued by him if he actually ever were to be mayor would be to allow kids into firehouses under supervised conditions to slide down the brass poles, what few of them were left—to hell with regulations.

From Leavenworth, McCabe cruised down the western side of Russian Hill to the Climax at the corner of Green and Polk. It was a warm

August evening. A sociable, gregarious crowd milled around outside the bar, mostly a mix of Caucasian and Asian—from their early twenties to mid-thirties—lots of slashed and tattered jeans, the women turning up their cuffs to flash more of their ankles, the men with fitted white shirts, long sleeves rolled up. Hairdos were dialed down, sleek and controlled, offsetting the distressed denim. A few people recognized him. He threw around some conversation, handed out copies of the *Foghorn* and gave out campaign buttons. There was much verbal effluvia; the valuable insight, the brief and to-the-point conversations were like green acorns in the desert.

The crowd's sexual appetite began stirring his own latent desires. McCabe could sense the substratum of the extended human mind whether it was a cluster of people talking in a park, a neighborly crowd outside a bar, or an entire city. He believed that the collective mind melded with the biosphere—plants breathed out oxygen and humans breathed it in. He could feel the hot happiness of an obliging crowd on a warm evening on Polk Street in a city on the west coast of America as well as the melting glaciers that endangered the Arctic polar bear. All living things were one, divided only by lack of self-knowledge and collective misunderstanding, he thought.

Noë and Zoë were standing by the bar drinking champagne. Noë was dressed in a teal mini-dress, azure pumps with red soles, a white pearl necklace, rosy coral lipstick. She wore a compact leather backpack filled with campaign buttons and copies of the *Foghorn*. Zoë, six inches shorter, wore a black spaghetti strap dress lined up just over her breasts. Her pumps were sparkly grey anthracite, complimenting a black Tahitian pearl necklace. McCabe lightly tapped Noë's shoulder, skimming his hand down her arm. She exclaimed animatedly, "Hey, we were getting concerned!"

McCabe joked, "You didn't look all that concerned to me..."

"Well, we were," said Noë, now giving him a clipped professional smile. She ordered a glass of champagne for him. "There are a lot of people who want to meet you. Come on, we'll introduce you around." Over the next hour, McCabe spoke to almost everyone inside the Climax. Many took a campaign button, pinning them to their lapels and dresses, some to their purses.

Leaving the Climax, they hit the Lush Lounge, then several more bars and cafés, giving out the last of the campaign buttons. Shanghai Kelly's at the corner of Polk and Broadway was the final hole for their bar crawl. Laid back and divish, a blue-collar crowd possied up the place—carpenters, electricians, contractors, a few police and firefighters. With the next drink, McCabe reached his limit—hearing the first hint of his own slurred speech.

They eased out of the bar onto Broadway. McCabe whistled down a cab. "You guys want a ride somewhere?" he asked nonchalantly, opening the back door for them to climb in.

Jumping in the cab, neither Zoë nor Noë replied to his schoolboy question. The driver wore a black turban matched by a Bin Laden beard, probably from the Punjab. Turning round in his seat he shot a quick glance at Noë and Zoë who were whispering to each other. "Where to *wenches* and *wangsters*?" he asked in a lilting British accent.

Noë blurted, "We have a surprise for you!" Zoë snickered.

McCabe looked archly at their smooth legs and hitched-up dresses. "What might that be?"

"Take us to the Beat Museum on Broadway," instructed Noë self-assuredly. She serenely put one hand on Zoë's leg, her other lightly on McCabe's knee. "Are you up for something literary, McCabe?"

"A book launch?"

"*Hah!* Not exactly. There will be readings. I think you'll like it, won't he, Zoë?"

Zoë smiled enigmatically, "You actually think he'll listen?"

The cab sped through the Broadway tunnel, crossing over Columbus to the strip clubs—past Satan's Cellar, Nymphia, Eager Beaver, Snatch, Taste Her, Maiden Lane, Deeper, Slut Robots, and lastly, Happy Ending. The strips clubs had been around since the early sixties, a jagged evolution from the old Barbary Coast days of gambling halls, opium dens and black-stocking bars.

The cab stopped in front of a three-story brick building that housed the Beat Museum. A maroon-colored 1949 Hudson with a wood-paneled dashboard was displayed inside the museum's plate glass window, the same year and model car that Kerouac as Sal Paradise and Neal Cassady as Dean Moriarty, manically drove back and forth across the country in *On the Road.* Sadly, the faithful Hudson never made the subsequent 1951 trip to Mexico. The car had been thrown over for a '37 Ford Sedan with the "right-side door unhinged and tied on the frame." Some claimed a happy ending for the Hudson—the specimen sitting in the Beat Museum window was a magical transmutation of the fictional version, having miraculously survived the junk yards and metal crushers, now placidly parked in a North Beach museum.

A reproduction of Kerouac's draft of *On the Road* hung in the Beat Museum window—a partially unwound one hundred and twenty-foot scroll of tracing paper that Kerouac had cut to size and taped together. Next to the scroll, a poster displayed three naked women sitting primly on a couch each reading a book that barely concealed their breasts. The poster announced, "THE NAKED LADIES BOOK CLUB PRESENTS—*The Wild Party*—a narrative poem by Joseph M. March." The bottom of the poster informed of yet another Naked Book Club erotic reading later in the month from Anaïs Nin—the *Delta of Venus* and *House of Incest.*

Inside the Beat Museum was an old turnstile through which a five-dollar admission allowed the run of the place. McCabe flipped a twenty to a sallow man at the counter, bought three tickets and put the remaining five dollars in a donation jar. Beyond the turnstile they walked through a reproduction of a 50s Beat writer's bedroom. There was a single bed stand, a chipped mirror and dinged lamp, a scratched up desk, vintage typewriter, a couple of plain wooden chairs, and a wall of paperback books—pulp novellas—from the 40s and 50s. There were obscure titles like *Jesus Was a Beatnik* and *Sin Time Beatniks.* There was also David Goodis' *Dark Passage*, subsequently to star Bogart and Bacall hanging out just above McCabe's cottage. The lurid covers paraded steel jawed men and scantily clad women depicting a corrupt, unsentimental and sensual world—often dealing with taboo subjects like juvenile delinquency—*Blackboard Jungle*, *Teenage Mafia*, *Jailbait*, *Sex Gang*, *Gutter Gang*, *Teen Temptress*, *Zip-Gun Angels*, *The Black Leather Barbarians*—lesbiana—*Spring Fire* and *We Walk Alone*—racism—*Nigger Heaven*, *The Whipping*—and drug addiction—*H is for Heroin*, *Junkie*, *Marihuana*, *Reefer Club.* In all, bleak one-liners, cryptic pronouncements and depressive endings were the norm.

Beyond the Beat writer's room a red arrow directed them upstairs to the "Naked Ladies Book Club". Female voices floated out into the corridor. They took some of the last remaining seats at the back of the reading room, the audience a mix of couples and singles. In the front, three naked women looking to be in their late twenties sat on a red leather sofa, their legs loosely crossed, taking turns reading from Joseph March's *The Wild Party.* Behind the women were curtains of green velvet. One woman was a fine breasted Bonnard, blur gold hair, wearing fifties style reading glasses—another, red-haired, a full-figured Botticelli, strong thighs, buxom, expressive-lipped, licentious—the last, of Mongolian descent, a slim legged Modigliani, high cheekbones, small breasts, long dark hair, distant. A waiter passed among the audience taking orders for wine, beer and sodas.

Initially, Joseph March's 1926 poem had been considered too racy for publication. It was not until 1928 that he was able to find a publisher for a run of 750 copies. It was *The Wild Party* that influenced William

Burroughs to become a writer. In turn he opened the door for other Beat writers. Joseph March was the first Beat writer a generation before Beat cohered into a recognizable cultural phenomena.

The women took turns reading stanzas from *The Wild Party.* They were already well into the poem—an extended description of an increasingly debauched, candle-lit party:

> The candles spluttered, their flames were gay;
> And the shadows leapt back out of the way.
> The party began to get going.
> The laughter rang shriller.
> The talk boomed louder.
> The women's faces showed flush through powder;
> And the men's faces were glowing.
> The room was hung with streamers of smoke.
> It billowed, curled,
> Swung, swirled,
> Poured towards the candle flames
> And broke...

Minutes later, with the reading finished, the women stood up to polite applause, clasped hands and demurely bowed, baring their shaved nakedness without irony or self-consciousness, then disappeared behind the velvet curtains.

McCabe, Noë and Zoë walked downstairs through the Beat bedroom, running their fingers over the '49 Hudson and back out into the cooling Broadway night.

"Are you up for that?" asked Noë, pointing across the boulevard at a former Gold Rush assaying office where miners used to bring their nuggets and gold dust, tested for purity, and exchanged for hard currency.

"That?" asked McCabe, staring over at the two-story impenetrable brick fortress with octagon towers and lancet windows.

"Yeah, I bet you've been in there, haven't you?"

"*Ah...*" he muttered disconcertingly.

"The truth, McCabe!"

"On opening night, members of the press were invited, so naturally I..."

"I knew it! You're so obvious," exclaimed Noë. "I've never been inside."

"Neither have I," said Zoë colludingly.

McCabe gazed edgily across the boulevard.

"Oh come on, McCabe, are you afraid to go in there again?" goaded Noë.

"Have you guys forgotten? I'm supposed to be running for mayor!"

"You're not going to be asked to assume the position. From what I understand, the women hold the controls and do it to themselves," Noë simpered. "You might even pick up the kink vote."

"A large portion of the voting public, no doubt," he replied sarcastically.

"We'll just take a peek, come on," urged Noë. She grabbed McCabe's hand, Zoë the other and skittered across Broadway. In a nearby police car, Officer Downer slunk low like a curled snake hidden beneath a desert rock, observing Noë and Zoë on their chattering four-inch heels, pulling along a befuddled McCabe.

Downer instantly recognized McCabe and scowled at him from the darkness of his cruiser. McCabe had ridiculed Downer more than once in his column for his petty meanness, cynicism and detachment, vilified throughout North Beach. Like the flickering of a snake's tongue, Downer gave them a quick lick of his siren, then hit them with a spotlight. McCabe was brought up short. Noë and Zoë froze, embarrassed. Broadway was a dangerous thoroughfare to jaywalk, particularly at night with the live music, gangsta DJ promoters, and strip clubs that attracted a randy, drinking, carrying crowd. Downer was jubilant, yelling to himself, "Got you, McCabe, arrogant prick! Your little chickies were scared out of their panties!"

Downer watched them continue down the street to the old assaying office. Over the front door was a pink neon sign, "SLUT ROBOTS." A group of inebriated conventioneers was just leaving the establishment. McCabe cracked them a smile. They ignored him, instead casting libidinous looks at Noë's and Zoë's high-heeled sculpted legs.

A grizzled pony-tailed doorman in a purple coat and gold tie called out in a staccato voice, "Come on folks, see what's inside! The Penis Flytrap, the Titan and the Trespasser doin' hard core, deep probin' g-spot sex! Guaranteed female orgasm with the hottest high tech, custom built sex machines! Come and look at the scariest of all, Fuckzilla! And for you romantics, the Double *Je Taime*! For the ladies man, the Mojo and the Dominate Her! Porn star sluts! The whore at your door! Cruel mistresses! Bratty schoolgirls! Or if you want—the cheerleader next door! College girls coming hard on the Drilldo! Multiple orgasms on the Intruder MK2! Discipline by the Spanker! And for you virtual reality kinksters, we got pixelated playmates—virtual sex partners—3D porn—bumping and grinding—make 'em tall or short—Brazilian or bald—big boobs—big butts—your favorite nipples—whatever your imagination desires—you're the carnal controller!"

"And if that doesn't satisfy your appetite, tonight we have a special feature for you, Zen Dicks—the world's very first sex robot! Always turned on and ready to play—or just talk dirty! A super-horny Siri! Program your own customizable personality—have her anyway you want—from Frigid Farrah to Wild Wendy—and she can even simulate orgasm for you Annihilators and Pile Drivers!"

"And if you're still not satisfied we have an entirely new feature! Girl-on-girl wrestling, oiled up and ready for a take-down! Tag teams and one-on-one! With a special strap-on round!"

The barker suddenly dropped his alpha spiel, recognizing McCabe, lowering his voice, "*Ah*—McCabe? Hey man, what's goin' on?"

McCabe had known Wolfe Barker for years. He had worked the Broadway strip for a couple of decades, was known to deal a little coke on the side, knew everything about Broadway and everyone on it. He had witnessed the six month turnover of strippers like the change of seasons, the police captains come and go, seen a rougher crowd move in, and with it the occasional gang fight, knifing and random killing. He was king of all he surveyed. McCabe high-fived him, "Wolfe, good to see you, man! My friends would *ah*—like to take a quick look. Curious to see what's inside." Noë gave McCabe an irritated look, putting it all on her.

Wolfe yelped, "Sure, whatever you want! Your friends will have a naughty time! *Ha, ha!*" He gave McCabe a conspiratorial pat on his back, *sotto voce*, "Although with these two, they might get some depraved ideas what to do with you later, Old Stick!" Wolfe called out to the ticket counter at the bottom of the stairs, "These guys get in free. Enjoy McCabe." He motioned them in with a courtly faux manner, "Ladies."

The bordello bar was jamming, a mixed crowd of professional men and women who could have been at any of the many financial district hangouts a few blocks away. McCabe ordered three barrel-aged cocktails.

Zoë felt the need, gesturing at the stairway where the bathrooms were located, "I'll be back."

"Have fun," said McCabe with knowing amusement.

Reappearing a few minutes later from the *tinkleatrium* and much relieved, Zoë declared, "I can't believe the signs to the bathrooms!"

McCabe feigned ignorance, "What do you mean?"

"At the top of the stairs the sign pointing left says 'Men'. The sign pointing right says 'Ovaries.' And the sign on the door to the woman's bathroom says 'Sit Down', so I checked the Men's door…"

"Yeah I know, 'Stand Up'. I hope you choose the right door!" snorted McCabe.

Across from the bar was a doorway with a garish purple neon sign—"Sex Machines." With a leavening of trepidation and excitement, they ventured into the Slut Robots panopticon, a dozen or so rooms arranged around a central well each housing a unique sex machine operated by a female "engineer." Each space had a distinct theme: high school classroom, saloon, pool hall, pirate ship, Victorian parlor, medieval torture chamber, speakeasy.

A separate room with wrestling ring was filled with a roisterous crowd, featuring women tag teams, well-endowed, one team in lavender, the other in fushia string bikinis. The winners could have their way with their submissive opponents by means of extra large purple strap-ons—and could double snake if they so desired.

At the Penetrator Room, there were about forty people studiously watching a mechanized driver, a red plastic vibrator on point. With a contented vibratory purr it slipped in and out of a barely adult, blonde-haired vixen. The other machines were variations of the Penetrator except for the human hamster wheel. In each, the woman remotely controlled her machine's vaginal impulses with a Bluetooth remote. Only the Double Snake did more than vaginal.

Leaving Slut Robots, McCabe sucked up a deep lungful of evening air, wondering if they had just witnessed a small slice of hell. The night had chilled. Foghorns blew in the distance. Noë and Zoë leaned into him for warmth. They crossed over Broadway, passing the now misty neon strip clubs signs, then walked up Grant skirting the crowd spilling out of the Saloon. At Caffé Trieste neighborhood regulars were still congregated in Poets Plaza listening to a street band playing Django Reinhart gypsy tunes—jazz guitar, bass, mandolin, fiddle and violin.

They walked past Ideale, Tupelo, Maggie McGarry's and Grant & Green. Redolent marijuana, jumpy bluegrass and raw rock'n'roll mixed in the air—all the bars a stage. On Green Street were the last of the blue-collar Italian joints—Sodini, Columbus Café, Gino & Carlo, Belle

Cora—each within stumbling distance of the other. Patrons clustered just outside drinking and smoking, breathing in a pungent Italian bouquet of garlic and basil.

McCabe was greeted effusively at Gino & Carlo. This was the bar that a generation earlier had given shelter and sustenance to another *Clarion* columnist often compared to him. For nearly twenty years his predecessor inhabited a four top table in the back, holding court, churning out a thousand words a day on Irish culture, booze, his mistresses and random failed marriages. Ripped from the typewriter as evening approached, it was frantically bike-messengered to the *Clarion* building, often arriving after deadline. WiFi McCabe, writing his column from another North Beach haunt, had never missed a deadline.

Leaving Gino & Carlo, they were riding the dragon. "Where to?" said McCabe, nothing particular in mind.

"Shouldn't we have one last drink?" Noë asked, feeding the beast.

Zoë, mirrored Noë, the alcohol taking her, "We've never seen your place."

McCabe, alcohol raptured himself, grinned with feigned hesitation, "*Hmmm*—do we cab it or walk?"

Noë and Zoë declared simultaneously, "Walk!" At Filbert and Grant, they ascended the irregular steps—deep stairs, shallow stairs, narrow stairs and wide—a spasmodic test of unsettled equilibrium and unsteady physicality.

Pausing at the top of the stairs, McCabe was surprised—for the first time in his life he needed to catch his breath climbing Telegraph Hill. Trying to mask his heavy breathing, he asked, "Ever been in Coit Tower? I know the caretaker."

"Somebody lives in the tower?" replied Zoë, doubting his assertion.

"Yeah, there's an aerie at the top."

Coit Tower was like a phallic exclamation point—!—its fluted shaft lit with red spotlights. It rose 180 feet to an observation deck that offered 360-degree views of the city. McCabe pulled out his cell phone. "See that." He pointed at a small lit window in the corona of the tower. "That's where Zack lives." He punched in a number.

"Zack, it's McCabe. I'm here with a couple of friends. Can I show them the murals?" He turned to Noë and Zoë, "We're in!" Shortly, the lobby lights came on. Zack was in his eighties sporting a ragged grey beard, wire rim glasses, a worn Brooklyn Dodgers baseball cap, blue work shirt and jeans. He was a wisp of a man, his voice high pitched and chipper, imp and elf in equal measure.

"Evening, McCabe, who're your pals?"

"Noë and Zoë," said McCabe, caressing their arms.

"Well, come on in, ladies! Enjoy the murals, but don't get lost in them—a few have and were never seen again! *Ha ha!* When you leave, just turn off the lights, the door will lock behind you. See you, McCabe. Ladies."

The walls of the lobby were decorated with New Deal murals, 4,000 square feet of frescoes, paid for by the Roosevelt administration. Twenty-five artists earned $25 to $40 a week, working independently of each other, designing and painting murals of industry, commerce, and the struggling masses determined to make their way through the Great Depression. The murals were integrated into the gun-slit windows, doors and alcoves of the tower's circular lobby. The fresco style was simple but time-consuming, applying wet plaster of marble dust mixed with slaked lime. All the color pigments were ground by one artist to assure uniformity, building up the intensity of the color for as long as the surface remained moist. Some claimed they could still smell the wet plaster.

They traveled the ring of murals, taking in socialist realism of 1930s Americana—steel mills, canneries, docks and chemical plants. They encountered a phalanx of grim faced miners striking for higher wages and safer work conditions—the scent of Bolshevist revolution. Placid murals of Central and Imperial Valley's agribusiness gave them a pause.

Rounding a corner, they looked down on Depression Era tent dwellers panning for Sierra gold. Further on, farm workers picked apricots, apples and grapes. Round another bend, hundreds of oil derricks pumped Kern County crude. The unsteady trio slipped by a muralled library where they scanned the headlines of *The New Masses* and the *Daily Worker*, catching Kenneth Rexroth reaching for a book on Oscar Wilde. They skirted a law firm, stole by the Federal Reserve Bank, briefly toured the Pacific Stock Exchange, then witnessed a traffic accident and armed robbery. Just down the street they encountered a pickpocket and policeman, and in the final scene crossed paths with a lonesome cowboy.

Completing the circle, McCabe turned off the lights, the lobby door slamming behind them. They stumbled down to his lair embraced by the chilling fog.

CHAPTER TWELVE: MAINTAINING

The strawberry sunrise flooded McCabe's sinner sanctum.

He warily squeezed out a pre-caffeinated peek at his devil's den. His cell phone rang on the bed stand, caller ID indicating it was Max. The fellatiatrixes were gone—the bedding primly pulled up as if after a peaceful night of sleep, no evidence of equilateral tri-coupling. Squad Car was curled up at the end of the bed, his head buried beneath his paw. McCabe tentatively reached out for his cell as if it might conceal an IED.

"Hey Max, why so early?" queried McCabe, raspy voiced.

"You gotta get ready!"

"For what?"

"For tonight's debate," Max sputtered, pummeling McCabe's tenderized brain.

"Oh..." was all McCabe had the strength to muster.

"McCabe, you OK? You sound bad."

"Long night, that's all."

"Well get your ass down here! We gotta prepare for tonight!"

"I know everything I need to say."

"Yeah? Affordable housing, tech invasion, transit, schools, parks, police?"

"I'm going to speak to journalism."

"Journalism!? You're running for mayor!"

"Who cares? We're running a newspaper—not for mayor."

"Whatever, get down here now!" shouted Max, ending the conversation.

It was an arduous climb up the Filbert Steps. McCabe's hellacious hangover overwhelmed the erotic reflections on the night's *Bacchanalia*. But, in a few days time the memories of his debilitating hangover would disappear, distilled to the erotic bedroom scene with Noë and Zoë—contentedly recalled for the rest of his life.

He grasped the wooden railings like a broken old man. ***Oh God, I'm paying a price.*** As if cast out of paradise—where the bluebird of happiness sits on your shoulder and parrots fly overhead—trouble finds us all.

He slowly made his way down to Grant. Trieste beckoned. He bought a hair of the fog—a double espresso and a bottle of water—went back out to Poets Plaza and sat down on a granite bench. It was still early, few regulars around. Anchored to the cold hard stone, he tried to recalibrate. The consequences of the previous evening could wait to be sorted out. Right now clearing his head was paramount. Life was an ebb and flow of his strengths and weaknesses. A hangover gave his weaknesses the upper hand. A severe hangover was a complete route—not much better than staying in bed all day.

He absently watched the pigeons pecking about the plaza. The gold crosses atop the twin spires of St. Francis church gleamed in the morning light, no peregrine falcon waiting to snatch a pigeon or parrot. McCabe closed his eyes trying to visualize the day running up to the debate. Usually his hangovers began to ebb around noon, gone by five, back to normal by early evening. It was getting there that would be the Augean challenge.

"McCabe?" It was Loki, the BDSM goddess giving him a deeply concerned look. "McCabe, what are you doing?"

He wearily opened his eyes, "Hey, Loki," but couldn't manage another word.

"Hard night?"

He winced, "Didn't seem so at the time..."

Loki sat down beside him, showing pleased concern, "You've been naughty, haven't you?" She whispered reassuringly, "Maybe this will help. Close your eyes…" She serenely pressed his temples, nursing him, murmuring in his ear, "Just maintain, rehydrate. Smile. It'll be fine."

McCabe drifted for a hundred heartbeats. Upon opening his eyes again, Loki had taken flight. He stood up and stretched, more limber than before. He crossed over Broadway into Chinatown. Midst the chatter of Cantonese, he waded through shoals of people shopping the produce, fish and meat markets—oranges, tangerines and apples stacked high—freshwater and saltwater bass, eels, frogs, live shrimp, red rock cod with oversized eyes, roasted duck on hooks, dried shark fin, braised fish maw, dried cuttlefish. No one made way.

McCabe negotiated the throngs to Waverly and the Wong Fook Hing Book Store, then crossed the alley to the Buddhist Association building. Three garish red banners hung from the campaign headquarters balcony boldly proclaiming "McCabe for Mayor". A fourth banner in Cantonese phonetically spelled out McCabe's name in three characters. It literally read "Good Luck Bird"—a big joke at campaign headquarters—"Good Luck Bird for Mayor".

Most of the merchants on Waverly had "McCabe for Mayor" signs in their windows in appreciation that McCabe, though not of Asian descent, had located his campaign headquarters in the heart of Chinatown—and as importantly in the Buddhist building. Each lunchtime and early evening, the good karma flowed—free deliveries of food from Chinatown diners and cafes, dim sum teahouses and hot pot restaurants—spring rolls, fried rice, dry garlic spareribs, salt and pepper squid, sweet and sour pork, crispy skin duck, ginger beef, moo shu pork, crab rangoon, ants climbing tree, sesame chicken, kung pao chicken, monks jump over the wall soup—dozens of different dishes.

McCabe scaled the tunneling stairway of the Buddhist Association building. In the 50 watt luminescence a saffron blur floated his way.

A Buddhist monk squeezed by and giggled. McCabe grimaced, then remembered Loki's admonition to smile. At the second floor landing he slowly opened the door to the campaign headquarters, feeling curiously distended.

Like a splash of cold water, April exclaimed, "Tom, good timing! We were just about to sit down and discuss tonight's debate."

"McCabe," boomed Max from across the room. "You look whipped! What have you been up to?" Other *Foghorn* reporters scattered around room stared at him, smiling, quietly laughing.

McCabe, irreparably frazzled, felt dream naked, "Morning, morning," he said gamely with a forced smile, nowhere to hide.

"Hey, McCabe, morning!" It was Zoë, cheery as a robin, radiating unusual joy and vitality, or was she blushing, unborn children in her eyes?

Noë walked up behind her, "We have a press release for tonight's debate." She handed it to him, flushed, "We need your ok."

There was not a touch of irony or sarcasm in their voices, not a hint of their earlier states of lubricious dishabille but a few hours ago. The press release was titled, "McCabe Comes out Swinging." ***Were the Freudian implications intentional?*** He gave them an inquiring look, probing their out-of-sight minds. ***Come on guys, give me a sign.*** Nada.

"Fine." said McCabe tentatively, off-balance. "Curious title." There still wasn't a clue that Noë and Zoë had been wild-ass naked, riding him like a Sybian, sharing their flavors of love.

McCabe spent the next several hours at the center table with April, Max and other reporters who were grounded in city issues. Land use went to the architectural critic, city finance to the business reporter, crime to the police watch reporter, landlord/tenant issues to the housing expert, public transit to the transportation maven. There was an extraordinary wealth of expertise and information bundled in the campaign, a hundred years of combined reporter experience—a cram-down of facts, numbers, and names. But it was all going into a black hole, not into McCabe's retentive brain.

As the campaign moved forward, it had taken on the actual appearance of a candidate intent on winning—when in fact nothing had changed from the original premise—running for mayor as a means of financing a newspaper. And with that purpose still uppermost in his mind, McCabe had other designs on the debate. He would not be bothered by the minutiae of city government—not vie with the other candidates to show who was most informed about city operations. He would focus on journalism and democracy.

His hangover began to ebb, but more slowly than anticipated—its dead weight vying against the countdown to the debate. He needed to get home and anchored, then showered and dressed. He had arranged to have April escort him to the debate. All the other candidates were married, including the lesbian candidate, and would have their partners present. As he was leaving campaign headquarters, Noë and Zoë approached him like two rabbits at a bunny hop. McCabe gave them a perplexed, self-conscious smile.

Noë laughed paso doble, "It's cool, McCabe. We just wanted to leave you alone. You needed to concentrate. We weren't trying to be mean. Say hi to Squad Car."

"And the parrots," Zoë chimed, so reserved compared to their earlier threesome reel.

McCabe took his time walking back through Chinatown. The markets were no longer packed. The produce trucks that had earlier blocked traffic were gone. City buses ran smoothly and unobstructed.

He crossed back over Broadway into North Beach. At Poets Plaza, Socrates Salonica Sarfatti, a hyperactive, theoretical—and theatrical physicist—UC Berkeley's only "outdoor professor"—was conducting his weekly seminar. Sarfatti challenged the universe with the dialectical primacy of the Idea. He came out of the 60s counter-cultural revolution and "question authority" academia. His was the most popular seminar offered at Berkeley—required to be held outdoors anywhere in the Bay Area—except in the event of bad weather—really, really bad weather. Only then did he grudgingly take his class indoors. Students were on the honor system not to travel to the professor's seminar in a car—and many of the locations were inaccessible by car anyway. The professor had held classes on his houseboat in Sausalito, in the abandoned Alcatraz prison yard in the middle of the bay, in the Mt. Tamalpais amphitheater north of San Francisco, at the summit of Mount Diablo in the East Bay, in Sproul Plaza at Berkeley itself, and even occasionally down south on the Peninsula at joint seminars in the Quad of rival Stanford University. But of all the spots in the Bay Area, Socrates' favorite was Poets Plaza where he could spin the universe like a top and offer up his ironic post-quantum model of consciousness. Today, the students sat on the Plaza's granite benches, others in chairs pulled up from Caffé Trieste. Protocol permitted, encouraged drinking wine during the seminar, and if you brought a particularly good bottle to share with the professor and fellow outdoor enthusiasts, Socrates was known to activate his inner Stardrive and power straight through Einstein's general theory of relativity to the farthest reaches of the multiverse. His speculations were like stardust in the solar winds–particularly if fueled by the likes of Chateau Lafite, Margaux, Latour, Le Pin or even better, Montrachet or Romaneé-Conti. Socrates was a high Burgundian, accented by his rakish black beret which he always wore to his outdoor seminars. A number of empty bottles of Bordeaux shared space-time with the students on the granite benches.

Professor Sarfatti, his arms outstretched like a gnarled vine, took off on an electromagnetic rip, "I want us today to consider string theory. Can someone give us a definition?"

A student jumped at the opening, "All subatomic particles—protons, neutrons, electrons and the smaller particles they're made up of—quarks and so on—and all forms of energy—are constructed of strings—infinitely small building blocks that have only a single dimension—length—but not height or width."

"And what else?" asked Socrates the free radical.

Another student joined in, "String theory posits that the universe is multi-dimensional. We all can observe four dimensions." He picked up an empty wine bottle. "This inhabits three dimensional space. And the time we took to drink it gives us four observable dimensions. String theory suggests ten dimensions—so the other six—well look around you. Do you see them? They can't be detected—at least not sitting here."

"And?" questioned the professor unprepossessingly, fiddling with his scholarly black glasses

"Well—the strings vibrate, right? In multiple dimensions, kind of like the experience I had once playing my guitar in the Angeles Forest. And depending on the nature of the vibration might be observed as matter—like the wine bottle—or light—like the refraction of the sun off the bottle—or gravity," letting the bottle drop from one hand to the other. "Depending on the vibration, it might appear as matter or energy. All forms of matter and energy are the result of the vibration of strings."

Socrates clapped his hands delightedly, pleased with the student's explanation. And the use of the Bordeaux bottle was an excellent pedagogical touch. He stroked his greying goatee, countering, "But were it that simple, no? It never really is, is it? The scientific dialectic is inexorable. From the pre-Socratic philosophers' cosmology to our very own moment sitting here in this plaza, physics undergoes continual refinement and change—red in tooth and claw—collaboration, competition and combat. Was it not Heraclitus who said, 'You can never step in the same river twice?'"

Professor Sarfatti believed the universe had ordered and understandable meaning, an unalterable truth, that included our own thoughts and intuition, allowing for the interplay of consciousness and the physical world. He could describe the cosmos mathematically, yet often explored

CHATEAU LAFITE
TRIESTE

beyond those parameters. He lived within and beyond his own quantum equations—he was the living embodiment of Niels Bohr's observation that a physicist is just an atom's way of looking at itself. The professor was thought to be a bit outré at times but nonetheless quite sane—weaving an interdisciplinary tapestry wrapped within quantum consciousness and time, matter and energy.

"The question is: *what is the question?* Is string theory a single theory? Anyone care to take up the baton?" asked Socrates, careening his liminal engine through the students' imaginations. "As the Mad Hatter said to Alice, 'If you don't know where you're going, any road will get you there.' So how deep does the rabbit hole go? Anyone?"

A student tentatively raised his hand.

"Yes, Democritus?"

"Well, aren't there a bunch of different string theories—with different numbers of dimensions and the characteristics of the strings themselves—open loops, closed loops—even intertwined loops—all of them as plausible as the others—but having contradictory sets of equations to describe the same phenomena?"

"That's a fair enough description of where we're at right now. So has anyone proposed how to reconcile these apparent conflicting versions?"

Democritus, whose pre-Socratic namesake had propounded an atomic theory of the universe, raised his hand again, saw he still had the floor, "Some think that the different versions of string theory might simply be describing the same phenomena from different perspectives, right? So they came up with a unifying theory—the 'M-Theory' which stands for membrane. And here's where I kind of get lost. They brought all the string theories together by saying that strings are one-dimensional slices of a two-dimensional membrane vibrating in multi-dimensional space."

The professor took the virtual baton back, "Good, that's right! So with the 'M-Theory' the underlying structure has been established. It's consistent with all string theories—and consistent as well with?" The professor looked round the group, "With…?"

Silence. "Come on! Someone! It's right in front of your nose!"

McCabe called out, "Our own scientific observations of the universe?"

"*Ah hah!*" Socrates laughed seeing McCabe, pleased by the Jungian synchronicity of his sudden appearance. He gestured at him, "This people is Tom McCabe—a columnist who many of you have probably read at one time or another—now a candidate for mayor—and definitely not a student of physics. But he is an astute observer—and that, my friends, is why he knew the answer—and why communication can be faster than light!"

Apart from teaching in and around the standard model of particle physics, Professor Sarfatti was also famous for his counterintuitive theory on retrocausality—a superluminal universe created from the future in which events that have not yet occurred can effect action in the present. Socrates shot the arrow of causality both ways, seeing the one-way flow of time as a stubbornly persistent illusion between past, present and future. His retrocausal model posited a role for future events in the present, joining a long line of thought going back to the enchanted forums of the Platonic world—our own lives being organized around final ends and goals waiting to be discovered. Socrates viewed the Pythagorean theorem, Michelangelo's Sistine Chapel, the architecture of Mozart's symphonies, Einstein's theory of relativity as having their origins at least partially in the future. The universe was created by intelligent design, a mind creator programmer living far in the future pulsing Telos into the Now, sending quantum signals—like the thunder of Zeus on Mt. Olympus or the prophecies of Cassandra from within the halls of Troy—future mind perceptions—accurate, but rarely understood, that only a few with particular genius could decode—images projected back from the future event horizon—all the world a Shakespearean hologram. A true exercise in free will, understanding destiny and fate, required a sense of the back-from-the future effect on the present. Our decisions might be preordained, but we still have to go through the paces, and that, Socrates believed is what gives our volition meaning.

Leaving Poets Plaza, McCabe's mind vibrated in a nano-tizzy from the mystico-illuminati of Sarfatti's cosmic ratiocinations and the uneasy sense of an inchoate presence seeking him out. Today it came with a bonus—his hangover had precipitously vanished from his own membrane. As he continued walking up Grant, "As Time Goes By" riffled through his head. He was drinking a bourbon whiskey straight up at Rick's Café in the old Medina:

You must remember this,
a kiss is just a kiss,
a sigh is just a sigh.
The fundamental things apply
as time goes by...

He shook off thoughts of Bogie and continued his quantum adventure back up Telegraph Hill, then looped down the Filbert Steps to Napier Lane.

He had wanted to grab a nap, but there wasn't time for anything but a shower. As he was toweling off there was a knock on the front door. April. The sight of McCabe, a towel loosely slung round his waist, gave her an erotic jolt, "I love your outfit!" she laughed, kissing him and reaching her hand underneath his towel, giving Tweedledum and Tweedledee the gentlest squeeze. "Oh, the twins are freshly shaven I see!" It was only one night of lovemaking years ago, but she still took liberties.

As he finished dressing, tightening the Windsor Knot on his tie, he took one last look in the mirror. There were feint dark circles under his eyes. ***An hour or two more, and I should look normal***, he thought to his mirrored self.

The debate would be televised at the San Francisco Art Institute located across Columbus on Russian Hill. It wasn't far, no more than a twenty minute walk. As McCabe and April left the cottage, the parrots swarmed, shouting out a newly minted "McCabe for Mayor" fight song:

Maaaacaaaab,
Maaaacaaaab,
Taaa maaaan
Faaa taaa jaaaab!

The parrots flitted from tree-to-tree, escorting them down Napier Lane, up the Filbert Steps and down to North Beach.

Like a lonely sentinel, the Art Institute's Spanish colonial bell tower beckoned. A foreboding swept over him. ***Never send to know for whom the bell tolls***, thought McCabe, John Donne emerging again from Ward's earlier admonition during the Vesuvio conspiracy. For the first time in the campaign he felt genuine fear. He went silent, worried that he might come off as the Fool. "Don't worry, you'll do fine," said April reassuringly, sensing his unease.

The curious entourage crossed over Columbus to Chestnut Street, then continued up to the Art Institute. In the courtyard an Andalusian fountain splashed Sierra water over earth-toned Moorish tiles. There were several Ginkgo trees that now swarmed with Air Marshall McCabe's parrot air force. Off to the side of the courtyard colonial wooden doors opened to the auditorium where the debate was to be held. In the foyer, campaign literature, house signs, buttons, bumper stickers, and position papers were being handed out by volunteers.

Although eight people were running for mayor, only the four leading candidates—the mayor, city attorney, president of the city council and McCabe, given his name recognition and presumed voting draw—had been invited in order to structure a coherent debate. McCabe was the last of the four candidates to arrive. The three others were animatedly talking to clutches of people, their spouses and partners by their sides, complicitly collaborating, agreeing with anything anyone had to say.

McCabe had the curious role of the spoiler. He was the wild card. The grass-roots demographics were vague on him. Whether you were right, left or center, on name recognition alone, he might be pulling votes from the your base.

Moreover, the city had an unusual system of voting that avoided a second election if no candidate received a majority. Instead of having a run-off among the two top vote-getters, voters in the general election could chose an order of preference among any three of the eight mayoral candidates. The person coming in last would be eliminated and his or her second and third preferences allocated to the remaining candidates, then the next person was eliminated, their second and third preferences reallocated until someone reached a majority and was declared the winner.

The system was called "RCV"—ranked-choice voting—or "IRV"—instant run-off voting. The supercomputers tabulating the votes could quickly count the votes cast in the initial round, then eliminate the last candidate, tabulate the votes again, eliminate the next-to-last candidate, retabulate until a majority winner was determined, thus avoiding having to go to the polls a second time in a run-off election. And it was IRV that made everybody nervous about McCabe. He was popular throughout the city due to his long-running column, resulting in unusually high positives and low negatives.

McCabe was given a seat at the far end of the table on the auditorium dais. The mayor was given the middle. McCabe assumed he was an afterthought—a nuisance who had to be given a spot—presumably to speak last.

He peered out into the audience, a pastiche of opaque shadows. He could vaguely discern human forms through the glare, but beyond the bare outlines, their features were indistinguishable.

The moderator for the evening was also a columnist, a political commentator who worked for the *Harbinger*, a rival to the *Clarion*. He had a narrower beat—city hall—unlike McCabe who often wrote non-political columns on cultural events and personalities in the city. The moderator worked for a more conservative paper, his leanings were necessarily similar to his publisher. As fellow-columnists, their camaraderie would normally override any political differences.

McCabe leaned back in his chair, realizing his position on the dais might actually be an advantage. His morning may have started out like a train wreck, but now the tracks were cleared and he was comfortably ensconced in the caboose. Others would pull the debate along for a time.

The moderator introduced himself, setting out the ground rules for the debate. There would be three minute opening statements for each of the four candidates. Next would be a series of eight questions. Each candidate would be picked randomly to give up to three minute answers to two of the questions. Then the others could jump in for one minute responses and rebuttals. The debate would end with three minute closing statements. The moderator looked to his right and nodded toward the city attorney sitting at the opposite end of the table from McCabe.

Let the train leave the station, thought McCabe. The city attorney composed himself as if preparing to burst out of the starting block.

The mayor gave McCabe an unsettling side-eye stare.

CHAPTER THIRTEEN: THAT'S DEBATABLE

McCabe had slowly adjusted to the auditorium glare. He doodled on a note pad penciling out a drawing of the parrots circling over the city. At the back of the hall he could discern the Diego Rivera fresco that had inspired the Coit Tower muralists. Through the wall of light he could now pick out April in the oscillating shadows—and then to his consternation, Noë and Zoë sitting on either side of her like bosom buddies at a reunion dinner. A moment later, there was the distended call of his name, "Mr. McCabe? Mr. McCabe?"

A surprised look appeared on the three women's faces. They shifted uneasily in their seats. McCabe was mystified, ***What's got them so agitated?***

"McCabe, McCabe," came the snappish voice again, more insistent. April surreptitiously gestured toward the podium. The audience snickered with half-suppressed laughs. In a star beat, the pulsatile ball of his inner mind's eye refocused, turning to the moderator.

"Mr. McCabe, please, we're starting with you. Three minutes," said the moderator, his solicitous smirk masking malicious glee at having sucker-punched the flummoxed competitor columnist. The mayor piled on, cutting a ruthless smile, his flickering eyes sending McCabe a nasty mind twitter, "For all those shitty columns you wrote about me! He got you good—FOOL!"

McCabe stood up, teetering between order and disorder, stability and collapse. "*Ah...*" He looked out on the now indistinguishable sea of faces—April, Noë and Zoë had slipped beneath the surface. ***If my first words fail, the remaining will be of no avail.*** But in another beat, the synchronic rhythm of his brain took hold, reorienting from the moderator's blind-sided blow back to coherence.

"Yes, thank you for that thoughtful introduction," said McCabe, looking over at the moderator with a sarcastic smile, ***You dick-head!*** then shakily launching into his opening:

> "You'll probably hear pretty much the same thing from my colleagues tonight—affordable housing, schools, infrastructure, police, unfunded pension liabilities. They'll tell you how Houdini-like they're going to extricate us from all the challenges facing our city.
>
> So allow me to walk a different path that goes to the essence of democracy and self-governance.

Regaining a measure of control, he continued:

> In 1774, two years before the Declaration of Independence, Tom Paine outlined the 'essence of liberty' as self-governance by informed and empowered citizens maintained by their representatives. Thomas Jefferson, building on Paine declared: 'The only security of all is in a free press. The force of public opinion cannot be resisted when permitted freely to be expressed. The agitation it produces must be submitted to. It is necessary to keep the waters pure.'
>
> Jefferson knew that the promise of freedom and democracy couldn't be done on the cheap. Instead, look what we have now—half hour news comprised of commercials and twenty minutes of twittered entertainment. Failure to cover local government cuts off the people—government operates unseen—major stories go unreported as

investigative reporters are let go and reporter-to-population ratio declines. You do the math.

We will be governed or will we govern ourselves? This isn't about print versus digital, it's about sustaining a free, vibrant, adversarial press. Freedom of the press is only as strong as we demand it to be, a fearless press being the best friend a democracy can have.

The crisis in journalism is a crisis in self-government. It's imperative to have strong journalistic institutions to bolster self-governing societies. The First Amendment will preserve the press only if we insist that it do so. It takes an act of will—the sustained trust and public confidence of the people and that of our elected representatives—to insist on media that actively sustains journalism. Instead, we are in free-fall collapse, newsrooms dissolving before our eyes, bureaus shut, papers stripped for parts—our right to know under sustained political threat, some politicians labeling the best friend of democracy, the enemy!

In the immediate aftermath of World War II, two Republicans—Eisenhower in Germany, MacArthur in Japan—made it a priority to create a strong and free press, so much so that both insisted that newspapers be free to criticize the postwar efforts of the occupying powers themselves. They understood that the first order of government is a free press—to foster, as Walt Whitman said, a 'daily communion' between newspapers and its readers. A viable press is among the highest duties of a democratic state—and so it was that Republican Ike birthed more papers than any other American.

When our country first came into existence it was the unassailable belief of congress that papers be delivered through the post office virtually free. Madison actually wanted free delivery, but a small charge was imposed to protect local papers from the onslaught of the large. Through massive subsidies the post office became the instrument of mass communication—the vehicle for basically free delivery of newspapers during the early years of our Republic—birthing a free press that forged the American experiment. Government understood the importance of arming its citizens with knowledge—not a cornucopia of guns.

As a columnist covering this beautiful city, I've made every effort to keep people informed—and I hope as well thoughtfully entertained—and in so doing, helping to make certain that we are not governed, but govern. If we need to create new systems out of old media models to get you the news—the real news—we must do it, the same way Jefferson and Madison did after the American Revolution and Eisenhower and MacArthur after World War II in Germany and Japan.

The sharp deterioration of press freedom must be reversed. Freedom requires sunlight. As mayor I will assure open government and insist the media get into the sinews of city hall operations—and armed with that knowledge, each of you and all of you make the informed decisions and I will be your servant in carrying them out and governing this city.

Thanks for hearing me out.

McCabe dropped like Icarus back into his chair. ***I'm not hearing any applause? Was it that bad?*** Then applause came from the area where he knew April, Noë and Zoë were sitting. As well, some others in the audience applauded—a smattering here and there.

The moderator was utterly baffled, "*Ah*—thanks, Mr. McCabe, for that existential analysis of journalism. Glad we're still breathing, you and I!" He followed with a rhetorical slap, displeased that McCabe had gone completely off the reservation, "Now, let's have someone who'll speak to the actual problems of San Francisco." He gestured to the other end of the dais at the city attorney, "Dennis Cabrerra—who as the city's chief lawyer has been forced to defend some of the most far-out actions and laws that any American city has ever managed to enact."

Cabrerra had been running the city attorney's office of two hundred lawyers and paralegals for years. There had been no newsworthy scandals or screw-ups. He hardly looked Hispanic despite his last name—baby blue eyes, impeccably dressed, polite, steady and amiable to a fault. He had few enemies. Some even considered him white bread.

He stood up and began his opening remarks:

Thank you one and all for coming here tonight.

As city attorney, I represent every city agency, the mayor as well, and our city council. In that capacity I've come to know how everything runs in this town—from the airport to the port—our parks and streets—our police, hospitals and schools.

San Francisco creates some pretty far-out stuff in the eyes of the rest of the nation, and I've been there to keep those programs alive—the first city to issue marriage licenses for gay couples, outlawing automatic and semi-automatic weapons, right-to-die legislation, medical marijuana dispensaries, our municipal clean energy system, free health care for the less fortunate among us, declaring this town a Sanctuary City, and most controversial of all capping our city's population on this tiny peninsula we call home. I mean, do we really want a million people living in our town and another million commuting here each day? All this creates controversy—lots of it—and I've ably defended each and every one of those initiatives—pursued challenges all the way to the US Supreme Court—parried legal threats from the state—countered public utilities trying to choke us with their monopolies. These initiatives are about freedom, a liberal-libertarian freedom. You can smoke what you want, marry who you want, demand 100% clean energy, and if you're struggling with a terminal illness, be allowed to leave this world with dignity and not go bankrupt.

My efforts have been about giving us greater liberty even though in a town like this everyone assumes politics is about increasing government intervention in our lives. But actually, being allowed to marry whom you want is about expanding freedom and loosening government regulation. Being able to buy medical marijuana—and legal recreational marijuana–is the freedom to try homeopathic remedies or just to relax, to which many other parts of the country attach a negative moral judgment and have outlawed. And if you're concerned about the kinds of energy we develop and its impact on our planet, you should be able to buy clean energy, freeing yourself from the utilities that have never provided any real choice. As well, if you slipped across the border to work here and employers knowingly hire you because your labor is needed to run our economy, you ought to be free to live a normal life without being threatened with deportation over minor, non-violent infractions of the law.

He's like a scarecrow claiming credit for raising the sun in the morning, smirked McCabe.

All these things are about life, liberty and the pursuit of happiness. You could call San Francisco a very conservative town in this respect. We're libertarian in our social values and live by the golden rule—do onto others, as you would have them do onto you.

I am fully prepared to run our city government. I know it intimately as city attorney—and at the same time, I will defend and expand the liberties that make our city so unique and wonderful.

Thanks again for coming here tonight. I hope I can have your vote for mayor of this utopian town.

Loud applause followed. The moderator looked over from the lectern, "Thanks, Mr. Cabrerra. It doesn't get any more San Francisco than that."

The next candidate to speak was the city council president, head of the local Green party, Rose Kim. Kim conveyed a quiet, beatific charisma. She was lesbian, of Korean descent and had married her partner several years before when gay marriage was first allowed in the city. After a brief introduction, diminutive Kim stood to speak:

> Good evening, everyone.
>
> Let me briefly tell you my philosophy of government because if you don't have a philosophy, then you're just a hack…

She glanced at the mayor dismissively—

> whose primary goal is to climb the political ladder, figuring out what lily pad you're going to jump to next.
>
> As an urban dweller, I believe our happiness derives from our neighborhoods and social trust between neighbors. Government must do what it can to build and enhance that trust. If we create and maintain sustainable neighborhoods and support and encourage families, we increase all our happiness, and just maybe trust in our city government as well, rather than simply flinging the door open to tech companies without consequence.
>
> As mayor my top priority will be to push back against the automobile—prioritize public transit and all forms of bike and car sharing—the city acquiring a fleet of electric, self-driving, on-demand vehicles—and some that run purely on hydrogen. Let's close off and reconfigure streets—turn pavement to parks—remove car lanes and curbside parking—widen sidewalks—encourage car-free households and walkable neighborhoods. You shouldn't have to use your car for more than minutes a day, if that, not hours, otherwise, we'll have *Carmageddon!*

This should be matched by a police force that gets out of its cruisers to walk and bike our streets, building relationships in our communities—Zen cops connected to the neighborhoods, particularly for our youth so that they understand what's across the "blue line".

And I will push for distributed solar and wind energy generation. What's that mean? It means homes and businesses would be energy independent, generating on-site sustainable energy for our electricity needs, feeding what's not used during the day back into the grid, and in return receiving credits for energy use at night when the sun doesn't shine and the wind doesn't blow—each home a virtual power plant. Ultimately, it will free us from the utilities that undermine our clean energy initiatives in order to protect their carbon energy monopoly. There is no greater transformative opportunity than each of us becoming our own renewable energy providers at grid parity. And we will go below grid parity—our homes and businesses will generate solar and wind power below the average cost of carbon generated power. You'll sell it back to the utilities and they'll become distributors of your excess energy. It will be a Rooftop Revolution equivalent to earlier revolutions in human history! We will generate green prosperity—increase the happiness, freedom and well-being of all—the democratization of everything in a collaborative commons!

If we have the imagination and collective will, we can do all this and more. Your vote is critical in this endeavor. Thank you so much, and please feel free to come speak with me after the debate.

As applause rippled through the auditorium, the moderator quickly moved on, "And now let me present the last of tonight's candidates." He nodded solicitously, "Ladies and gentlemen, the mayor of San Francisco—Galen Newman. Mr. Mayor, please."

The mayor, GQ looking, had orchestrated the quickest turn-round from a sex scandal—with the wife of his closest aide—that McCabe had ever seen, even though it had occurred in San Francisco where sexual peccadilloes were given wide European-style latitude. The political fallout had an unintended consequence—laying to rest the rumors that he was a gay blade. Now his petite blonde wife, who some had first thought a beard, sat transfixed in the audience waiting for him to speak. The mayor stretched his arms as if to embrace the world:

> Tonight my colleagues' remarks have been directed at the death and life of American journalism—as well—the cutting-edge laws enacted by me that our city attorney has been called upon to defend, and a vision of an urban green utopia. But, do any of those pipe dreams actually tell you anything about the state of our city? It's newspapers, it's progressive law, it's green. Do you have any better idea of what's actually happening in our city government than before my esteemed opponents spoke?

McCabe smiled ruefully. ***The benefit of going last.*** The mayor looked out at the audience and let his criticism of McCabe and the other candidates sink in. He laid his hand over his heart:

> You should know the truth. So let me tell you about the viability and solvency of our city. We're ticking toward a reckoning. Detroit is already living the apocalypse—New York, Chicago are moving in that direction. Let's be honest—we're using budget gimmicks that obscure the true extent of the city's money problems. We're utilizing opaque accounting methods, fiscal sleight-of-hand, cobbling together schemes that make it look like our budget is balanced when in fact our fiscal problems are worsening, including billions in pension obligations which we lack the means to cover in full.

Have any of my three worthy opponents tonight dared mention our looming financial crises? No, they spin moonbeams and spout philosophy, but that won't run our city. And the reason my opponents haven't talked about the hard choices that confront us is because they either don't know how to get us out of this mess, or simply want to ignore it, hoping for some kind of miracle that will never materialize without firm, realistic leadership only *I* can provide!

I had nothing to do with our unfunded municipal obligations agreed to years ago. And since then our situation hasn't improved all that much despite the recent false prosperity. We can't avoid this conversation any longer—the time to evade hard choices is over. If you switch horses now, it'll all be that much harder to reverse our state of affairs.

What must be done? We all pretty much know the answer and that's why I've declared budgetary "martial law." We're obligated under our city employee contracts to pay some of the highest salaries in the country—and some of the most generous pension and health care benefits as well. Now maybe a hundred million here, a hundred million there, doesn't sound like a lot when our federal government is running trillion dollar deficits, but it is, my friends. So, I've been working with our municipal employee unions to get them to agree to some difficult concessions, because if they don't, all those generous public pensions and other unfunded liabilities they're clinging to so dearly will eventually sink. I can furlough employees, or lay them off, but there's only so far you can go before city services become so degraded you won't want to live here. And we can try to raise some fees and taxes, make some work longer hours, have workers pay more into the system. But that won't cover the system's true costs, merely postpone the day of reckoning as we continue to slide further into debt while at the same time passing more and more bond issues just to cover basic operations.

That's our financial state in a nutshell. I give it to you straight. And I hope you'll give me both your confidence and your vote this November.

Thanks one and all for showing up this evening.

The mayor received a solid and lasting round of applause. But McCabe's columnist antennae sensed an underlying unease. It was the widely-held perception that the mayor was spending most of his time preparing to run for governor, which if successful would allow him to abandon the city's financial mess and leave someone else holding the bag. The mayor had never been a hands-on administrator. He left it to others and shied away from confrontation. Putting all that together, it was hard to see how he was going to solve anything. He needed a second term in order to seek higher office and flee the city—and everybody knew it.

Thereafter, the debate moved into the question-and-answer period. The rules of engagement were benign. Each candidate was given two questions drawn from a bowl—and any other candidate could do a follow-up or simply ignore the first answer and provide an independent response of their own. McCabe had no interest in trying to stick an oratorical knife in anyone. He realized from his opening statement this was not his forte—debating with knives. He simply wanted to come across as a serious enough candidate to generate the monies to run the *Foghorn* and cross the finish line in a credible fashion.

He was lobbed two easy questions, the first on waterfront development, the second on police staffing. Both were areas he had covered many times in his column. He knew most of the port staff and the details of the controversial projects fronting the bay. He knew as well many of the police brass, as well as dozens of cops on the beat. He answered both questions with a command of facts remembered from his columns. The other candidates' follow-ups went their own direction and he was not attacked. On the questions asked of other candidates, McCabe did a follow-up on only one—supporting the tearing down of O'Shaughnessy Dam and restoring Hetch Hetchy Valley which in the eyes of John Muir matched Yosemite in its Sierra magnificence.

His fellow candidates took whatever shots they could at the mayor. He was the one who would have to go down for any of them to win. McCabe could save his digs for future columns that would reach a much wider audience. It was a one-way hit—the mayor had no way of fighting back. Better to take on the mayor at one's leisure from *McCabe's Corner* in Vesuvio, where you got to land all the punches and stick in the shiv however you liked.

The debate only reinforced McCabe's wonderment why anyone would want to run city hall. He couldn't remotely imagine being mayor of the town.

CHAPTER FOURTEEN: QUANTUM CANDIDATE

With the passing of Labor Day and just two months to the election, McCabe began looking beyond the vote on the first Tuesday in November—returning with the parrots to the old ways of practiced synchronicity. He began getting up later in the morning, anticipating the mayoral campaign would now be narrowing to the two front-runners—the mayor and the city attorney. He could seamlessly slip back into his previous life style, making sure there was enough money coming in to keep the *Foghorn* running and salaries paid. He would continue in the mayoral marathon but no longer break a sweat, cruising to the finish line in the middle of the pack.

He rolled over in bed and looked at the clock—6AM. He could sleep a few more hours—fantasize being entwined with Noë and Zoë or best of all imagine that the race was over and his former equipoise returned. His cell phone rang—bluntly reminding him there was still more foolishness to endure.

"Hey, Max."

"Did I wake you up?"

"Good surmise."

"An early rise makes an extra day, McCabe."

"Why would we need an extra day?"

"According to today's papers, you're leading in the polls!"

"What? You're screwing with me!"

"Well, you are and you aren't. There are four of you bunched together. You're actually five points behind the mayor who's at twenty-two percent, the city attorney is second at twenty, you're third at seventeen percent, Kim is in fourth at sixteen."

"So? We're not leading. What's the concern?"

"When you factor in ranked-choice voting from instant run-off, you're leading! If the vote were held today, you'd be the goddamned mayor!"

McCabe sat up in bed, his Noë-Zoë erection gone flaccid. "How's that?"

"There are eight candidates running and as each round eliminates someone, their second and third choices are distributed to the remaining candidates, right?"

"Yeah?"

"The polls show you're the most popular second and third choice, which means that starting out, as long as you're in the top four or so, the second and third choice votes from those progressively eliminated will go to you more than others, and you'll slowly rise till you have a simple majority and win."

"That's ridiculous! How the hell did this happen?"

"Who else has squadrons of wild parrots screaming his name all over town?" Max's laughter did not go down well.

"That's not funny, it's a disaster!"

"Maybe being mayor could work for you, it might..."

McCabe cut him off in mid-sentence, "Don't even think of going there man! We had a plan. Everyone's got a job till Election Day. That's it!"

"*Hah, hah!* It worked too damn well! We didn't factor in instant runoff voting. You're gonna be mayor! Just what you never wanted! *Hah, hah, hah!*"

McCabe's tried shaking off the bizarre news, at a complete loss, "Can you meet me at Trieste?"

"Sure, Mr. Mayor. You're de boss man now! *Hah, hah, hah, hah!*"

Iolanda was working the morning shift at Caffé Trieste. As McCabe approached the counter, she reached across and gave his cheek a maternal pinch. "*Buon giorno, Bello.* Here so early! Is everything going well? Miss *la dolce vita*?"

"I may never get it back, Iolanda." It suddenly occurred to him his wan observation might somehow prove accurate—*la dolce vita* transmuting into pathos.

Iolanda pushed a double espresso, a bacci of lemon on the rim, across the counter. She patted his hand, "*Bello,* men are sharpened on men, like knives on a stone. A bar of iron continually ground becomes a needle."

"That's not exactly *la dolce vita.*"

Iolanda burst out laughing, "Vino in small gulps, knowledge in large!"

Max came into Trieste, sporting a big shit-eating grin, "Your Honor, thinking about your inaugural speech yet?" He bought an africano and joined McCabe back outside on Poets Plaza.

McCabe shook his head in unalloyed disbelief, "Now what do we do? How do we get out of this mess?"

"McCabe, are you sure...?"

"No dammit! We stay with the original plan. For Christ sakes, we're not supposed to be leading!"

Max shrugged his shoulders, giving McCabe a disappointed look, "So the race has shifted in your favor. So you win—become mayor. If you were publishing the *Foghorn* to give people jobs, think of the patronage you'd have as mayor."

"You're making me feel like crap."

"Like the selfish prick you really are," joked Max.

"Like the selfish prick I am..." McCabe's voice trailed off, contemplating the present situation. ***It's those crazy Buddhists on Waverly. They did this. How else could this absurdity be happening?***

Max pulled McCabe back from his drift, "It's okay, man! We were slammed! You left the *Clarion*, helped us out when we needed it. It's truly appreciated, and..."

"Enough, Max! I simply don't have the fire in the belly to be mayor even if it was handed to me on a platter. I just don't see it." He gazed dispiritedly across the plaza. ***Maybe I'm just a coward.***

"Alright, but if you keep doing what you're doing, you're gonna win."

"Good point! Hell, I'll take a trip, come back after the election."

Max gave him a squinty look.

"I'm messing with you! *Hmmm*, let's go to the temple."

"The temple? You're not Jewish!"

McCabe chuckled, "No, no, the Buddhist temple above campaign headquarters."

"Why there?"

"I'm not sure, but I gotta hunch. We gotta go to headquarters anyway."

"Mind telling me what you've got in mind?"

"I don't really know, but the answer may start there."

"The Tao is the way, *huh*?" joked Max.

"Who the hell knows?"

Leaving Poets Plaza, they walked through Chinatown to the Wong Fook Hing Bookstore, then crossed over Waverly to campaign headquarters. No one had arrived yet. They grabbed the bottle of peanut oil from their earlier visit several months before, then walked on up past the Kung Fu Martial Arts Foundation to the top floor and knocked on the Buddhist Association door. The same wizened monk appeared at the portal.

McCabe smiled gamely, "*Ah,* we're..."

The monk interrupted him, "No need to explain. Please, you are most welcome." As they entered the room, the monk assessing the bottle of peanut oil, said cryptically, "If you are not truthful to yourself and to others, you will be wasting those prayers on the Buddha. You must be willing to give up what you are in order to become what you would be. You cannot force the Zen."

McCabe nodded in apparent agreement.

Max gestured toward the donation box, McCabe dropping in some bills. Following the same ritual from their earlier visit, McCabe poured peanut oil into the onyx bowl resting in the Buddha's hand, floated a small candle, and lit it with a taper. He closed his eyes and tried to reflect.

Max sensed the campaign beginning to ebb, musing to himself, "We're wishing away a win. We could have had the run of city hall!" He quickly blinked and left McCabe to his cerebrations.

After a time, McCabe looked up and whistled out some air. "I think we just entered a new path."

"To where?" asked Max walking back over to the Buddha.

"Beats me, away from city hall I hope."

"Do you have any idea what you're doing, McCabe?"

"Not a clue!"

Back downstairs at campaign headquarters, there was now a gaggle of supporters and *Foghorn* staff. Everyone was electrified at the poll numbers indicating McCabe would win under instant run-off voting. This was huge. It would give the campaign momentum that would send him to city hall—unless something went awry.

McCabe walked over to speak with John Nattos and Bruce Alaska who were sitting at their desks overlooking Waverly. "Hey guys, can Max and I speak to you privately?"

Outside on the balcony McCabe queried Nattos, "Whatta you think?"

John laughed uproariously, the rusting iron balcony shaking tremulously. "Remember when we first talked about your strategy? Not to win, going against everyday experience and common sense—reversing normal tactics—making sure your campaign failed? You're obviously in some kind of political warp where everything you've been doing has actually helped you become the front runner. You found a natural way of politics, aligned yourself with it as opposed to forcing it. You don't care about winning. You actually don't want to win! All the normal forces of classical politics don't work on you! You're a duality—McCabe and anti-McCabe. You unknowingly achieved some kind of strange alignment and made this explosive jump! And now you're the damn front-runner! It's astounding!"

"And ridiculous!" added Bruce cracking up. "Probability, uncertainty, complementarity, entanglement. You're a quantum candidate! Spooky!"

"So we reverse course," said McCabe vaguely.

"What's that supposed to mean?" asked Max, "What do we do different?"

"Try to win?" joked McCabe.

Nattos and Alaska exploded in more laughter. Now the balcony really began to shake.

McCabe grumbled, "It can't be that difficult to lose can it?"

"Shouldn't be," laughed Max at the absurdity of the question. "You could ground the parrots, no more of those flying monkeys campaigning for you!"

McCabe mused on that suggestion. ***Doubt I could get them to stop now. They're having way too much fun.*** "Change the emphasis of the *Foghorn*—de-emphasize the neighborhood pieces," he said brusquely.

Later that day Max reluctantly made an announcement to the *Foghorn* staffers to switch the subject of their articles away from the neighborhoods—produce a "more balanced and pragmatic" point-of-view. Give the downtown corporate interests and tech giants a good share of coverage. Start writing about celebrities and throw in a high-society gossip page, including pictures of all the swells at their expensive charity balls. Keep the articles short, no more than five hundred words, nothing in-depth. Run lurid crime stories on the front page. Bury neighborhood pieces in the back. Start publishing poetry—bad poetry—really, really bad poetry. Add a little kink as well—free ads for escort and sensual massage services.

Around noon, with the campaign ostensibly reoriented, McCabe left Chinatown and walked over to North Beach Restaurant still puzzling over how to reverse the tide. He sat down at an outdoor table and ordered a Cabernet. Customers streamed into the restaurant, many stopping to say hello. With the polls showing him winning in instant run-off, people's attitude had undergone a subtle shift, now more formal and respectful. Yet here he was working to secretly undo his lead, to intentionally falter in the home stretch. The crosscurrents put him in an ambivalent mood. But as he parsed it, his covenant with the *Foghorn* staff hadn't been broken. Only the unexpected lead in the ranked-choice polls had confounded the underlying premise of the campaign. A mid-course correction was needed to stay on point, seemingly an easy thing to accomplish. Yet it was still a subterfuge, as only a few actually understood that McCabe had no desire to win. Virtually everyone outside the *Foghorn* believed he was intent on capturing the office of mayor and taking his place atop the city's political hierarchy.

McCabe drank from his glass of Cabernet, closing his eyes to the mid-day sun. Moments later a glass of tawny colored Brunello touched down on his table. As he turned to thank the waiter, Luciano Peroni sat down next to him, "*Bello*, congratulations! I don't believe it! You're actually winning! What kind of strange magic did you pull?"

"*Hah*, hi, Luciano," said McCabe, startled at the garrulous intrusion into his blissful blend of red wine and sun. "Yeah, under ranked-choice I'd win, but not straight up."

"Who cares, *Bello*? The point is you'd win, no?"

"Yeah, assuming the polls are correct."

"Then what are you doing here, drinking wine like some old man slouched in his chair? You gotta be out there, protecting your lead. Drink all the wine you want later."

"Aren't I allowed a brief moment in the sun here? And it's your wine I'm drinking."

"I appreciate you drink my wine, *Bello.* And as mayor I expect you to order lots of it for your city hall parties. You'll be the best salesman I got! *Hah, hah!*"

"So that's why you're backing me," McCabe joked. "I need to tell you something about my campaign..."

Luciano sputtered. It was rare for anyone to get in more than a couple of sentences before he countered with a gale of words. "*Bello*, don't tell me, you need more money? Haven't I done enough for your campaign already?"

"Yeah, of course, but..."

"*Bello*, business is slow. It's not like a few years ago when I could afford to pour money down political rat holes!"

This time McCabe riposted, interrupting, "*Nah*, it's not more money I need."

Luciano brightened, "*Ah*, why didn't you say that in the first place?"

McCabe gave Luciano an exasperated look. "Hey, I'm trying to here. Look it, there's no way I actually want to be mayor, *ah...*"

"What? What?"

"I don't want it, never did, this was supposed..."

"What, are you crazy?"

"No, no, Luciano, I mean it! I never wanted to be mayor. I've enjoyed the break, starting up a newspaper, seeing the city in a different light."

"*Bello*, you run for mayor like it's some kind of experiment!"

"When you put it that way, I guess it is."

Luciano slapped his forehead as if trying to ward off a mosquito, "For the love of God! You're ahead in the race in one of the most beautiful cities in the world—as nice as any city I have ever known in Italy! And you want to walk away?"

"Yep."

"Just give it up?"

"That's right."

Luciano pondered McCabe's curious confession before finally breaking the silence, "*Bello,* it's your life. Let's drink to something real—your father—a friend, a good man who didn't give a damn about politics. He didn't waste his time on it like you and I. He loved your mother, and even though you're kind of nutty, raised you well. He built a business, grew a few grapes, loved wine and good food. It's been twenty years since he died. Look what he left me with—you, McCabe!"

They clicked their glasses, the big alcohol wines heating their palates, the herbal flavors lingering long after they swallowed the viscous vinifera.

CHAPTER FIFTEEN: REBEL YELL

Rosé light flowed into McCabe's bedroom caressing his face like the hands of an angel. He made it to campaign headquarters by ten, Trieste cappuccino still in hand.

Max motioned him over to his desk. He was typing an article on the sea lions that followed the seasonal anchovy run into San Francisco Bay—"Harbor Master Threatens Sea Lions with Electrocution".

"Sea lions?" asked McCabe, confounded.

"The harbor master wants to *zap* 'em, keep 'em from climbing up on the docks."

"We're supposed to make the campaign less sympathetic! How am I going to lose the damn race if we appeal to people's sympathies? No easier way than to write about cruelty to animals."

"Your *diktat* yesterday wasn't well received. It caused a bit of a rebellion."

"How's that?"

"One word: 'integrity'. You're acting worse than Snellgrove, like the pigs that took over *Animal Farm*! No one here wants to write vapid pieces on celebrities, crime and corporatism! Come on, we were doing good stuff on the neighborhoods! It's what we love doing! You know that! You might as well just kill the *Foghorn*!"

McCabe exasperated, his voice cracking, shot back, "Well, maybe we should! The campaign was the cover for starting the newspaper, not the other way around! I'm not supposed to become mayor now am I?" He lashed out uncontrollably, "Look at us. You got me in a totally strange place! I'm the bad guy? We were going to create jobs after the *Clarion* lay-offs, not turn me into a pol!" McCabe realized that several of the *Foghorn* reporters were honing in on his tirade. "I love newspapers as much as anybody in this room. Guess what? It worked better than anyone could have imagined! Too good! That's not what was supposed to happen! We all know that!"

April slipped her way into the mash-up. Without her usual touch of tenderness she reproached McCabe, "Tom, it may have started out that way, but it's a real paper now!"

"And a good one!" cried Robert. "We can't just turn around and trash it! Let us write what we want! That was the deal, McCabe!"

"That's right, it's our paper as much as yours!" yelped Joyce, now the *Foghorn*'s cannabis editor.

Max shrunk back, knowing this was brewing, hoping it wouldn't erupt as it had.

There was a stunned silence. Max was right, he was acting worse than his old boss—their old boss—Snellgrove. Through collective enterprise and shared imagination they had built a thriving paper in just a few months, covering more neighborhood issues and news than the *Clarion*. They had exhibited integrity of purpose and consistent, quality writing. Freed from a for-profit paper, now working for a non-profit or actually no-profit paper that largely ran off public monies, everyone had been unshackled to write unbound. Many had done their best writing in years—some in their lifetime.

In fact they had been so successful that the subscription-based *Clarion*'s circulation had fallen by 25 percent. The *Clarion* had even filed a complaint with the Department of Elections claiming the *Foghorn* was just a regular newspaper with less than 10 percent of its content actually devoted to campaign ads. The claim was rejected on the grounds that the masthead made clear who the publisher was—McCabe for Mayor—as well as McCabe's front-page column and his full back page political ad for mayor. If McCabe wanted to publish a paper that downplayed his candidacy, but carried articles that implicitly underscored his own point of view about politics and the city, it was his right to do so under the First Amendment—even if it was mostly taxpayer money that financed it.

April wasn't done with her excoriation, "There's got to be a better way, Tom. You don't need to destroy the paper to do it! Let the *Foghorn* do its thing! It's a sentient being now, it's got a life of its own!

Can it get any more embarrassing, being slammed by April in front of everyone? thought McCabe. His colleagues' distraught expressions were truly unsettling.

April continued to pound away, venting emotional frustrations that had been immured for years. "They've done an outstanding job—haven't they?" she asked rhetorically. "We helped get you what any normal candidate would want—a lead in the polls! Sure you got us work after we were laid off. And it's pretty damn cool what we're doing. But don't ask people to go against their grain and put out a lousy paper! Would you start writing idiotic columns for the twisted reason of assisting someone to lose, rather than win?"

Max tried tempering down the conversation, "Yeah, McCabe, there's got to be other ways than taking out the *Foghorn*. And what would your volunteers say if they heard this conversation? They think you're in it to win."

McCabe threw up his hands, surrendering, "All right, all right. It's your paper—*our* paper. Do what you want. Play it like we're still trying to win. We'll find another way. But come Election Day, the money runs out. So if you got something to write, do it now, 'cause I don't see how we can keep it operating after that!"

Noë, professional in her demeanor, without the slightest hint they had ever engaged in wild-ass sex, took over the lead, "So let's have lunch—you, me, Max, and Zoë. If you really want to drop in the polls, do it surgically. Don't destroy the best thing in your campaign. In fact you might even be able to give the *Foghorn* a boost while taking down your poll numbers."

"Really?" said McCabe sarcastically. "Now the paper runs the campaign? This puppet is going for a walk! I need to clear my head!"

Noë calmly replied, "Well if fresh air is what you want, how 'bout we grab some sandwiches and meet at Washington Square?"

"See you around noon," said McCabe, still incensed, relieved to be leaving. "*Ciao.*"

Zoë called from across the room with a dispirited look, "*Sayonara.*"

McCabe rolled his eyes. ***Aren't we being melodramatic?*** As he walked back out on Waverly, he looked up at the Buddhist Association nameplate above the front door, mystified, then sauntered down the alley into the din of Chinatown.

CHAPTER SIXTEEN: WASHINGTON SQUARE

At noontime McCabe emerged from Chinatown having engaged in a dozen fractured sidewalk conversations. A clutch of parrots spied McCabe walking across Columbus Avenue to Molinari's Delicatessen in North Beach. The parrots peeled off, covertly following him, if out of curiosity or concern was hard to tell. They alighted on the crosses of St. Francis Church across from Molinari's—a dangerous maneuver given it was also a favorite spot for red-tailed hawks and peregrine falcons.

Molinari's was floor-to-ceiling Northern Italian décor—bottles of Chianti, hanging salami and swinging sausages, shelves lined with cans of anchovies, sardines, salt-packed capers, bags of dried porcini mushrooms, bottles of olive oil and balsamic vinegar, dried Umbrian chickpeas and lentils, cans of espresso, boxes of biscotti, panettone, amaretti cookies and crostini. There was a long glass case filled with Italian cheeses and charcuteries. Next to the meat case was an aged cutting board running the length of the counter for making sandwiches. The air was so pungent it could induce an Italian accent even in a native son hailing from Tupelo, Mississippi.

McCabe ordered a prosciutto and mozzarella sandwich with basil garlic spread and sweet pickled bell peppers. Luca Signorelli, the owner

TOSCANA cured
Molinari COPPA HOT
Molinari SALAMI fennel
100 YEARS
MOLINARI
SALAMÉ
Frigidaire
OLIVE
S.B.

of the deli, made the sandwich, drizzling olive oil from the sun-dried tomatoes on the bread. He cut and wrapped the sandwich in parchment paper, bagged it and handed it over the counter, taking McCabe's money. "*Grazie*, Mr. Mayor."

As McCabe left Molinari's, the parrots, uncharacteristically silent, flitted along behind him, jumping the outdoor ficus trees that lined Columbus. McCabe was still unaware of being tailed, his mind consumed by the *Foghorn* rebellion. He walked past North Beach Restaurant. This noon Luciano was not standing outside—a relief. McCabe wasn't in the mood for one of his harangues. At Union Street, the regulars playing liars dice outside Original Joe's and Tony's Pizza greeted him as he passed. McCabe crossed over into Washington Square, the parrots now jumping ahead of him, alighting in the Lombardy poplar trees growing in the center of the park. The trees had begun to change colors to autumn yellow. The parrots' bright green plumage and cherry heads were easy to discern. McCabe gave them a loose salute. They settled into the poplars and quietly observed.

People languished on the grass eating their lunches. Sunbathers, some women topless, lay on blankets in the dappled light. A few dogs scampered about. Mothers pushed their baby strollers. The park's gardener absently watered some jasmine plants. Fred, a bicycling police officer rode slowly round the park paths. He had the best job in the city, a bike cop in North Beach. He underscored it with the sardonic exhortation, "Many are called, but few are chosen." De Forest, an aging blues man strummed his guitar. Several elderly Chinese men sat on benches reading Cantonese language newspapers. A few down'n'out folks splayed on the grass. Pigeons pecked at bald spots in the turf.

And across the street was a peregrine falcon, perched motionless on a spire of Saints Peter and Paul Church.

Noë, Zoë and Max were already in the park, eating their sandwiches. McCabe joined them on the grass, greeting them tentatively. As he sat down, Max dissolved into laughter, "The ladies have come up with a creative proposal. It's called, 'McCabe's Clean City Program'."

Noë nodded approvingly, "Yeah, so your campaign theme is 'Clean, Green Streets for a Livable City,' right?"

"That it is," said McCabe warily.

"And you've always said that you gotta start with clean, cause without that, you can't really get a handle on safety or greening—like that first bit of graffiti leading to progressively deteriorating neighborhoods unless you fix it immediately, correct? So we do a cleaning demonstration—something that will grab media attention—and at the same time sidelines you as a viable candidate. It'll look like a campaign stunt that wasn't well thought out and backfired."

"What do I do, dress up like a clown and steam clean the streets?"

Noë touched his knee, "No, something more intimate."

"What?!"

Zoë whispered puzzlingly, "More titillating."

"How's that?"

A Frisbee floated over them and alighted in the grass.

Max pulled a dandelion from the turf, "Look, you want a drop in the polls. We think we have an easy way of doing it, taking you out of contention."

"If it doesn't?"

"Oh this should, this definitely should," chortled Max.

"Well, what is it?"

Zoë replied tentatively "Well you *ah*..."

"Come on." said McCabe. "What is it?"

Zoë overcame her initial reluctance, "Well, you talk about clean streets all the time..."

Noë added, "Yeah, you're actually kind of obsessive about it."

"Maybe I am. Why would the media pay any attention, much less report on my little obsession as you call it? Who's gonna come to a press conference on that? The media isn't gonna want to hear me talk to that."

"They will if you're taking a shower," ventured Zoë.

"A shower!?"

"Yeah, we can ask that no one publish *ah—ah*—a full length picture of you..." said Zoë hesitantly.

McCabe replied in mock relief, "Oh, thank God for that! But that'll look idiotic, me standing in a shower setting out my program for clean streets! Stupid and boring! Mostly stupid! Is that all you guys have been able to come up with?"

Max joked, "Remember what Mark Twain said, 'Clothes make the man. Naked people have little or no influence on society.' There's more, McCabe, there's more. Listen to this!"

Noë added obligingly, "Zoë and I will be in the shower with you!"

"We'll be shampooing our...your hair while you talk about your program! The Clean Team!" said Zoë, animatedly.

Max laughed uproariously, "It's classic! Right up there with the shower scene from *Psycho*! That'll get you headlines and a drop in the polls for sure! They won't exactly be showering you with votes after that, and it won't hurt your reputation as a columnist. Everybody knows you guys are mad as a March hare. It's just a wonder how you got a lead in the polls in the first place. "

"That's demented!" sputtered McCabe. "Preposterous!"

"Exactly!" said Max exultantly. Then he had another thought, turning to Noë and Zoë, "Are you guys OK being naked with McCabe? That's definitely not part of your job description."

An indecipherable smile crossed Zoë's lips, "McCabe, would you be ok getting naked with us?"

"Would you let it all hang out with us, *hmmm*?" needled Noë, enjoying the inside joke.

McCabe looked down at the grass, hoping Max wouldn't pick up on their drift, "I've got nothing to hide..."

Noë choked back her laughter, "And with us in the scene, they'll crop the pics at a strategic height, so for once your little Tommy Gun should be safe from over-exposure!"

"You got *cajones*, McCabe," punned Max, taking a large bite of his sandwich.

The peregrine falcon launched from the spire of Saints Peter and Paul Church, scattering the parrots helter-skelter over the rooftops of chiaroscuro North Beach.

CHAPTER SEVENTEEN: SHOWER POWER

The Clean Team press conference was set to be held in the bathroom of McCabe's cottage. Given the compact dimensions, the invitees were limited to a representative from a local newspaper—naturally, the *Foghorn* from McCabe's own campaign—as well as one television station, KINK—and one radio station, KFOG. Neither Noë nor Zoë objected to being filmed naked—as long as all taping avoided their breasts, and most certainly no full frontal nudity.

It was now only two weeks till the election. The Registrar of Voters had mailed absentee ballots several weeks before. Given that half the citizenry voted absentee, the message that McCabe the candidate was a goofus ideally needed to hit the voters a few days before the absentee ballots were mailed. As it was, two weeks of absentee voting had already occurred, but that seemed an inconsequential concern.

Not a word was said about a shower to any of the invited reporters—including April—not one little drop. McCabe would be making a statement about his "Clean City" platform and the "initiatives" he would undertake as mayor to make this top priority program a reality. This all seemed uneventful and in most cases no one would have showed, but now that he was the presumed front-runner, his words and policies suddenly became important.

The press conference titled "McCabe Comes Clean" was scheduled for noon. KINK's TV truck arrived on upper Montgomery and snailed down the narrow street to the top of the Filbert Steps. Out jumped KINK reporter Miles O'Riley, a cameraman behind him. Miles, disoriented, squinted at the street sign to see which way the street numbers ran. He rolled his eyes, "Man, it's down in that jungle somewhere," pointing at Filbert's switchback stairs that disappeared into the Grace Marchant Garden. "Come on, watch out for pythons and jaguars!"

A block below where the Filbert Steps ended on Sansome Street, a radio reporter for KFOG, Charlie Horn, drove up and parked. Packing his miked equipment, he grunted up a set of nearly vertical metal stairs to a concrete landing then continued along the winding wooden stairway to Napier Lane.

Miles and his cameraman emerged from the overgrowth above Napier at the same time as Charlie Horn from below. Miles and Charlie knew each other from multiple assignments covering the San Francisco political scene. They both sensed something unusual was afoot—the vague invitation and most puzzling, the location on the back side of Telegraph Hill, off the Filbert Steps on wooden-planked Napier Lane, inside McCabe's cottage.

They walked down Napier and through McCabe's front gate. Squad Car greeted them with a soft "*Meow*," and scrambled up the stairs guiding them to the front door. There being no doorbell, Miles pulled the woodpecker knocker, its long black beak *tap-tap-tapping*, gently rapping, on McCabe's front door. Max greeted them, appraising their bewildered faces, "Good to see you, guys! Glad you found this place! Come on in!" No one appeared to be inside the house other than Max.

"So where's McCabe?" asked Miles. "Don't tell me he got lost trying to find his own house in this briar patch?"

"Fellas, give me a moment," smiled Max enigmatically. "We're still waiting for April from the *Foghorn*. I'll be right back." He disappeared into the bathroom. The reporters stood in the hallway, befuddled. If this was about "Clean San Francisco," why not at McCabe's campaign headquarters or some iconic outdoor location? Max reappeared, closing the bathroom door behind him, "Alright, give us a few moments, McCabe will be ready for you guys, shortly..."

"In the bathroom?" asked Miles, pointing incredulously at the door. "In...in...*in there*!?"

"Actually, Miles, it is in there. Never attended a press conference in a bathroom? It's not all that capacious—but you'll all fit in there just fine."

"Come on, Max, you're kidding right?" said Miles, laughing edgily, his gleaming white teeth taking on a tiger-like snarl. "We're gonna listen to McCabe in there? I don't care how 'capacious' it is! It's a damn bathroom! Are we all gonna sit on the pot? Or is it McCabe who's sittin' on the pot?" Then a shower was turned on, the sound of water hitting the tile floor. A man began laughing, joined by peals of female laughter. Wisps of steam crept out from under the bathroom door.

Miles perked up, electrified, "This I gotta see!"

At that moment, April arrived, not bothering to knock on the door, out of breath, notebook in hand.

Max cued up the presentation: "Well, alright then, now that we're all here, let the press conference begin. On behalf of the 'McCabe for Mayor' campaign, I welcome each of you to his home for an intimate 'McCabe Comes Clean' press conference. If he is to become mayor, he wants you to understand his inalterable commitment to his campaign pledge of 'Clean, Green Streets for a Livable City.' First, you gotta have clean, cause without clean, you're never get to get safe and green. The tipping point is clean. From there everything follows. And, I want to remind you cynical souls of the press, all life is performance, is it not? Every action determined by relationship and context? Well, keep that in mind, because it may not look it, but I assure you, McCabe is a rational man about to do something that may look anything but rational, but in

SB

fact is! You figure it out—or don't. Here are the rules for this, *ah*—this press conference. Each of you can ask a few questions with a follow-up. April, as representative of our *Foghorn* newspaper gets to ask the first question—then Miles, then Charlie. Oh, one other thing—regarding the ladies in there, perhaps it's best if there are no shots below the shoulders. You'll understand shortly. And as to McCabe, nothing below the waist. And if you do, you gotta blur it! *Ha ha!* You'll soon see why!"

Like an impresario, with a touch of the absurd, Max slowly opened the bathroom door, "I present you: 'McCabe Comes Clean!'" Steam billowed out like fog pouring through the Golden Gate. Molecules of fragrant shampoo infused their olfactory senses, momentarily disorienting the intrepid reporters. A voice like an ancient god beckoned them through the mist, "Come in, come in, don't be bashful!"

The steam cleared. There stood McCabe, Noë and Zoë, shining and naked, joyfully shampooing each other's hair. The reporters were aghast. Miles eagerly barked out to his cameraman, "*Fa–fa–*film it, *film it!*"

April exclaimed, "Oh, Thomas, what on earth?" Then staring at Noë and Zoë, "Oh my, what are you girls doing? You're being taped!"

"Hey, April," cried Noë effervescently.

Zoë gave April a buoyant wave of her hand.

McCabe laughed irrepressibly, "Is that your first question, April?"

Barely regaining her composure, April tried to proceed with a sense of decorum, "Let's see. Well, so tell us what's this all about? Clean streets, is it?"

McCabe gurgled deliriously, "Exactly. I wanted to make a point today about what my administration's priorities will be if I'm elected mayor. Why is it that our streets are so dirty? Look at our commercial corridors—graffiti, gummed-up sidewalks, overflowing trash bins. As citizens we interact more with our sidewalks and streets than any other element of our city—more than police, fire, parks, public health, schools. This is where the soul—*ha ha*—and the sole, '*s-o-l-e*', interacts with city most often—on our sidewalks and streets. So shouldn't this be an administration's highest priority? Clean streets? To which everything else is related and interconnected?"

For the briefest of moments the logic of McCabe's response made everyone disbelieve he was actually showering with two young women. But, the suspension of disbelief quickly evaporated as Miles jumped in for the next question, "Look, McCabe, clean streets and all that are great, but really, what exactly are you trying to accomplish here? Don't you think this manner of making your point is a bit—*ahhh,* over the edge? I mean is anyone gonna take you seriously, showering with two women at a press conference?"

"I take your point, Miles, I truly do," enthused McCabe. "But really, this is about substantive policy." McCabe wagged his finger sarcastically, "It's about how we make our city more livable and where we begin to do that—where we put our priorities in an era of shrinking budgets, while protecting our frontline workers from layoffs and furloughs."

Charlie Horn, mike in hand laughed incredulously, "*Ah* yeah—ok. San Francisco may be a liberal and tolerant town, lots of far-out, colorful characters and all that. But don't you think the voters might find this scene a little over-the-top?"

McCabe picked up a bar of soap, lightheartedly sliding it over Zoë's pear breasts, "Strange? *Rub-a-dub-dub!*"

Seeing a fat pitch down the middle, Charlie had no choice but to swing away, "So are Noë and Zoë, your campaign managers—the women you're showering with—are they slated for positions in your administration if you're elected?"

"Positions? Well, of course," enthused McCabe, as the water coursed over his chest. "The campaign that showers together, positions together!"

Severely testing her professionalism, her anger at low boil, April asked, "Tom, so what will be your first steps in initiating your "Clean Streets Program" once you become mayor?"

McCabe mustered a serious demeanor, as Noë shampooed his hair and Zoë soaped his thighs, "Well, *ah*, the first thing I'm going to do..." Zoë slid the bar of soap over his buttocks. "The first thing..." Noë slapped his ass playfully. "The first thing is to appoint an advisor for my 'Clean Streets Program', to coordinate the various city departments on making every street in the city clean, safe and green." Noë pressed into him, her breasts against his back, continuing to enthusiastically shampoo his hair. In the background Charlie Horn was giving color commentary on the naked shower antics, and the TV cameraman was freely taping everything, not abiding by the agreed-upon restrictions—no breasts—*no breasts!* And definitely not McCabe's *hard drive!*

Miles pitched McCabe another question, "So how do you think the public will react to the 'Clean Streets Program' you're presenting today? Might your message get lost in this soap opera of yours?"

"I hope the voters out there will see this as good, clean, innocent fun, and take seriously my 'Clean Streets Program.' Government may not be able to give you much these days, but at least the streets should be as clean as we are right now!" McCabe flipped the bar of soap in the air for emphasis. "We need to clean from the summit of our city hills," McCabe soaped Zoë's breasts metaphorically, then moved down to her thighs, "to our commercial corridors and boulevards"—then her ankles and feet—"and every street and alley in between!"

Miles couldn't possibly leave that unharvested, followed-up, "I'm not clear why you're doing this? You lead in the ranked-choice polls. It seems counterintuitive, taking a risk like this. Why do something so unorthodox? Normally the person leading in the polls plays it safe. This isn't exactly a prudent way to protect a lead is it?"

"Unorthodox? Am I hiding anything? I'm being completely transparent! I can't think of a better way to highlight my commitment to clean streets than to have a press conference in a shower!"

Max interceded into the splish-splash. "How about one more question.

April, why don't you close it out?"

April, her poise starting to break, haltingly asked, "Tell me, Tom, how do you see the final two weeks of the campaign going? Are you pleased to be doing so well? Are you still confident about your chances of winning?"

"I'm confident that I'm doing the right thing to achieve my goals of running for mayor. I can walk away at the end of this, win or lose, feeling good about myself. I've made a genuine effort to make my campaign financing as clean and transparent as possible. You gotta make constant efforts to stay clean! Just like today!"

April fled the bathroom, embarrassed and distraught.

Miles shook his head in wonderment, "McCabe, this is the damnedest thing I've ever seen anyone do running for public office! I hand it to you, this is a YouTube moment! This'll go viral! But I'm sure not clear how this is gonna help you win! But it's your show, what the hell!" The cameraman turned off the light on his video camera.

Charlie Horn wrapped up his radio coverage, "You've heard it from the cleanest candidate for mayor, Tom McCabe! As we begin the final sprint to election day, this is steamy Charlie Horn for KFOG, reporting from McCabe's shower in his super-clean cottage on the twilight side of Telegraph Hill."

As Charlie turned off his mike, Noë snuck in the last word, "Alright, now that the press conference is over, anyone want to join us?" She beckoned with her index finger, "Come here, Miles! You too, Charlie Horn!"

CHAPTER EIGHTEEN: BELLO HOW COULD YOU?

The six o'clock evening news on channel KINK led with McCabe's aqueous press conference, extinguishing the usual mayhem leads. A good minute was devoted to the shower scene. McCabe, Noë and Zoë were presented with the barest impressionistic blur, naked to the world.

KINK's story opened with a shot of Miles walking down Napier Lane commenting on the baffling press conference invite, then a shot walking through McCabe's garden. Even Squad Car made a cameo appearance leading them to the front door. The shower scene began with a head shot of McCabe, then steamy shots of Noë and Zoë, followed by Miles' question about the propriety of the shower, the camera slowly teasing the viewer with ever more exposed shots until the barely blurred nakedness of the three was revealed. Almost nothing was said about McCabe's "Clean City Program" other than at the very opening of the piece, after which it was shots of soaped-up flesh and shampooed hair, together with Miles' tongue-and-cheek commentary.

McCabe became an overnight reality TV star featuring his own shower show. From there it went viral—Twitter, Reddit, YouTube, Facebook—across the Pacific to Weibo, over twenty million views—then repurposed and rebroadcast on talk radio. By that evening Google was showing hundreds of links. The comments on the KINK website took up more than eighty pages, close to a thousand people. The commentary ran the gamut from outrage to the tolerant, with thumbs up and thumbs down votes running more-or-less even. The unscientific analysis indicated mostly shrugs with a shrill negative element balanced against a few who saw it as comedy and farce, as did Michael Savage, the Bay Area conservative radio talk show host of *Savage Nation*. Many assumed that McCabe must have grievously wounded himself as a candidate for mayor. The question asked by many was why he had engaged in such a stunt when everything seemed to be going his way? Some even speculated that McCabe was dissatisfied at the poll numbers showing him winning only through ranked-choice voting—he wanted to win outright on the first ballot, not on the fifth or sixth, and had engaged in the high-risk maneuver hoping to catapult himself to a first ballot majority.

That week, the *Foghorn* put out its own front-page article written by April titled "McCabe Presents His Clean Streets Program." It featured a black and white shot of Noë and Zoë from the neck up shampooing McCabe's hair. The emphasis was not on titillation, but on policy and programs, mixed with before and after photos of gum-encrusted sidewalks now steam-cleaned, mechanical street sweepers sucking up litter, early morning water trucks spraying commercial corridors. Even though the *Foghorn* as a campaign newspaper was supposed to seamlessly carry out campaign strategy, it was no longer playing on the same team as McCabe. It had kept to its editorial integrity, eschewing the obvious entertainment value of the press conference, sticking with policy and prescriptions for cleaner streets. Max figured that the television and radio coverage would be the lasting impression in voters' minds. The *Foghorn* didn't need to highlight the erotic buffoonery, and thus kept peace on the staff, which refused to participate in cratering McCabe's campaign.

By the following day, coverage had spread across the globe from Paris' *Le Monde* to Hong Kong's *South China Morning Post*, even to

San Francisco's sister city, the *Shanghai Daily*. Then came the backlash. McCabe had some explaining to do, summed up by one word, "Why?" This deceptively facile question was not, however, a simple matter to answer when the actual strategy was to *lose* the campaign. There were many McCabe supporters who felt let down, even betrayed at what appeared to be a silly PR stunt that had little substance and potentially calamitous results. McCabe had not anticipated this permutation—those most loyal to him now saw themselves as victims taken in by an insurgent campaign that had made a fool of itself, snatching defeat from the jaws of victory.

McCabe attempted to clarify his antics as injecting some humor into the mayoral campaign—a mere dalliance. Phone calls to the campaign headquarters continued to pour in like a pineapple express storming in from Hawaii.

He shifted to contrite. But that still didn't quell the uproar.

The last bullet in his chamber was simply to apologize, even though the strategy had been to evaporate his support. But as McCabe parsed it, there weren't many people who actually deserved an apology. His contributors could only give a hundred dollars. And the writers for the *Foghorn* were on salary. The only group that deserved an apology were the volunteers. They had given their time in the sincere belief that his was a campaign to win, unaware of its true nature and purpose.

Within a few days, other news crowded out the shower story. The downpour of criticism began to pass. But there were still supporters who had not yet had their say, particularly Luciano Peroni at North Beach Restaurant. Several evenings after the shower show McCabe dropped by the establishment. He ordered Luciano's Brunello. At twenty-five dollars a glass, it was not only outrageously expensive, the restaurant was parsimonious with a pour as well. A martini glass was used to measure a standard five-ounce pour, the pour not to exceed its height. If Luciano wasn't at the bar, the bartenders often gave over-pours to their favorite customers. If Luciano happened to witness an evident over-pour, he would invariably challenge it. And Luciano was always right. When the martini glass was set beside the wine glass, the wine would be a quarter inch, sometimes just one-eighth of an inch higher than the rim of the martini glass. Always more. Luciano had never made a miscalculation.

Marilyn was working the bar, requiring the dexterity of a gymnast. The wine selection was presented on shelving behind the bar, four shelves high. The male bartenders could barely reach the top shelf to pull a bottle. Marilyn could only reach the second. There was no movable ladder for the higher shelves. She simply vaulted onto the back bar's marble counter to reach bottles on the upper shelves, then adroitly dropped back down to the floor. She carried out the feat in seconds. Once she determined where the wine was located, the jump, grab and drop was a mere afterthought. She had never lost a bottle.

Marilyn gave McCabe a flagrantly generous over-pour of Brunello. It nearly reached the rim of the wine glass. He acknowledged the pour with a conspiratorial smile. As he settled into the bar, a voice boomed out from the owner's table in the corner of the dining room, "*Bello*, what are you doing? Over here!" It was Luciano. McCabe scrupulously carried his glass of wine to Luciano's table. Marilyn anxiously watched the scene develop, realizing she was about to be busted for the over-pour. As he set down his brimming glass of Brunello, Luciano immediately reckoned McCabe's out-of-character shuffle. He scowled over at Marilyn, "*Bella*, you're going to ruin me! Bankruptcy will be your fault!" Then he gave McCabe a merciless look, slamming his hand down on the table, causing rivulets of wine to flow over the rim of McCabe's glass, "*Bello*, what's this? Taking a public shower with your campaign managers? Are you nuts?"

McCabe's Brunello continued shivering in the verbal storm. "It wasn't public, Luciano, it was in my house."

"Not public!? Your house!? It was on TV, on the radio, in all the newspapers. My wife says it's even on YouTube. She thought it was hot!

She said it was some of the best soft porn she's ever seen!"

"What I meant was..."

"Not public!? You think it was private? They showed everything! Everything! The ladies too!"

"They blurred it."

"Blurring?" Luciano wagged his little finger, "They even showed that!"

"In your imagination, which is coming up short!"

"Why? Why would you do such a thing? Do you know how many calls I got! I look dumber than prosciutto for supporting you!"

"A year from now no one is going to remember who you supported. You've contributed to every politician who's waltzed through the door. No one is gonna remember."

"But right now they do! What am I supposed to tell them? That you went temporarily insane? That showering with your female campaign managers is just one of your strange little habits?"

"The mayor slept with his aide's wife and he's still in office," rejoined McCabe. "Schwarzenegger had a love child with the family maid. Willie Brown got his campaign manager pregnant. Hell, he was married too, and she had the child! Barely caused a ripple in the press."

"Willie gets away with everything! You're not Willie, *Bello!*"

"Luciano, it's over, done! Relax!"

"Relax? Relax? How can I? You're gonna give me a heart attack! I treat you like a son! I give you big respect, arrange a huge—*huge* fundraiser! Did you think of people like me before doing that?"

"Well..." said McCabe, thrown off balance by Luciano's onslaught.

"No! No you didn't! I know you, McCabe! You just went ahead and did it! As usual, thought of no one but yourself!"

"It was just a shower! I didn't rape and pillage!"

"*Bello*, it was almost as bad!" Luciano shook his head in disbelief, "Almost as bad!" He paused, then down-shifted, "You told me you didn't want to be mayor, but this! This! You embarrassed us all!"

"Admit it, originally you never thought I had a chance! So what have you lost? I'm the one taking the hit, not you!"

Luciano's intensity began to dissipate. "You and two women in a shower! On TV! What would your father think? I've never heard of anything so stupid!"

"And harmless," added McCabe. "Can you imagine me being mayor, Luciano? Me as mayor?"

"You're as good as anyone. You just don't have the ambition."

"I'm not that needy."

Luciano laughed, "I can see that, at least not in politics!" Then he added, almost as an after-thought, "Be careful, *Bello*. Don't fool yourself! And who is the easiest person to fool?" He chuckled to himself and raised his wine glass, "To whatever comes next, *Bello*. I wish you the best."

"To whatever comes next," said McCabe relievedly, believing the final chapter of his campaign was now a foregone conclusion, "to whatever's next."

Luciano took a drink of his wine with a curiously knowing detachment. Then his eyes narrowed, unnerved at the circular red wine stain on his lamb white tablecloth.

CHAPTER NINETEEN: WORKERS IN THE VINEYARD—MATTHEW 20:1-16

McCabe owned a small hillside vineyard above St. Helena in the Napa Valley. By late October his Cabernet grapes would normally have been harvested and contentedly fermenting in the barrel. But this year the spring and summer had been unusually cool. Bud break, flowering and fruit-set were late, the grapes had ripened slowly in moderate summer temperatures. Veraison—the point at which the grapes turned from green to purple had occurred in mid-September rather than early August. Now, the first big storm of the season was rolling in from Hawaii, a pineapple express loaded with water; the deluge would decimate the fruit.

Pickers were scheduled for the day after Halloween. Even though the election was only a week away, the grape harvest provided an excuse for McCabe to leave town. Normally the candidates would be in manic overdrive, spending twelve, fourteen hours a day campaigning—working the phones, knocking on doors, leafleting, hitting bus stops in the morning and late afternoon. But not candidate McCabe. He was the father of a vineyard in which Mother Earth was ready to produce her harvest. This was the closest he had come to ever being a parent.

His house was perched 1,700 feet above the Napa Valley, bathed in the cleansing breath of Oak, Madrone, Bay Laurel and Douglas Fir.

His drinking water flowed from a spring that ran year-round from volcanic fissures deep in the earth. He had spent many hours working his mountain property, building nearly a mile of rock walls, ringing his house in terraces. In the winter he pruned his fruit trees—pomegranate, persimmon, apple, peach, pear, apricot, fig and olive. He also tended his herbs—rosemary, thyme, oregano, and his English and Spanish lavender. As he engaged in his mountainside chores, the city gradually peeling away, he emerged from his urban chrysalis. At that altitude, the ultraviolet light produced a radiant energy that converted into vitamin D. The reserve of energy quickly dissipated back in the city where as a columnist, he effectively worked every waking moment—and all the food, wine and occasional sex that went with it. If he missed his days in the country, he began to feel ill-tempered and out-of-balance. His skin began to pale. His eye sockets darkened. He began to die a little.

McCabe took off for the Napa Valley on Halloween day in his green convertible Mini Cooper. The car didn't throw thunderbolts, but was ideal for parking on Telegraph Hill where space was at an extreme premium. It could be folded in almost anywhere, and cornered as firmly as grabbing a stripper's pole.

He cruised over the Golden Gate Bridge with the top down, drops of moisture falling on his head from the fog condensing on the bridge. At Novato, he turned off Highway 101, drove past the old town of Sonoma to Highway 29 that ran the length of the Napa Valley. After the town of Napa, he entered the heart of the valley and the premier viticultural areas—the Yountville Appellation, and further along the winery-rich Oakville and Rutherford Appellations—bringing him to the stone bridge at the entrance to the town of St. Helena. He drove down Main Street past the limestone buildings now housing art galleries, restaurants, jewelry stores, an old movie theater, and McCabe's favorite, the used bookstore, Main Street Books. He stopped at Sunshine Market and picked up some prosciutto, carpaccio, marinated olives, Humboldt

Fog cheese, focaccina and calamari vinaigrette.

Provisioned, he drove to Madrona Avenue, and with confident momentum along the twisting road into the Spring Mountain Appellation. Just above Langtry Road his house came into view. The home, all of redwood, was married to the mountain, ringed with rosemary and lavender drenched walls of volcanic rock.

Leaving his car, a vinegary odor engulfed him. Just across the road Keenan Winery had finished harvesting its grapes, distributing the remains of its crush—the lees, grape skins and seeds—around its vineyards. It was a natural fertilizer, fermenting on the ground and giving off a redolent but not unpleasant smell.

He walked down the river-smooth stepping stones to the graveled patio by his house. An old swing hung from a massive live oak, its bark suffused with lichen. The sheltering branches spread over a long feasting table made of staves from a redwood fermenting tank, deconstructed many years before. More stepping stones wound down from the patio to a small pool just above his Cabernet vineyard, almost erotic in shape.

The view opened not merely beautifully, but sublimely to the Napa Valley, bracketed by undulating ridges of Oak and Douglas Fir. At the foot of Spring Mountain lay the town of St. Helena, barely perceptible through the profusion of street trees. Only the spires of St. Helena's many churches emerged through the canopy of the village forest. Beyond St. Helena lay a sea of vineyards in varying swatches of green, mixed with snatches of yellow and orange—vineyards ready to be picked, still green, while varieties that had already been harvested, mostly Chardonnay, having begun to turn. Wineries and farmhouses dotted the vineyard landscape—one part plan, two parts accident.

McCabe pulled out a key hidden in the leg of the table and unlocked the door to his house. The cabin interior was a country cousin to his cottage on Telegraph Hill—madrone floors, a cross-hatching of beams in a cathedral ceiling, skylights. The redwood walls gave the interior a warming hue that shifted in light and shadow as the sun moved across the sky. There were hundreds of books and records, Indian mortars and pestles by the fireplace, bowls of arrowheads, original Audubon prints, Navaho rugs, a shelf of hand-blown bottles, mid-century furniture—a shabby genteel look. A guest room and small bathroom was off to one side of the living room and on the other side McCabe's bedroom and a second larger bathroom. Just outside his bedroom was a gnarled Black Mission fig tree, its pendulous branches bending with ripe figs that rubbed sonorously against the house in a strong wind.

Immersed in private thoughts, he laid out his meal on the patio table. Adding to his repast, he picked some black figs with their dense pink flesh, a silky soft and creamy Comice pear, and a Golden Delicious apple with its fine and smooth buff-colored fruit. As the final act, he uncorked a bottle of Chardonnay and poured himself a glass, enjoying the self-sufficiency of a part-time, semi-recluse.

Perfection, like a seventh day palace in time.

An avian opera played out about him. A swooping flight of swallows performed arabesques counterpointed by a languid buzzard gliding overhead. A rafter of wild turkeys gobbled maniacally from the protective shadows of the nearby forest. Pitying turtle doves cried in the peach trees. A piliated woodpecker pounded out a deep tom-tom beat from a hollow oak. Scolding blue jays screeched from an apple tree. A charm of iridescent hummingbirds probed the trumpet vine on the side of the house. Band-tailed pigeons winged nervously over the vineyard towards the forest refuge.

Playing in the background by the corner of the house was the gentle humming of a honey bee hive in the hole of a declining oak.

As he took his first sip of wine, a car peeled off Spring Mountain Road into his driveway. ***Who the hell is this? Is there no solitude?***

"Hey, McCabe!" called out Noë breathlessly, jumping from her car. Then Zoë sheepishly emerged. McCabe's jaw dropped wide enough to allow a swarm of sneaky fruit flies into a tasting room of a winery. "We thought you might want company!"

McCabe was momentarily flummoxed, "You guys? What a surprise! How did you find this place?"

Noë gushed, "Google Maps led us right here!" She looked out over the valley, "My god, it's so beautiful, I can see why you escape here! I have house envy!"

Zoë said gently as a spring brook, "We missed you. Hope we're not intruding."

McCabe laughed and embraced them, "No worries. Sit on down, let's get a few more plates and wine glasses."

As they drank the Chardonnay and finished off their meal, the Halloween moon, blood red from the smoke of gathering forest fires, began its rise over the valley. The forest around them began to darken. Across the valley the shadows cast from the western ridge of the Mayacamas Mountains inexorably climbed to the crest of the eastern hills above the Silverado Trail. Several miles below, the siren from the St. Helena volunteer fire department rang out. In the forest a clan of coyotes howled back, answering the call of what seemed a coyote-in-distress wailing from the valley floor.

McCabe, mellowed, offered liquid dessert, "Why don't I crack another bottle and crank up the hot tub?"

Noë and Zoë brightened like Venus rising.

He walked down to the terrace below the patio, turned on the hot tub's gas heater, which activated with a "*Thruuuump.*" Returning to the house, he uncorked a bottle of Cabernet produced from his grapes. The wine smelled of black currants, herbs, and of the mountain terroir—Franciscan sedimentary rocks, mostly sandstone and conglomerates—as well as Napa–Sonoma volcanic formations. He swirled the wine to the rim of the glass, inspecting the thin viscous sheets of wine flowing back down the sides of the glass— shimmering, high alcohol legs, reminding him of his father's sage observation, "The better the legs, the better the wine."

With each draught of wine, they floated higher above the valley.

A great horned owl began a courting cadence, *hoo hoodoo hooo hoo*, then a longer *ho hoo hoo hoododo hooooo hoo*, quickly answered by a female owl in a higher pitched, *guwaaay guwaaay.*

Below the patio, fingerlings of mist rose from the hot tub. Inside the house they stripped. Noë and Zoë wrapped towels around themselves leaving their contoured asses uncovered, gingerly walking barefoot down to the hot tub. McCabe grabbed a towel and walked bare-ass from the house to join them. His buttocks were sculpted from walking the roller-coaster hills of San Francisco, his arms muscled from building the rock-walled terraces on his hillside property.

They eased themselves into the hot tub, buffeted by jets of massaging spring water. A pair of lizards skittered by. The Halloween moon turned creamy as it inched along the Milky Way. A rapture of crickets chirped round them. Time was converted by their wine-fueled high, released into transports of delight, longing and desire.

Later in bed, they languidly stroked each other to sleep.

In the pink light of morning, McCabe found himself dreaming in Spanish, a language he had learned in college and spoken intermittently in his travels and in working with the Mexican stone masons on his property. Until now, he had never dreamt in Spanish. He could sense he was struggling to wake, realizing that he was in a lucid dream that seemed to be holding him against his will. Then the dream released him from the somnolent effects of the night's wine erotics. Noë and Zoë lay on either side of him, their backs to him, oblivious. Low voices in Spanish drifted in from the vineyard. He thought he had escaped his Spanish language dream. The bedroom looked real, every book properly shelved, the towels from their hot-tubbing lying on the floor, their clothes thrown over the chairs, the bathroom door slightly ajar, and perched on the open window sill, a curious blue jay staring him down.

Dammit, I'm awake! realized McCabe, overcoming his now receding dream. He bolted up in bed. ***Shit, the pickers are here!*** He threw on a pair of jeans, grabbed a work shirt from the closet, slipped on his shoes, no socks, and hustled out of the house and down to the vineyard. Four pickers were standing next to a flatbed truck, empty half-ton containers securely strapped to its bed. The driver was standing by the the truck smoking a cigarette, conversing in Spanish with the pickers.

As McCabe approached, the driver called out, "*Qué pasa*, McCabe?" His dream flashed back, like a quantum pulse from the future event time horizon, now decoded, then evaporated. Reality settled and cohered. "*Buenos días, buenos días*," said McCabe simply, greeting the men.

There were supposed to be six pickers, not four. Each worker had a curved picking knife. They wore threadbare cotton shirts, dusty jeans and straw hats. He asked the pickers where the remaining two workers were, but they had no idea. McCabe pointed at a nearby set of terraces above the main vineyard. He instructed them to start there, then move to the other rows of the vineyard, working down the western edge to the bottom, the truck to follow them as they finished off their rows. They were to leave unripe fruit, any bunches showing signs of mildew and stems stripped of grapes by the songbirds and turkeys. And no leaves. They had heard the same instruction many times; it made no difference. Some workers picked fast and clean, some slow, some messy. They were paid by the job and picked according to their personalities.

The workers each took a picking box that could hold up to forty pounds of grapes. McCabe climbed up on the bed of the truck. As the pickers approached the truck, their hands balancing the full box of grapes on their head, he grabbed the box in one smooth pull, flipping the grapes into a bin, then throwing the empty box back to the picker. Periodically, McCabe sorted through the grapes, removing leaves and stems, his hands turning sticky purple from the grape juice. After several hours, he took a break. The driver, who was sitting on a stone wall reading a Spanish language newspaper, listening to Mexican radio, took over for him while he returned to the house.

Noë and Zoë were still asleep, blankets down to their waists. He peeled the blankets further back to gaze at their striking nudity, sparking an unquenchable desire to return to bed. He sat down on the edge of the bed and stroked their backs, slipping his grape-juiced hand between the warmth of their honeyed wetness. They moaned contentedly. The evening's wine and heated hot tub play had sapped their energy, wanting nothing more than to drift in and out of sleep in the serene warmth of the bed.

McCabe went back down to the vineyard. A fifth man had arrived and was picking with the others. Each man took a row of about fifty vines, beginning at the end farthest from the truck, at each vine dropping to one knee, reaching into the trellised canes, quickly slicing off the bunches into their box, even bunches of no more than ten grapes. Each grape was precious. Most remarkably, the pickers didn't wear a glove on the hand that held the bunch to be cut, even though the grape knives were razor sharp. The first time McCabe worked a harvest, he cut his hand badly, and thereafter always wore a glove. That the pickers could work through the day without cutting themselves was testament to their dexterity and surgical abilities, particularly when both hands were buried in the vines—and all the while carrying on distracted conversation with fellow pickers in parallel rows.

McCabe returned once more to the house, made coffee, relaxed, the harvest going smoothly. He gazed over the valley, his mind wandering over the landscape. Noë and Zoë were still out. ***What light-weights***, he mused.

When he again returned to the vineyard, a sixth man had joined the other pickers.

In the early afternoon they completed picking, having harvested a little more than four tons of grapes. The bins were filled over their brims, but would consolidate as the truck drove to the winery. He paid each of the workers in cash, two hundred dollars. The daily wage during harvest was good, higher than normal. Even though they had completed the picking in five hours, they were paid for an entire day. The first man paid was the last to arrive, and the second paid was the next-to-last to arrive. They both received the full day's wage. The remaining pickers complained among themselves—if the last to arrive received a full day's wage shouldn't they receive more for working longer hours in the increasing heat of the day? McCabe demurred. He had promised a full day's wage and that was what each would receive; the last as the first and the first as the last, Matthew 20:1-16.

The truck eased out of the vineyard, its load of grapes gently quivering with each bump and turn in Spring Mountain Road.

CHAPTER TWENTY: BUDDHIST CURVEBALL

With a week to the election, the polls showed McCabe's support eroding, the number of undecided voters increasing. However, unlike some earlier polls, these lacked a certain transparency as there was no indication of a voter's second and third place choices. It was rare if not unheard of for a candidate who didn't come in first in the initial ballot count, to win through ranked-choice voting. But instant run-off was still largely experimental in the United States. It existed in only a few jurisdictions of the country, its implications and possible scenarios were largely unknown, particularly where there was no clear front-runner, the first place votes spread among a handful of candidates.

The venue for McCabe's election night close-out was still undecided. With a reasonable expectation of winning, a large space would be reserved, but if the expectations were modest, a smaller venue such as neighborhood café or bar would suffice. McCabe preferred a spot somewhere in North Beach. A larger space devoted to acknowledging one had lost was worse than a smaller, intimate space where you could party with your friends, while the winner could bask in the glory of a victory night cattle-call.

Max suggested Capp's Corner. Capp's was a rarity in North Beach, still serving old style Italian fare—a plate of antipasti, minestrone, green salad and beans brought out in self-serve communal bowls, a basket of bread, entrée, dessert and coffee. Located at the corner of Green and Powell, Capp's exuded the spirit of the old Barbary Coast—a saloon-restaurant—gruff bartenders tending about a dozen regulars plunked down on red vinyl bar stools. There was a podium by the doorway where a hostess greeted guests. In acknowledgment of modern day media, two big-screen televisions showed baseball, football, basketball or golf—sometimes football on one screen, golf on the other. An antique mirrored bar was lined with red wines, whiskeys, vodkas and liqueurs. A Lou Gehrig Louisville Slugger hung just above the cash register, once used on unruly dissolutes. The walls were covered in kitschy San Francisco memorabilia—black and white sketches of long gone but not forgotten bartenders, faded autographed photos of local boxers, baseball and football legends, a smattering of pictures of Joe and Norma Jean DiMaggio who often ate there in the mid-50s. At the rear of the dining room a neon beer sign clock was stuck permanently on "Earthquake Series Time"—5:04—the moment the October 17 Loma Prieta earthquake hit on the opening minutes of the 1989 "Bay Bridge" World Series. The dining room had a score of four-top tables covered with red-checkered tablecloths, and a couple of long communal tables. Veteran waitresses in bowling shirts, still sporting the ponytails of their youth, served the patrons in an entertainingly brusque, charmingly rude manner—as McCabe had described them in his column.

For the night in question, the campaign reserved Capp's for twenty-five hundred dollars, then upped it to five thousand, including free drinks. McCabe figured a few hundred people at two drinks each could be covered by what remained in the campaign account. Why not blow the remaining campaign funds when the point was to lose, particularly since most of the drinks invariably would be consumed by *Foghorners*—paid for by the city?

On Election Day, McCabe rose early and walked to the polling station located at the top of Union and Montgomery. An entourage of parrots hopped from tree to tree ahead of him, heralding, "*Maaacaaab, Maaacaaab!*" Just outside the polling station, they alighted in a flowering red eucalyptus tree continuing to screech his name. Across from the polling station he noted a "McCabe for Mayor" sign in the window of Spediachi's Market—a technical violation of the election law that required all campaign material to be more than one hundred feet from a polling station.

As McCabe began to fill out his ballot, blue-headed Athena, leader of the pack, fluttered into the polling station and perched precariously on his shoulder, eliciting panicked cries from the polling workers. "Athena, what are you doing inside here—get out!" Athena furiously flapped her wings, maniacally bobbing her head up and down, ignoring McCabe's entreaties. Her eyes pinning, she hopped onto the ballot, locked onto the marking pen with her beak and dropped it by McCabe's name, "*Voooot Maaaacaaab! Voooot Maaaacaaab!*"

"Give me back the pen, you little terrorist!" McCabe filled in the space by his name.

Satisfied her mission was accomplished, Athena bolted from the polling station rejoining her cherry-headed cousins in the eucalyptus tree, continuing to shriek, "*Maaacaaab! Maaacaaab!*" McCabe dropped his ballot in the ballot box and hurriedly left the polling place, flummoxed at Athena's dissonant intrusion into the solemnity of the voting process.

Where the hell is the rest of the flock? McCabe wondered. Political blogs observed that at many polling stations throughout the city, clutches of parrots screamed McCabe's name for hours on end. Bloggers joked the parrots were in egregious violation of the prohibition against campaigning within one hundred feet of a polling station. As there were hundreds of polling stations throughout the city, many with bunches of parrots screaming outside, it was apparent every available parrot throughout the Bay Area had come to town on Election Day to help support McCabe. There was even a contigent of colder clime monk parrots that flew in from Portland to join in the festivities. The parrots had either not gotten the message he was planning to lose, or didn't care, one hundred feet or no.

At Caffé Trieste, McCabe bought an espresso and settled in at Poets Plaza. Regulars streamed by, many stopping to chat, wishing him well. Most assured they were voting for him. If McCabe were running for mayor of North Beach, there would be no way, short of premeditated murder that he could not win. Publicly showering with a couple of female campaign workers was an inconsequential indiscretion in that part of town.

From Trieste, McCabe walked down to campaign headquarters in Chinatown. What would normally be a ten-minute walk took almost an hour as he talked to numerous people along the way who stopped to greet him. As he walked onto Waverly, he was surprised to see a crowd milling outside campaign headquarters, mostly elderly Chinese men, smoking and chattering in Cantonese, several offering him Chinese cigarettes.

Upstairs in the headquarters, a ten-person phone bank was calling prospective voters urging them to get out and vote. Hand-held "McCabe for Mayor" signs were being hammered together for volunteers to wave at major intersections throughout the city. A long industrial table was devoted to precinct captains who were preparing packets of polling data for going door-to-door, getting out the vote. Several volunteers were on the phones directing people to their nearest polling station, others were fielding calls about polling irregularities. It all appeared—at least to the volunteers—as normal Election Day frenzy.

Noë and Zoë were on the phone talking to reporters and fielding calls from campaign workers. Max was at the back of the room, calmly reading through the final issue of the *Foghorn* that had been distributed a few days before, as if to give it some final *ex post facto* edits.

For McCabe, the job was done, the ruse accomplished. Seeking some solitude from the inevitable election night bedlam, he slipped out of headquarters. It was around noon according to the massive clock on the face of old St. Mary's Cathedral at Grant and California. An Ecclesiastical verse below the clock face warned brothal-bound Barbary Coast boys, "Son, Observe the Time and Fly from Evil."

He headed up Grant past the Chinatown vegetable stands, trinket and tee shirt shops to Columbus and onto Fisherman's Wharf. At Aquatic Park he climbed over the grassy knoll to the Marina Promenade, then followed the shoreline path all the way to Fort Point at the base of the Golden Gate Bridge. Streams of joggers and bicyclists passed him by, many greeting him with a wave of their hand. Windsurfers plied the bay, seagulls chased fishing boats cleaning their catch, harbor seals popped their heads from the ruffled bay waters.

McCabe took his time returning to North Beach, then slowly walked back up Telegraph Hill, turning over in his mind the many scenes from his campaign. At Montgomery and Filbert, McCabe gave cardboard Bogart in the *Dark Passage* building a hard look, fantasizing he had finally earned his respect and would be acknowledged. Bogie stared back, cooly impassive.

Most of the houses along the Filbert Steps had "McCabe for Mayor" signs. It was the densest patterning of his house signs in the city. They all supported their neighbor, yet McCabe didn't even believe in his own campaign for mayor—a charade that would come to a close tonight. There was always a reckoning to be had when you played such a false role, more so when you actually got people to believe in you, right down to those who put campaign signs in their windows. But it would seem he might escape without consequence.

At Napier Lane, house cats snoozed along the wooden planks, barely opening their eyes as he walked by. Squad Car was sleeping in the garden

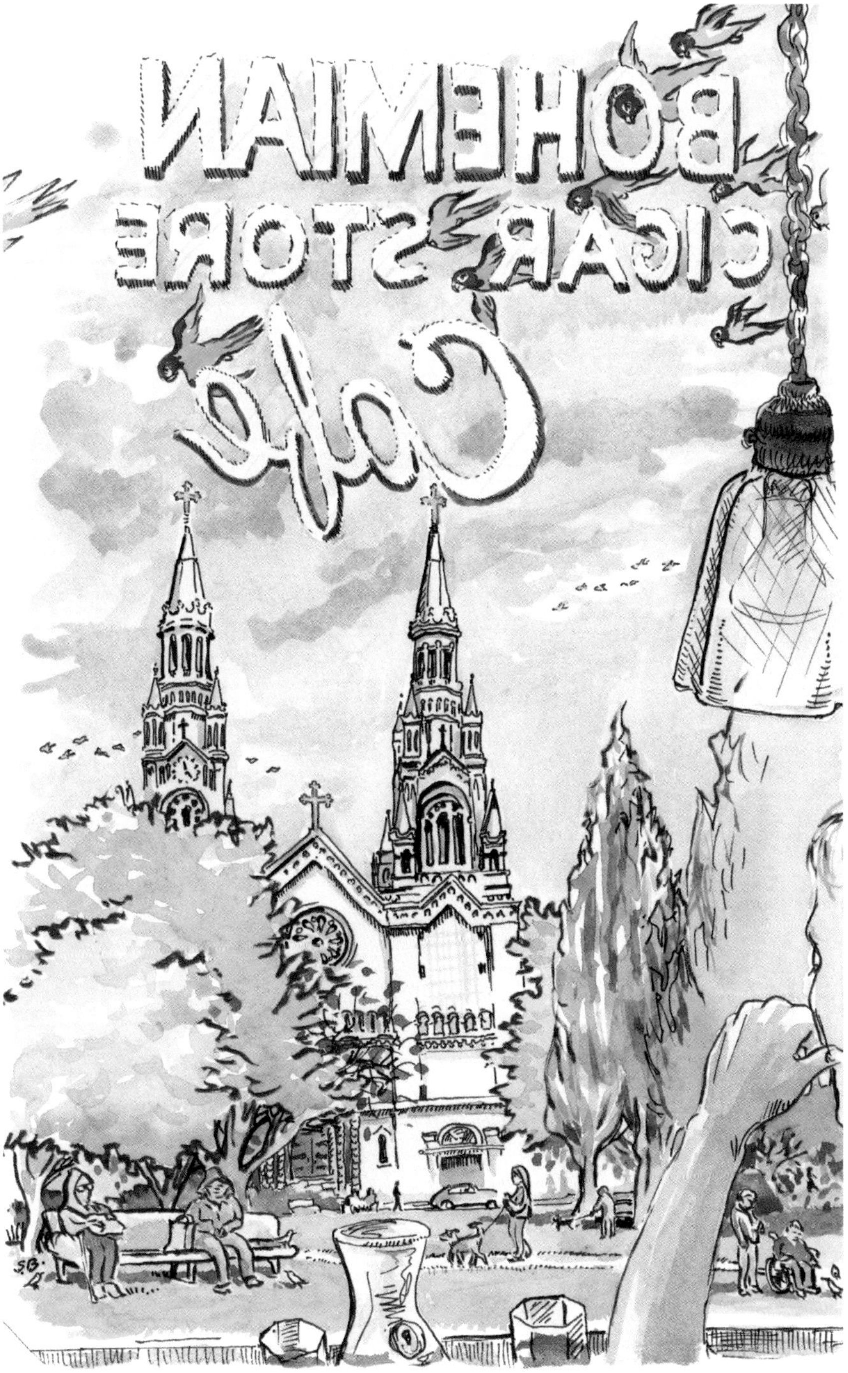
BOHEMIAN
CIGAR STORE
Cafe
S.B.

under a loquat tree, the late afternoon undisturbed by the parrots not yet returned from campaigning around the polling stations. The cat lifted up its head ever so slightly as McCabe came through the garden gate, it was too perfect a day to do otherwise. Inside his house, McCabe poured a glass of Zinfandel and went out onto the porch, letting his mind wander over the white-capped waters to the tinder dry East Bay hills. He had certainly succeeded in getting out of his comfort zone. Now he was worried if he would ever get it back.

He showered, put on his usual, formal outfit–white shirt, red tie, clean pair of blue jeans, blue blazer and his high mileage walking shoes.

He strolled down the hill to meet Max for dinner at Mario's Bohemian Cigar Store at Union and Columbus. Mario's no longer sold cigars. It was now a funky hole-in-the-wall, broken-down bar. There were a dozen barstools set against a dark wood interior, busted wooden floor, chrome dinette tables stuffed in its corners. The split-door entrances on Union and Columbus were propped open with a couple of banged up bistro chairs. A cross-breeze circulated the burnt bread smell from panini and focaccia sandwiches prepared behind the bar in a small wood fired oven.

Max sat at a corner table looking out on Washington Square Park and Saints Peter and Paul Church. He was scrolling on his laptop, drinking wine from a hexagonal tumbler glass. As McCabe pulled up a chair, Max poured him a glass of wine from a carafe of Malbec. "You look worried McCabe! The race is over, pal. We're fine!"

"I'm not exactly feeling the liberating qualities of ending my run for public office," teasing his olfactory senses with the fat wine's chocolate and blackberries. McCabe had always been polyamorous with many and diverse red wines, its sensory gratifications equaled only by the wet taste of a woman.

Max sensed McCabe's brief untensing, "Come on, do what you want! Go back to writing your column. Try some fiction. Travel. Trip out. Spend some time at your place in Napa. You're a free man!"

McCabe shook his head concernedly, "There's something out there—I can't put my finger on it—a premonition that won't let me in." The ancient Greeks believed a select few were given the ability to either know the future or understand the language of animals. McCabe had mastered inter-species communication—at least as to the parrots. But perceiving the future, clearly he had not. Only Noah had mastered both—and that was before the ancient Greeks.

"Well, you'll know soon enough," shrugged Max. "Come on, let's order some food." Max raised his glass, "To the end of the campaign," then with a touch of irony, "and to your uncertain future!"

After finishing dinner, lightheaded from the robust Malbec, they walked across Columbus to Capp's Corner at Green and Powell.

The dining area at Capp's had been cleared of tables, opening up a space for people to stand around and watch the election results on the big screen TVs. There were already about fifty people, mostly *Foghorners* and campaign volunteers, milling around the bar looking at election results coming in from the rest of the country. The polls would close in less than an hour. As McCabe entered Capp's, people greeted him warmly, their enthusiasm unnerving him, as he fully expected it to be apparent within the hour that he had lost the election. Nonetheless, he put on a game face, smiling self-confidently, engaging and garrulous. Noë and Zoë came over, kissing him with the briefest, possessive brush of their lips.

By the time the polls closed, the room had swelled to a hundred people, spilling out onto the sidewalk. The campaign's election night drink budget had been soundly breached, but it was assumed once the election results began coming in, the crowd would quickly thin. No one gave the order to cut-off free drinks; no one was actually paying attention. There were no TV trucks outside Capp's as they were stationed at the election night venues of the two mayoral candidates running first and second in the polls—the mayor and the city attorney.

At precisely eight o'clock, the affiliates of the major TV stations switched back from nationwide to local coverage of the mayor's race. Within a few minutes, the first tabulated absentee ballots were thrown up on the screen. The vote was spread thin, the mayor in the lead with just 25 percent, the city attorney next at 22 percent, the city council president at 19 percent, McCabe at 18 percent, the minor candidates sharing the remaining 16 percent. The absentee votes were thought to favor the mayor, who had made significant effort to lock up votes early, putting serious resources into getting his supporters to vote absentee. The absentee ballot results elicited groans and a marked slumping in the crowd. McCabe smiled stoically. It was going down just as planned.

A half hour later, with all the absentee ballots tabulated, the results were little changed, though McCabe had switched places with the city council president at 19 percent, the mayor widening his lead, having picked up 2 percent now at 27 percent, the city attorney remaining at 22 percent. A few people began to filter out. The local TV affiliates aired coverage of the mayor and city attorney campaign headquarters, each of them expressing guarded confidence. Absentee ballots which made up about 50 percent of votes cast, often didn't reflect voting on the day of the election and tended to skew conservative.

More people left Capp's. Noë and Zoë sat at the bar, dispiritedly watching the returns, occasionally glancing over at McCabe. Max circulated through the diminishing crowd, joking, reminiscing, and periodically checking with McCabe.

An hour later, about half of the votes actually cast that day had been reported, combined with the absentee ballots, totaling 75 percent of votes. Surprisingly, McCabe had picked up a point, an increase to 20 percent, the mayor dropping by a point back down to 26 percent, the city attorney now at 23 percent and the city council president, 18 percent. Only a quarter of the votes were left to be reported and they would be from the southern and western-most parts of the city, their polling stations furthest away from city hall, taking the longest to deliver the ballot boxes to the Department of Elections. The percentages were expected to move against McCabe as those areas of the city were more conservative and family-oriented, not considered particularly enamored of him, unlike the more liberal eastern areas of town where he lived. It was however, the area where the parrots had flown the most sorties, screaming out his name.

McCabe breathed easier.

Around 10 o'clock, all votes had been tabulated, the percentages held steady, still showing the mayor in first place, three points ahead of the city attorney, 6 points ahead of McCabe, 8 points ahead of the city council president. Even though the mayor had only received a little more than a quarter of the first ballot vote, two of the local TV stations projected him the ultimate winner, while the two remaining local stations analyzed the vote figures as presaging the race having come down to the mayor and the city attorney, but as yet too close to call. As there were eight candidates for mayor, the Department of Elections would begin by eliminating the last place finisher, redistributing their second and third place votes, then eliminate the next-to-last place finisher, until one candidate passed the 50 percent mark.

Only twenty or so stalwarts remained at Capp's. Max resignedly walked over to McCabe, "Looks like it's pretty much over—I think it's safe to say you're out," the barest hint of disappointment in his voice. "Do you want to say something before this place is completely empty?"

"Yeah, I suppose I should," he responded, wanting nothing more than to go home and crash.

Max whistled for quiet. McCabe stepped into the middle of the dining area. The room fell silent:

> Thanks you diehards, who stuck it out this evening. Two stations have called the race for the mayor, the others are holding back. Even

> with ranked-choice voting, the candidate who comes out ahead on the first ballot normally maintains the lead through whatever number of rounds it takes to get to a majority. So if history is a guide, the mayor has won re-election and I congratulate him. Although I have to say, the city attorney isn't far behind, so if I wake up in the morning and the city attorney is in fact the winner—I congratulate him, too!

A few laughs scattered about at McCabe's hedged congratulations to the two leading candidates. Sam Zinella, owner of Capp's Corner, turned off the TVs, hoping to inject some lightheartedness back into the room—silencing the constant broadcast reminder that McCabe's campaign was doomed. Sam yelled, "We should all congratulate you as well, McCabe!"

Amid the laughter and clapping, McCabe resumed:

> I'll tell you what, I congratulate everyone who ran for mayor! We all contributed to a democratic dialogue about the future of the city—quality of life issues, neighborhood preservation. Open dialogue is the most important element of all—win or lose. We acquitted ourselves well, put out the best paper west of the Mississippi, and as Max loves to say, didn't lose a dime!

People whooped and clapped acknowledging Max.

> And of course we should recognize the city for underwriting the *Foghorn*. That was a pretty sweet deal I think we'd all agree. To everyone who worked on the paper, those who are still here and to those who have understandably gone home, that kind of journalism hasn't been seen in this town for years. There were no sacred cows—much easier to do when you have no advertising other than

your own campaign. But the deal is done. Tomorrow we disband this ragged army of journalistic vets and loyal volunteers and go back to civilian life. The battle is over and we all—each of us—need to move on to the next stage—or should I say adventures that await us. Thank you again! No regrets. And I hope you all feel the same way too!

Let's enjoy one last round of drinks on the campaign!

Those remaining pressed round him. April, despondent, cried on his shoulder, "I thought you actually had a chance, I know you didn't want it, but the rest of us did! You would have been a wonderful mayor, Tom!" She left disconsolate.

Max embraced him, "That was one hell of a trip, McCabe, as good an ending to my career in journalism as I could have asked! Let's get together in a couple of days and talk."

Noë and Zoë hugged him uneasily, "We love you, McCabe," murmured Noë.

"We do, we really do," breathed Zoë.

McCabe sensing an underlying turbulence, laughed nervously at the hidden dissonance, "You guys made it a whole lot different! More than I could have imagined!"

Noë began to ask him a question, "Do you have time after this, there's something we'd like to talk to you about..." Her question was deflected as a camera crew from KINK burst in, Miles O'Riley in the lead.

McCabe emitted an audible breath of frustration, "Hey, Miles, shouldn't you be over at the mayor's campaign headquarters sucking up to him?"

"What? Haven't you been watching the ranked-choice vote!? They've eliminated the last candidate and you picked up a coupla' points on the mayor! And you're almost even with the city attorney!"

"You're kidding?" said McCabe. "It's some kind of anomaly! You wasted your time coming over here!"

Miles bared his incising tiger teeth, "McCabe, I don't know—there's a trend building here—the mayor is at 29 percent, you're at 24 percent; almost in second now—the city attorney has 25 percent!"

Sam Zinella turned the TVs back on. Indeed, Miles was right. McCabe had almost pulled even with the city attorney and partially closed the gap on the mayor. McCabe was dumbfounded, but it was probably as he surmised, a quirk in the redistribution of the bottom ranked candidates' second and third votes. Once ranked-choice voting moved onto redistributing the second and third place votes from the higher, less kooky candidates, the vote pattern would no doubt return to the previous percentages. A few people came into the restaurant, stared at the TV screens, ordered drinks, which were still being paid for by the campaign.

The seventh-ranked candidate, the naked yoga guy, was shortly eliminated, his second and third place votes redistributed. McCabe picked up two points at 26 percent, the mayor one point to 30 percent, the city attorney now in a tie with McCabe, also at 26 percent. Closing in on midnight, Capp's was beginning to jam.

Next, the sixth and fifth place candidates were eliminated. When their votes were redistributed, McCabe jumped by four points, the mayor and city attorney only by a couple. The mayor remained in first place, now with 33 percent of the vote, McCabe 30 percent, the city attorney falling to third at 28 percent, the city council president falling farther behind. Another TV crew crammed into Capp's startling everyone with their lights and cameras, raising tensions further.

With the elimination of the fourth place finisher—the city council president—McCabe was now comfortably in second place only two points behind the mayor who was at 36 percent, and 4 points ahead of the city attorney at 30 percent. Two more television trucks drove up to Capp's. Their reporters couldn't squeeze through the door and were forced to remain outside with hundreds of people, many following the returns on their smart phones.

The next person to be eliminated would be the city attorney, which would either take the mayor or McCabe over the 50 percent threshold to victory.

Noë and Zoë had squeezed in next to McCabe who was sitting at the bar, packed among his supporters. McCabe wanted to go to the bathroom and heave, his stomach churning like the barrel of a cement truck. ***Me in second place! And after the shower scene! How's this possible! This joke has gone on long enough!*** He considered that he was friends with the city attorney. He had the progressive cred and had treated McCabe with respect throughout the campaign—unlike the mayor, who had mocked him at every opportunity. If the city attorney's supporters followed the sentiments of the city attorney himself, what then?

Oh god! This can't be! Grant me a reprieve! Let the mayor keep his damn job! I sure as hell don't want it!

The results of the city attorney's redistributed votes flashed on the screen. McCabe had inched passed the mayor at 50.3 percent to the mayor's 49.7 percent. Assuming the few provisional ballots still remaining to be verified held true to the overall results—McCabe was mayor! Indeed, in short order all the local TV stations declared him the winner. Capp's was complete bedlam, in an uproar. Outside the restaurant a raucous crowd began chanting, "McCabe! McCabe! McCabe!" their shouts reverberating through the streets of North Beach. Several police cars blocked off the area, their flashing red lights contributing to the tumultuous scene.

Max, jubilant, yelled over to McCabe, "You gotta go outside and say something!"

Noë laughed ecstatically, the retrocausual revealing its hand in the current moment, "Yeah, McCabe, get out there before they riot!"

"This isn't happening!" stammered McCabe at the lunatic touch of a terrible surprise, quantum uncertainty come home to roost. "What the hell?"

Max pointed emphatically at the door, exhorting, "Get your ass out there, McCabe!"

Any sense of the rational was overwhelmed by the deranged scene of electoral revelation. McCabe waded through the crowd to the open door of the restaurant. Outside, reporters, as a pack of wolves, converged on him, throwing him a score of questions:

"McCabe, do the results surprise you?"

"How did you pull off such an upset?"

"Everyone thought you were done after your shower stunt! What does that say about the voters in this town?"

"Are you prepared to be mayor?"

"Do you think ranked-choice voting worked the way it was intended?"

"Anyone gonna' be your first lady?"

"Did the parrots have anything to do with your success?"

McCabe held up his hands more in defense than triumph, trying to silence the crowd. People called for quiet, the crowd calmed, then someone shouted, "Go, McCabe!" and the crowd roared again.

McCabe again motioned more emphatically for quiet, trying to gain some semblance of control:

> A few hours ago we were down to a handful of people here. I was ready to go home and try to get some sleep—but obviously sleep deprivation will be my lot!

There were more cheers and shouts—notes of the song of victory—

> I can't think of a more challenging time to be mayor of a large American city.
>
> Federal government support of our urban centers waxes and wanes like a harvest moon, while at the local level, our bonded indebtedness increases in tandem with our unfunded pension obligations.

> We are a dynamic neighborhood and business town—when in balance there can be a general satisfaction with the body politic—but we all know what the consequences can be when there is a great tech overreaching or for that matter—unwinding—as in the Dot.com implosion two decades ago or the financial meltdown just a decade ago.
>
> Our neighborhoods are us—they aren't someone else's. We can't be left holding the bag with the next financial earthquake, which are happening more frequently than the real ones. We must protect our neighborhoods now—make them sustainable—every hill and valley—every street corner and alley—diverse and family friendly—safe, clean and green.
>
> We're a strong city. In the history of our nation, no one suffered more devastation than San Francisco in the 1906 earthquake and fire—not even the Great Chicago Fire of 1871. Our town was reduced to rubble, but only a few years later we were celebrating the Panama Pacific Exposition and our return to greatness. If we could bounce back from that disaster, we can certainly find our way through any future economic uncertainty that puts at risk our city and our neighborhoods.

McCabe stopped and looked out over the irrepressible crowd—the cameras hot, the mikes suffocating:

> But you know, I'm fortunate! I come into office without the support of downtown. They put their clout and money on other candidates, so I'm not beholden to anyone but you! This won't be the most pleasant job in the world. You and I both know that! But I will try and do what's best for the city in the next four years, not what's best for vested interests. In the end, leaving politics would

> be easy—*very easy*—so I don't have much to lose, do I? The only thing at risk is your trust and loyalty, and I will do everything in my power to keep it!

The crowd whistled and hollered.

> I only ask one thing of you since you've put me in the mayor's office. Don't walk away now thinking your job is done. It isn't! We're all in this together. I can't do it alone. We hang separately or we hang together.
>
> My thanks to the other candidates in the race—the mayor, our city attorney, the city council president, and the other remaining candidates. I picked up a lot of second and third votes from my competitors. It means I owe not just the people who voted for me first, but also those who marked their ballots giving me their second or third votes.
>
> I should also acknowledge my pals on the *Foghorn*—at great sacrifice they pulled it all together and presented a coherent vision of what this city can be. And to all the volunteers who believed in me when others didn't, I thank you in ways you might not understand, but it comes from my heart! Being the most loyal of all to the campaign—you hung in there when I faltered.
>
> I'm humbled more than you know. This is a stunning turn of events. No one is more surprised than me!
>
> To one and all, young and old, all races and creeds, let's build that City on a Hill!

Amid the cheering and acclamation, McCabe glanced at his watch.

> I see there's still an hour till the bars close. For the good of this crazy town, let's get this party going! Drinks are on me!

There followed a tumultuous ovation.

CHAPTER TWENTY-ONE: GO DADDY GO

Capp's Corner served drinks up to 2AM closing time, ignoring the normal 1:30AM protocol that was supposed to allow patrons to finish their drinks and clear out. But tonight the cops were cool, despite their station being only a block away on Vallejo Street. The heat wanted to be on the good side of the incoming mayor. Revelers were nursing their drinks well past 2AM.

McCabe was hammered. Noë and Zoë spirited him to their car, leaving the hangers-on at Capp's to close the place. He slumped down in the back seat, trying to make sense of the past twelve hours.

Noë murmured to Zoë, "McCabe is awfully quiet back there." She looked over her shoulder, "Everything alright?"

McCabe mumbled, "I don't know—all those complexifying runs redistributing second and third place choices. This town is insane."

Zoë smothered a laugh, "You did the opposite of everyone else. With your name recognition and some other things, you just became mayor!"

"What other things?" he asked quizzically.

"Mostly those crazy parrots," replied Zoë, the slightest uncharacteristic asperity in her voice.

They crossed over Columbus and headed up Telegraph Hill. Noë, her hand on the wheel, snapped the reins, "Why don't we go to Coit Tower?

Take a look at the city you're about to govern, McCabe? *Hmmm?*"

"I'm whipped, I just want to crawl in bed and do the *Big Sleep*."

Zoë softly urged him on, "Come on, see if you look at the city differently now..."

Noë finished the sentence, "Now that it's yours."

McCabe was adrift, "What the hell, if you want, it's on the way." They drove up Lombard Street segueing into Telegraph Boulevard to the dimly lit circular parking area at the foot of Coit Tower. There were a couple of empty cars—no one to be seen—nothing stirred. They walked up the stairs to Coit Tower, then around to the grassy knoll that provided a panoramic view of the city—overlooking Downtown, Chinatown, Nob Hill and Russian Hill, the Golden Gate Bridge and Bay Bridge, Treasure Island and the East Bay.

Noë pulled out a ginormous joint, "Let's celebrate your victory!"

McCabe demurred, "I don't need anything more, I'm gone..."

Noë ignored his feeble protest. She lit the dagga, took a long toke, then handed it to Zoë. Taking a deep drag, she held the smoke in her lungs, then exhaled, the thin blue smoke, redolent and sensual, mixing pungently with the autumnal night air. Zoë handed the joint to McCabe. He looked at the herb as if it were some curious specimen.

"Come on, McCabe, you might not do this once you're mayor. You'll be even more uptight then," Noë exclaimed.

He put the doobage to his lips, muttering incoherent fifties jive, "Go, Daddy, go," then took a hit, infusing his chest with a heavy jolt of resinous ganja. He exhaled and coughed. Zoë was right, the city did look different, now morphed into an exotic menace—Moloch—a slumbering dragon, with a thousand flickering eyes of scaled light, its gestating tail bridging across the bay to the other side of the world.

"McCabe?" Noë was calling his name.

"This is heavy stuff we're smoking!" he joked, Noë and Zoë bioluminescent like the beginnings of a psychedelic sex trip.

S.B.

"We need to talk to you," added Noë, wrapping her arm round his waist.

"Hey look, you guys will get great jobs at city hall! No problem, guaranteed!"

"It's not that, McCabe," said Zoë stroking his arm, "We're..."

McCabe searching for space, repeated his assurances, "Really, whatever you guys want, I'll get it for you! You're set, I promise!"

Noë sloughed off his fraught pronouncements, "That night in August when we were all together at your place..."

"Yeah!" he smiled broadly, thinking he had escaped the dragon, "*Knock, knock, knockin' on heaven's door!*"

"It seems..." said Zoë, unable to finish the sentence.

So Noë did. "It seems, we're pregnant!"

Above McCabe, phallique Coit Tower shuddered and swayed as in an earthquake. Deep in the westerly sky a comet shot over the Golden Gate Bridge, disappearing on the Pacific horizon.

"We didn't tell you because of your campaign, but time is starting to run short," whispered Zoë, "and we're not sure what to do."

Addlepated, McCabe gasped, his diaphram constricted, "You're pregnant? Both of you? Me? On that evening? Come on, you're screwing with me! What're the odds of that!? You guys–*ah*–presumably get around a lot."

Zoë shot back with uncharacteristic heat, her self-possession gone, "We're not sluts McCabe! You may think we are, but we're not! We get around a lot less than you, from what we hear."

Noë, as a lioness protecting her cubs, exclaimed, "You guys have it so easy! You have sex with us. All you worry about is getting us pregnant! What an inconvenience! We carry them in our bodies, birth them, sustain them. God, the male species! Acting like we're the loose ones!"

McCabe convulsed, feebly shot back in a fever dream, "Each of you guys are evidently smoking for two—don't talk to me about being responsible!"

Noë ignored the woozy barb,"We're pretty sure you're the father!"

"Pretty sure? There are other candidates out there? Come on!" he pleaded, grasping for a lifeline.

Noë did the head shake, trying to evince a sympathetic smile, "We've compared notes on who we'd been with. Neither of us had done anything for a while. We were both at peak fertility. That's when we party more. We were all crazy that evening. None of us took precautions."

McCabe choked back, spinning with vertigo as the dragon let fall its prey, "Christ, if you knew this day! Now you're—you're *both* pregnant!?"

"We needed to tell you," said Zoë calmly as she could. "We can't remain tight in the bud much longer. We have to make a decision whether they'll be allowed in or not."

McCabe stared vainly over the phosphorescent city looking for an emergency exit from gravity and flesh. Moloch's psychotropic mirage had mercifully dissolved in the febrile air. "This is off the goddamn rails! Assuming I wake up tomorrow, we can try and disentangle this hot mess," he entreated, trying to maintain.

They walked back to the car without speaking, unbalanced by frissons of the illicit. Noë and Zoë dropped him off at the Filbert Steps with muted good-byes.

But McCabe was not alone.

From the *Dark Passage* building Bogie called out to him, finally giving him droll recognition after years of implacable silence, "We all lose Eden sometime, pal! You've eaten of the fruit that cannot be undone."

Taking Bogie's blow, McCabe—in the waist of an hourglass—weaved slump-shouldered down to Napier Lane, his neighbors' porch lights illuminating the way through decoherence to his cottage. The parrots tittered restlessly in the loquat trees. Squad Car, perched on the gatepost, greeted him edgily and darted up the stairway to the front door. Unmoored, he lurched up the stairs, fumbling with his keys. Inside, he kicked off his shoes, hyperventilating, trying to still the queasiness of his epic boner. He stared dolefully at the glittering spans of the Bay Bridge. A wave of nausea slid through him. He went to the kitchen and grabbed a glass of water. Above the sink, Charlotte serenely weaved her silken web.

McCabe soon would be the honorable mayor.

THE END

POSTSCRIPT: Last week, Athena, Blue-Headed Coneur and leader of the parrots of Telegraph Hill was taken down by a peregrine falcon over Washington Square.

Rest in peace, Athena.

—Thomas McCabe

I wish to acknowledge the City and County of San Francisco for its public campaign financing and ranked-choice voting legislation, which despite being subject to some comedic barbs, in actuality work reasonably well in the Cool Grey City of Love's own unpredictable way.

To the police of the North Beach Central Station–our beloved *Ess Eff Pee Dee.*

To the Telegraph Hill Dwellers which in the spirit of Jane Jacobs has helped preserve the neighborhood in which many scenes occur.

To the current management of Caffé Trieste, for allowing my return after seven years of biblical exile.

I wish to also thank, Christy Medellin, Jenny Luu, Jennifer Morla, Lyra Cruz, Giulia Pattini, Natasha Dennerstein, Veronica Moreaux, Le Tu Coleman, Lucy Samuel, Elisa Celli, Stacey Carter, Ryoko Tajiri, Sandra Garcia, Lori Sottile, Karin Velasco, Kathy Russel, Kathy Bruin, Susan Bearden, Susan Revah, Cyan Tolland, Keith Howell, Dan Keller, Bruce Hasson, Lawrence Ferlinghetti, Janet Clyde, Rebecca Peters, Ida Pantaleo, Ward Dunham, Marc Bruno, Gary Near, Raj Dutt, Scott Lyons, Michelle Zaffino and Nick Borthne.

And most of all, Charles Cunningham whose tolerance, good-nature and skillful artistry brought it all to fruition.

END NOTES:
Chapter 3: Vesuvius Eruptus

1. Author's Credits: Opening lines from several of McCabe's favorite novels and sonnets (See pages 37-39).

Lolita, light of my life, fire of my loins.
Vladimir Nabokov, *Lolita* (1955).

It was a bright cold day in April, and the clocks were striking thirteen.
George Orwell, *1984* (1949).

If you really want to hear about it, the first thing you'll probably want to know is where I was born, and what my lousy childhood was like, and how my parents were occupied and all before they had me, and all that David Copperfield kind of crap, but I don't feel like going into it, if you want to know the truth.
J.D. Salinger, *The Catcher in the Rye* (1951).

All children except one grow up.
J.M. Barrie, *Peter Pan* (1911).

Scarlett O'Hara was not beautiful, but men seldom realized it when caught by her charm as the Tarleton twins were.
Margaret Mitchell, *Gone with the Wind* (1936).

Time is not a line but a dimension, like the dimensions of space.
Margaret Atwood, *Cat's Eye* (1988).

It was love at first sight.
Joseph Heller, *Catch-22* (1961).

It was the best of times, it was the worst of times.
Charles Dickens, *A Tale of Two Cities* (1859).

In my younger and more vulnerable years my father gave me some advice that I've been turning over in my mind ever since.
F. Scott Fitzgerald, *The Great Gatsby* (1925).

How,,,,,,do I love thee,,,,,,let me count,,,,,,the ways.
Elizabeth Barrett Browning, *Sonnets from the Portuguese* (1850).

A screaming comes across the sky.
Thomas Pynchon, *Gravity's Rainbow* (1973).

A story has no beginning or end; arbitrarily one chooses that moment of experience from which to look back or from which to look ahead.
Graham Greene, *The End of the Affair* (1951).

Call me Ishmael.
Herman Melville, *Moby-Dick* (1851).

In the late summer of that year we lived in a house in a village that looked across the river and the plain to the mountains.
Ernest Hemingway, *A Farewell to Arms* (1929).

The Content is the Message (See pages 32 and 37).

ILLUSTRATIONS: